The Sweetest Scheme

JACQUELYNN HARBELL

Author's Note

Dear Readers,

This book contains:

- Steamy scenes
- A fake relationship that gets *very* real
- A swoon-worthy photographer with a dirty mouth
- A baker who finds herself tied up, in more ways than one

Read responsibly. Preferably with dessert.

With love,

Jacque Harbell

"The Sweetest Scheme" Official Playlist

- *The Ballad of Phil and Phyllis* – Oliver Richman, Joy Woods, & Grant Steller (Don't ask why, but this song is responsible for the last 10,000 words of this book.)
- *Photograph* – Ed Sheeran
- *Polaroid* – Jonas Blue, Liam Payne & Lennon Stella
- *Sugar* – Maroon 5
- *Sweet Pea* – Amos Lee
- *Taste* – Sabrina Carpenter
- *Too Sweet* – Hozier
- *Sweet Nothing* – Taylor Swift
- *Delicate* – Taylor Swift
- *Labyrinth* – Taylor Swift
- *Dive* – Ed Sheeran
- *Boyfriend* – Ariana Grande & Social House
- *Plot Twist* – Ashley Kutcher
- *How Not To* – Dan + Shay
- *Good for You* – Selena Gomez (feat. A$AP Rocky)
- *There's No Way* – Lauv (feat. Julia Michaels)

- *Hurt Somebody* – Noah Kahan & Julia Michaels
- *Sangria* – Blake Shelton
- *Ocean* - Martin Garrix (feat. Khalid)
- *Fallin' for You* – Colbie Caillat
- *Why Can't We Be Friends* - War
- *All I've Ever Known*- Eva Noblezada & Reeve Carney, from *Hadestown the Musical*
- *The Ruse* – Barlow & Bear, from t*he Unofficial Bridgerton Musical*
- *What Baking Can Do* – Jessie Mueller, from *Waitress the Musical*

To those who stuff their stresses into sweets, bury their bitterness in buttercream, or pack their problems into pastries—this one's for you.

Palmer

In and out. He doesn't need to see you. Nobody needs to know.

This will be the quickest setup I have ever done (without compromising the work, obviously).

I take a deep breath to steady myself, a difficult task while holding the bulky white box against my chest. I brace the heavy load against my body and ring the doorbell of the Barlow mansion. I'm not sure if the word *mansion* is adequate to describe the sprawling, white stone complex of buildings. The Barlow Estate, maybe? The Barlow Kingdom?

That feels right. The Barlows are as close as we get to royalty in Charleston.

An older woman answers the door and aside from not having a British accent, she looks like something straight out of Downton Abbey. She sees me holding the heavy box and brings me to the part of the house where they are holding the party. I can't tell if they have a dedicated ballroom—do people have those in real life?—or if they have simply cleared furniture from a large enough space in the house to make room for rows of wooden tables ornately decorated in white roses and greenery. Either way, most of the dedicated wedding venues I have seen look far less regal. The room is dripping in white roses from every visible corner.

The woman shows me to my table, where I carefully set down the box and start to unpack the tote bag with my supplies. At the center of the table, they have a large silver cake drum with a halo behind it made of more white roses. They have set the stage perfectly. I couldn't have asked for a more beautiful display for my work. And this is just the engagement party. Just close friends and family, they said. This would be but a small taste of what was in store for the main event.

The thought of what the actual wedding will be like—the wedding of the century, it is being called—makes me simultaneously giddy and nauseous. How can it be that I am the baker the bride chose, out of all the bakeries Charleston has to offer? And let's be honest, the Barlows could afford to go far outside of South Carolina, if they had desired. They could fly some Michelin-starred chef from France if they chose. And yet, they chose me.

Now, I just have to make sure I don't screw it all up by running into the groom or letting the bride know we used to sleep together.

I carefully slide the two-tiered cake out of the box and set to work. For a moment, the anxiety of being here and knowing *he* is here as well flees my body, and I lose myself in the process, as I always do. The base tier is tall—six layers of lemon chiffon with blueberry coulis and vanilla buttercream. The top tier contains layers of chocolate with espresso mousse and chocolate buttercream. Both layers are wrapped in pure white fondant that I meticulously painted with white flowers over a delicate lattice of green leaves. I center it carefully on the drum and inspect it for any flaws that might have appeared in transport. I carefully smooth a bubble out from the fondant with my icing spatula. I fix a smudge in the edible green paint with a clean paintbrush and some water.

I take the silver cake topper from the packaging and carefully stick the prongs into the top layer. It says, "Bennett & Grant" in pretty, silver cursive letters. My stomach gives an uneasy jolt as I make sure it is placed perfectly, to honor *the happy couple*.

I step back to admire my work. It looks perfect. Everything the client envisioned. Beautiful. Understated. Elegant. Just like the bride.

It makes me feel sick to my stomach.

I hear a soft *click*.

The unexpected sound pulls me violently from my focus. I turn to meet the source of the sound: a camera. And behind it, a man. He lowers the camera a little, revealing his face. He flashes a sheepish smile. And *my God*. He is gorgeous.

My whole body has felt coiled with tension since the moment I arrived, dreading the possibility of running into Grant. Knowing that if I did run into him, I would likely lose the best thing that has ever happened for my small business: the Barlow wedding.

But that all fades somewhere distantly into the back of my mind at the sight of the man behind the camera. He has a crop of dark brown curls atop his head, with the sides closely shaven. He peers at me with warm brown eyes—exquisitely sensitive eyes, turned downward at the outer corners. He wears a black button-down with the cuffs rolled to the elbows, with brown suspenders over his broad shoulders. I wonder to myself how he manages to pull them off so well without looking like an eighty-year-old man or a German yodeler. I have never seen anyone make suspenders look hot before. I can see the edge of a black tattoo etched into his light brown skin, just peeking out below the cuff of his shirt.

He holds the large, expensive-looking camera in both

hands, and I watch him look at the preview for the picture he just took. He smiles down at it, clearly approving.

The photographer for the party. I clear my throat and start hurriedly cleaning my supplies off the table.

"I'm so sorry," I say. "You want to take pictures of the cake. Let me move my things—"

"I wasn't taking a picture of the cake," he corrects me, his voice deep and warm. He looks from his camera to my face, his smile growing slowly wider. "Here, take a look."

My brows furrow in confusion. I drop my tote bag to the ground and approach him. He holds the camera out for me to see.

It's a picture of me, but it looks somehow unlike any other picture or reflection of myself I have ever seen. I look stunning.

No one has ever just pointed a camera my way and captured me in such a raw and beautiful state before. I'm not smiling or posing. I'm just inspecting my cake, as I have done thousands of times before, the faintest hint of a focused crease between my brows. My lips are just barely parted. The light from the windows reflects off my cheekbones and brings out the gold in my honey-blonde hair that I have pulled back into a claw clip. My eyes look impossibly green. I have always considered my eye color to be more of a dull, mossy green, not the bright and clear emerald, as in this photo. And this is just the raw photo—he has not even edited it yet.

I look up into his face, searching it. I shake my head in disbelief.

I begin to ask, "Why would you—?"

He grins. "I love capturing artists and their work. It seems silly, making art out of art. But I just love creative people."

I shake my head, a blush warming my cheeks. "I'm not an artist."

I would know. My mom is an actual artist. Sculptures and

paintings and drawings. She could make something beautiful out of any materials.

He gestures to the cake. "I would beg to differ."

I laugh. I'm not trying to be falsely modest. I know I can decorate a cake, otherwise I would not have started my business. But I wouldn't call myself an artist. Not like my mom is. And not like this man, who can pull the beauty out of someone with just the click of a camera.

"Silas Howell," he says, offering his hand. I reach my hand out and rest it in his.

"Palmer," I reply. "Palmer Sullivan. Sweet P Bakery."

His eyes grow wide with delight. "Sweet P is your shop? I've tasted your cakes before. They are amazing! Weddings suck significantly less when there's a Sweet P cake there."

I sputter out a dubious laugh. "Wow. I should have you write our next advertisement."

"It's true, though. Your cakes are fantastic. And wedding cakes usually suck. So dry. Never your cakes, though."

I shrug bashfully. "Well, I've only seen one photo so far, but I can see why they chose you as the photographer. Your work is amazing. Do you have a website or a social media page I can follow? So I can see more?"

He smirks. "You can see as much as you'd like. Do you want the wedding stuff or the real stuff?"

"The wedding stuff isn't real?" I ask.

He shrugs. "Pays the bills."

I know instantly and deeply what he means. Being in the wedding business can be a thankless task—dealing with people on one of the most important days of their lives, when expectations and anxieties are at their highest. But people will pay good money for quality when it comes to one of the most important days of their lives. So, while it may be thankless at times, it is the most lucrative part of my job. I may have more fun making a four-year-old's whimsical Elsa-themed birthday cake, but my living is made on the dreams of brides.

"I'd love to see the real stuff then," I reply.

And it is true—I would love to see more of his work. But there's an implication behind the words that sends a thrill through me. In just our short conversation, we've started drifting toward each other like there is a magnetic force drawing our bodies together. I realize I miss feeling like this—feeling that initial frisson of attraction shivering down my spine. He looks at me with such earnest appreciation that it draws an instantaneous, irresistible response from my body. My heart begins to race; my mouth goes a bit dry. This is what it feels like to feel wanted again.

If he likes me now, just wait until he sees me put some effort in. I know I can do better. I'm wearing black jeans and a black long-sleeve shirt with clouds of smudged powdered sugar all over them. I had put minimal effort into my hair or makeup this morning; I was not expecting to meet anyone of significance today. In fact, it had been my intention to be seen by as few people as possible.

I hand him my phone, with my Instagram profile left open. "Find me your handle?"

He smiles and takes the phone from me, adding himself as a friend on my account. I look down briefly at the screen, seeing the thumbnails with beautiful, vivid pictures lined in a grid pattern. I look back up at him, delighted.

"I can't wait to see more," I tell him.

"Me neither," he responds, and I don't think for a single second that he is talking about my cakes.

I force myself to draw away from him, to pull my body away from the magnetic force that has brought me within inches of him. To pack up my things and leave. This was supposed to be a quick setup, and I have spent the last ten minutes flirting with the photographer.

But *damn*. Who wouldn't want to spend ten minutes flirting with him?

A part of me is relieved to feel like this again. A part of me had wondered if I would ever feel like this again. Maybe time does heal all wounds?

I grab my bag and shoot Silas a dazzling smile over my shoulder before turning to leave.

Which is precisely when I run directly into him. Grant Foster. *My ex.*

I stumble backward, nearly tripping over my feet in the process. I look up into his blue eyes that have gone wide, as if he has seen a ghost.

Oh shit. Oh shit, oh shit, oh shit, oh shit.

"Grant," I whisper. My whole body freezes in pure, undiluted panic. *God, he looks good. Painfully good.*

His light brown hair is neat and styled. He has always been well-dressed, but I wonder if being around the Barlows has forced him to up his game. He wears an immaculately tailored gray jacket over light slacks and a crisp white dress shirt.

"Palmer?" he asks. He sounds dazed, as if he might be dreaming. Or having a nightmare, I guess. "What are you doing here?"

"I, um," I falter, looking over to my cake where it stands proudly on display, "I made the cake."

I fixate on my cake, trying to look anywhere but directly into Grant's eyes.

"You made the cake?" he asks incredulously. "For my engagement party?"

And hopefully your wedding, I think to myself, though I do not offer that information in this moment. I scramble for something, anything helpful to say. But there is nothing to say. I was an idiot for taking this job. I only brought this on myself.

A squealing noise slices through the tension between us, and we are joined by none other than Bennett Barlow herself, the heiress to the Barlow empire. The princess of this unfathomable kingdom. She looks unsurprisingly stunning in a fitted white knee-length dress with off-the-shoulder sleeves covered in white ruffles. The dress hugs her curves like second skin, and I know no amount of Spanx would ever make my body look like that in a dress. Her hair, so dark it is nearly black, is impossibly glossy and in perfect waves to her shoulders.

And you simply cannot look at Bennett Barlow without noticing the enormous—and I do mean truly gigantic—rock adorning her left ring finger. How can you miss it? I am certain they must be able to see it from the International Space Station. Does the woman not have carpal tunnel? How can she even lift that hand at all?

But Bennett Barlow looks like the kind of woman who works out. And not normal people workouts like running, but something cool and sexy like pilates or hot yoga. I am certain she has been preparing her entire life to wear a diamond ring like that.

I breathe in sharply and hold it.

"Sweet P!" she squeals, grasping me by the shoulders and shaking me from side to side with the force of her excitement. My brain rattles a little in my skull at the intensity of her greeting. "I'm so glad I caught you—*Oh. My. God.* Look at that cake! It's perfect! It's everything I imagined it would be. You have outdone yourself. Grant, isn't it just perfect?"

"Just *perfect*," he echoes, though he could not have said the words more sardonically.

She looks at him curiously, raising an eyebrow. She shakes her head, staring at him pointedly as if to say, *Sweetheart, you're being rude.*

"Grant, Honey?" she asks, hesitantly. "The cake is perfect, right?"

"Perfect," he confirms again, still sounding bitter. "Palmer's cakes are always perfect, though."

She looks at him in shock, as if she cannot believe how rude he is being. But then it hits her. The way he is looking at me. The way he knows my name without being formally introduced.

She looks nervously at me and back at her fiancé. "You two know each other?"

"She's my ex-girlfriend," he says, and the title hits me like a punch to the gut. As much as I don't want it to hurt, it still does, even a year later.

"Your ex-girlfriend is Sweet P?" she asks, sounding heartbroken by the idea.

He presses his lips into a thin line. He takes a deep breath through his nose like he's trying to gather every ounce of his patience before he says, "You know that's not her legal name, right?"

She rolls her eyes, as if this is a dumb question. I'm still marveling over the fact that I got through the entire consultation with Bennett weeks ago without her asking for my real name, happy just to call me "Sweet P," but I wasn't one to look a gift horse in the mouth.

"Of course I know that," she insists. "I just thought it was a stage name. Like Lady Gaga."

I press my lips firmly together to keep myself from laughing at the absurdity of the comment. Nothing about this is funny. But comparing me to Lady Gaga might just be ridiculous enough to break the last shred of my sanity.

Grant chooses to move past this comment and turns to me, fixing an accusing stare on me. I balk beneath it.

"Palmer, why would you agree to this?" he asks sternly. His tone is so patronizing it coils up some small, petulant animal inside me.

I shrug, though I feel anything but nonchalant about this exchange. "It was too good an opportunity to pass up."

He frowns deeply. "An opportunity to do what exactly?"

"To get close to Grant again?" Bennett asks, as if this is the most logical conclusion. But she doesn't say it meanly or accusing. She says it with her blue eyes wide and genuinely concerned, as if worried that I'm plotting to steal her fiancé. The thought of Bennett Barlow being threatened by me is so ridiculous it's laughable.

And I do laugh, though it doesn't seem to mollify either of them.

"No, no!" I insist, raising my hands in protest. "I'm not trying to get closer to Grant—"

"What else do you have to gain from this?" Grant asks, spoken like a true child of wealth. Not only did Grant grow up with wealthy parents, but he also makes fabulous money as an investment banker. And now he is marrying into riches beyond my wildest dreams.

This wedding is one of the highest-paying individual jobs I have ever received. How could I pass up a gig this momentous? How could I decline the exposure? This wedding is going to have 300 guests, celebrities included. This could potentially open doors to more high-paying jobs for my business.

But Grant is looking at me so coldly, so skeptically, and Bennett is looking at me with so much hurt and fear. I can see the mistrust kindling in their eyes. How do I tell them that this isn't personal? How do I prove to them that I don't want him back? Even though the latter might not be entirely true, if I am being honest with myself.

"I'm seeing someone!" The words burst out of me, loud and desperate, before I can think better of them. There is no logic left in me, only panic. I need this job. I can't lose it for such a stupid reason.

I continue, "Please, you don't need to worry about me. I'm happy, and I want you two to be happy. I promise, I'm not plotting anything. I'm not trying to get closer to you. I didn't want to run into you today. I only intended to bring my cake and leave."

Grant's eyes narrow. "You're seeing someone?"

I swallow hard, averting my eyes. "Yes, I am. You don't need to worry about me."

"What's his name?" I look up into his stern expression, and my brows furrow together. What right did he have to question me? Even if I was lying through my teeth.

"His name is—" I hesitate. And it's a terrible, awkward length of hesitation. It's so long a second that I might as well have stamped "LIAR" across my forehead.

A name, I think. *What is a name? Why can I suddenly not think of any name in this world for a man?*

I try again, as if a name will magically come to me, despite there suddenly being an endless blank pit between my ears where my brain used to reside. "His name is—"

I feel an arm slide over my shoulders, and I tense at the contact.

"Silas Howell."

There is a feeling like a wave of cool water washing over me at his voice, freeing me from the panic. He coolly offers a hand to Grant to shake, bobbing it up and down with a firm grip as he squeezes me comfortably into his side. I look up from their joined hands into Silas's face, gawking at the warm smile he casts on Grant and Bennett.

"The photographer," he offers, "*and* Palmer's boyfriend."

The look on Grant's face at this revelation is something I wish I could have bottled and kept on my shelves for the next time I'm having a bad day. He looks so stricken. So disbelieving. So jealous. His whole body tenses, and his shoulders square as if some primal instinct arises in him to fight for me. And while I know it is petty and silly and entirely unhealthy of me, the look delights me. Part of me still wants Grant to fight for me, even if the battle is long lost.

He's getting married, I try to remind myself. *I need to move on.*

But even if I haven't been able to move on in the last year, in contrast to his rapid and highly successful ability to do so, at least I will have this moment to hold onto. At least I know, from the immediate and visceral reaction he has to seeing me with someone, that a part of him still loves me. A part of him still doesn't want me to be with anyone else.

"You're the—" Grant says, pausing to inhale sharply, then starts again. "You're the photographer? And you two are—?"

"Dating," Silas confirms with a wide, genuine smile. Grant looks him up and down, from his dark curls to his shiny leather boots. His eyes linger on the tattoo.

"How long?" Grant asks. His voice is clearly meant to sound chill and mildly curious, but instead comes out through slightly gritted teeth. I grin a little in triumph. I snake my arm around Silas's waist, my brain finally catching up to the situation enough to play along.

"About a month?" I say, looking up into Silas's toffee-brown eyes as he looks down at me, as if we are asking each other, *isn't that right, Darling?*

"A month?" Bennett asks with some excitement, clapping her hands together. Apparently, all the fear she felt a moment ago regarding my plot to steal her fiancé has disappeared, leaving only her bubbly personality behind. "That's about when I hired you both! Did you meet because of *our* wedding? Wouldn't that just be so—"

"No," Silas corrects her quickly but not unkindly. "We met a while back on the wedding circuit. We got together after my little sister went in for a cake consultation. She is getting married this October."

The whole story comes to him so easily and naturally, I wonder if part of it is true. *Is his sister getting married in Octo-*

ber? Am I making her a cake? I wrack my brain trying to remember if I met a bride with the last name Howell who would be getting married in October. Nothing comes to mind.

"Oh, how cute!" Bennett gushes. "You two are like a wedding power couple! This is amazing. Isn't this amazing, Grant?"

Grant says nothing. His eyes are entirely fixed on Silas's face, where there is a coy, slightly smug smile pulling at the corner of his lips.

"Oh my God, I have a completely brilliant idea," Bennett says, squeezing Grant's arm, though he does not drop his gaze to acknowledge her. "We should double date!"

These words break Grant of whatever spell Silas has put him under, and he looks at Bennett with a dubious expression. "No, Benny, this is not—"

"It's settled!" she cuts him off with an eager squeak. "How 'bout next Friday? Y'all down?"

I am about to say *absolutely not* when I hear Silas say, "That sounds great!"

I shoot him a glare. I met this man ten minutes ago. Why is he trying to ruin my life?

Grant opens his mouth once more, as if to protest, when Bennett says, "It's settled!"

Grant clears his throat. "Benny, I—"

Bennett suddenly drops the enthusiasm from her face and her voice, as quickly as flipping a light switch. She looks pointedly and seriously into Grant's face, challenging him. "What's the matter? What's a little double date between friends? You two have both moved on, *right?*"

Grant's rebuttal is cut off abruptly in his throat. He presses his lips together as if to keep the words tucked away.

I realize, with the drop in her facade, that the peppy princess persona is an act. She is testing us. She wants us to prove that there isn't anything still between us. And I need to prove it, if I'm going to keep this job.

I squeeze Silas a little closer, wrapping my other arm around his waist in a hug. Somewhere in the back of my mind I register just how sturdy he feels in my arms.

"Of course," I say, with all the enthusiasm I can muster. "We would love to."

Bennett's alter ego returns as quickly as it disappeared. She drags her eyes from Grant's face to shoot me a dazzling smile. "Wonderful! I'll get us reservations at Chez Claire. Eight o'clock?"

I smile feebly, nodding. "Sounds great."

"Well," Silas says with some finality to his tone, "you have to get back to the bakery, don't you, Babe?"

I'm astonished at how easily the term of endearment rolls off his tongue, but I nod gratefully. I unwrap my arms from around him and straighten my tote bag on my shoulder. "Right. I do. Still have that wedding cake for tomorrow."

"Of course," he says, as if this is a detail he has known for weeks, as if we didn't just meet for the first time ten minutes ago. "I'll catch up with you later, then?"

I turn to leave, but he leans in before I can move. He cradles my face gently in one hand, and the action makes my entire body freeze, paralyzed in anticipation of what he is about to do. His thumb brushes my cheekbone before he plants a gentle kiss on my forehead. His lips are incredibly soft against my skin, and though he only maintains contact for a second, the spot on my forehead tingles in his absence.

I look up into his smiling face, a little dumbstruck. I make no motion to move.

"*See you later?*" he urges, and the tone is firmer, as if to remind me that I should be getting the hell out of this house while I still have the chance.

I reclaim the ability to move my legs suddenly and turn,

walking quickly and with purpose away from Grant, Bennett, and Silas without turning to look back. I can feel their eyes on me as I retreat.

When I make my way out the front door, I don't stop, not pausing to consider what just occurred. But my mind is reeling.

How are we going to pull this off?

CHAPTER 2

Silas

onfession time: I knew who Palmer Sullivan was the second I saw her.

Not by name, admittedly, but I recognized her. We have been circling each other, just out of reach, never actually meeting, for months—maybe even years, I bet.

I can't remember the first time I saw her, exactly, but I can recall the last dozen or so times I have seen her. She has made herself prolific on the wedding scene this past year. We have been hired for the same gigs so frequently that we might as well have set up a package deal by now. I can only imagine, based on how often I have seen her myself, the sheer volume of weddings she must have undertaken during this time. I have to admire the hustle, of course, but there is another small detail I can't possibly overlook about her.

She is, perhaps, the most stunningly beautiful woman I have ever seen in my life.

It was impossible to miss at first, but the constant and repeated exposure to her has somehow only compounded her effect on me. I would be at a venue, setting up my supplies or taking practice shots, and there she was—lining the dessert table with cookies or cupcakes or putting last-minute decorations onto a cake. I'd catch a glint of her golden hair from the corner of my eye, and when I turned to get a better look at her, I couldn't bring myself to look away. Even from across a room, she had one of the most remarkable faces I'd ever seen.

I had to force myself to look away eventually. I'm a professional, after all, and I have better ways to spend the hours leading up to a wedding besides gawking at another vendor.

But then, she just kept appearing. One wedding after the next repeatedly, until I simply began to assume that when I looked up at a cake table, she would be there. I realized, only recently, that I was starting to feel the faintest twinge of disappointment when it *wasn't* her.

It wasn't like me to let a beautiful woman catch my interest from afar for months and do nothing about it. After all this time, I knew I should have just done the logical thing and gone up to her to introduce myself. I had never had a problem approaching women before—they're just people after all, and I usually have no trouble starting conversations.

But Palmer Sullivan was also a professional. She always arrived promptly, set up her desserts quickly and efficiently with delicate, well-practiced hands, and got out. She was obviously a busy woman, her work in high demand. Watching her assemble her creations from across a room, there was something in the intense focus in her eyes and the rigid line of her posture that made her seem... unapproachable? But that wasn't the right word. Impenetrable? Also questionable.

Palmer seemed to exist in her own world while displaying her cakes, a world above all of us mere mortals. I didn't go up to her because it didn't feel right—to break her focus, to break into that world uninvited.

Until today, that is.

The Barlow engagement party was the closest I had ever

come, just ten feet away from her. So close I could see the bright green of her eyes as she looked over her work.

I was working myself up to finally do it, to put a name to that incredible face, but all I could seem to do was look at her.

I could practically hear my best friend Cal's voice in my mind mocking me—*Take a picture. It'll last longer.*

Defying all logic and reason, that's exactly what I did. I took a picture.

And now, here we are, from strangers to fake partners in less than ten minutes.

Everything had been going so well, too. One minute we're flirting, the next second I manage to entangle myself in a clearly messy situation involving the people paying my rent. Was it one of my smarter moments? No. Was it the kind of chivalrous act my mom would be proud of, if she were still here? Absolutely.

I just couldn't stand by and watch it happen—watch them gang up on her. It was like watching a baby deer stare into the face of the eighteen-wheeler as it was about to run her down. She bumped into the groom, and her whole expression changed in an instant. She went from this sexy, confident being into the meek, frail creature that visibly shrank beneath the stare of Grant Foster.

What a waste. I don't understand it. How does someone as vanilla, as cookie-cutter retired frat boy as Grant Foster get not one, but two of the hottest women I have ever seen? Bennett Barlow is not only exorbitantly wealthy, set to inherit the entire Barlow Hotel empire someday, but looks like she could win a fucking Megan Fox lookalike contest.

And Palmer redefines the word gorgeous. Bennett has the literal face of magazines, whereas Palmer's beauty is... unexpected. Bennett has the perfect symmetry and hourglass shape that only endless amounts of time and money can buy, yet somehow, Palmer is so much more interesting to look at. My job is to find the exact combination of lighting and position and camera settings that can bring out the best in someone. But with Palmer, it's like all the work has already been done for me.

And somehow, that completely conventional, soggy piece of Wonder bread convinced them both to fall in love with him.

The injustice of it all is enough to drive a man crazy.

When I heard her flailing to name a boyfriend that clearly did not exist, I became that imaginary boyfriend.

Now, why I agreed so enthusiastically to go on a double date with her ex and his new fiancée, both of whom are our employers, is a different question. That is probably something I should discuss with my therapist. Maybe it reflects some superhero complex I didn't know I had; some desire to save this woman again.

All I know for certain is that I do want to see her again. I already feel it like a craving.

When I'm in my car after the engagement party, I open my phone intending to call her, but my heart sinks when I realize I never got her number. *Damn it, why didn't I get her number?*

But I remember then that I gave her my Instagram handle. I open the app to several dozen notifications; the usual likes combined with new followers and message requests from brides. But there, toward the top of my inbox, is Sweet P Bakery. The message is just a phone number, followed by the words, "call me."

Yes, please.

I don't even wait. I save the number in my phone and call her. She answers on the first ring.

"Hello?" she breathes.

"Hello, darling girlfriend of mine," I say, my lips curving into an amused smile. "I've missed you."

She utters a surprised laugh. "Silas. It's you."

The way my name sounds in her voice is delicious. Addicting.

"It's me."

"What are you doing right now?" she asks. "Can you come by the bakery?"

"I think that's a great idea." I start the car and plug Sweet P Bakery into the GPS. "I'll be there in fifteen minutes."

"See you soon," she says before we hang up.

Fifteen minutes later, I park in front of a pink storefront with a white-and-green-striped awning, sandwiched between equally bright facades of blue and purple. The second I walk through the door, I'm hit with the most incredible smell. And I realize that it is also Palmer's smell—a decadent mix of vanilla and almond and caramel. It makes my mouth water.

The interior of the bakery is decorated in similar colors as the exterior—white and pink and pale, mint green. The counters and tables are white and gray marble patterns, and there is a wide display case with cupcakes, pastries, and a few ready-made, beautifully decorated cakes.

The woman behind the counter is scrolling on her phone when I arrive. Her brown hair sits atop her head in a messy bun with a pencil stuck through it. She looks up with a bored expression, but when she sees me in the doorway, she sits up straighter, suddenly at attention.

"Welcome to Sweet P," she says, though she sounds expectant, as if she suspects who I am. "How can I help you?"

"I'm here to see Palmer?" I reply as a question. "I'm Silas—"

She flashes a wide and entirely evil grin. "The fake boyfriend. God, you *are* freakishly tall. Palmer's in the back."

I resist the urge to laugh as she gestures to a white kitchen door behind her. I join her behind the counter, but as I'm placing my hand on the swinging door to the kitchen, she stops me.

"I'm Jenna, by the way." She reaches out to shake my hand, and I return the gesture. She adds, "Palmer's best friend and business partner."

I smile. "Nice to meet you."

She gestures to the door again, as if I'm wasting time, as if she wasn't the one who stopped me in the first place. I push into the kitchen.

Palmer's there at the center of the room, leaning over a silver worktable. She has a pink apron tied around her waist, and her black jeans are adorably smudged with white powder—flour or powdered sugar, I imagine. I realize with some amusement that she has an almost perfect impression of one delicate hand outlined over her back pocket—a perfect handprint traced over what I realize is an incredibly perfect ass.

She carefully pipes a pattern of tiny buttercream shells in rows onto a large white cake. There are two identical, smaller tiers beside it. When it's done, it will be a three-tiered masterpiece of old-fashioned buttercream. It's incredible. *She's* incredible.

She is also intensely focused and doesn't realize I'm there behind her. I stand mesmerized, watching her make art out of sugar, when I realize suddenly that we are not alone.

One of the big ovens in the corner slams shut. A man several inches shorter than me and thin, with cropped, sandy brown hair places a tray full of cake tins onto the counter. His jaw drops when he notices me standing in the doorway.

"Oh my God," he says with a slow smile. "If you don't want him, Palmer, I'll take him."

I'm tempted to laugh, but I am distracted when Palmer whirls on the spot. Her expression passes through a diverting series of emotions—surprise, delight, embarrassment, back to delight.

"Silas," she gasps, a little breathless. "How long have you been standing there?"

"About three minutes," I reply. "I didn't want to disrupt your work."

She shakes her head in surprise, laughing. "I'm sorry. I just get so focused. Sometimes I have no idea what is going on around me."

I believe it. All those times I saw her at weddings, nothing seemed capable of diverting her attention away from her work.

Palmer looks at the other baker, her expression a little desperate. "Evan, would you please—"

"Get lost?" he finishes, then breathes a very dramatic sigh. "I *guess*. I'm basically done, anyway. Take these out of the pan when they're cool, would you?"

"You got it," she replies, watching him carefully as he hangs up his apron and leaves.

As soon as the door swings shut behind him, she springs into motion, pulling two stools over to the counter closest to me and gesturing for me to sit with her.

She takes a deep breath, opening her mouth as if to speak, but no sound comes out. She tucks a stray lock of dark blonde hair behind her ear, glancing away from me as she searches for her next words. She crosses then uncrosses her legs.

"Where to begin?" I ask to fill the awkward silence.

She lets out a shaky laugh. "Where, indeed?"

"I guess it's safe to assume that Grant Foster is your ex," I begin.

She nods. "He is."

"And you agreed to make the cake for his wedding," I continue.

She nods again. "I did."

"And your motivation for doing so was...?" I ask, almost afraid to know the answer.

"The same as yours for taking the job, I imagine?" she retorts, a little defensively. "It's the wedding of the year. Maybe the century. I can't pass up that kind of opportunity for my business. No matter *whose* wedding it is."

The wedding of the century, I think. I consider for a moment how that must feel, for your ex to move on so spectacularly after you. I have a few exes who are married now, to —as far as I am aware—seemingly ordinary people. No heirs to any household names. No one who had ever been featured in a magazine's "Celebrities: they're just like us!" section before. She addresses the situation with such a distant, practical approach. I'm not sure if I would be capable of looking at the situation so logically, if I were in her shoes.

"You don't want him back?" I ask.

She winces at the question, as if it strikes a physical blow, and I immediately dislike this feeling, knowing I caused her pain. But it feels like a question that I deserve to know the answer to if I'm going to be involved in this charade.

She hesitates for just a breath, then says, "No."

I raise an eyebrow, unconvinced. "Are you sure about that?"

She shakes her head. "I *don't* want him back. We weren't right for each other. We didn't want the same things—"

"I'd feel better if it didn't sound like you were trying just as hard to convince yourself as me," I insist. She lets out a frustrated groan.

"It's complicated," she explains. "We were together for three years. I thought we would get married someday, but obviously, that didn't happen. We've barely been broken up a year. But I know now that we shouldn't be together. And I promise you that I didn't take this job as some plot to win him back. I really didn't. But it would be unfair to lie to you, so I'll admit that I'm not completely over him."

I nod, mollified by the confession. I believe her, even if it is not exactly what I want to hear. What I want to hear her say is, *that man is dead to me, and I'm ready to thoroughly move on, preferably with you.* But if I can't have that, at least I get honesty.

Feeling resolved, I say, "The goal then is to keep Bennett Barlow happy and convinced that you're not pining after her man for the next six months?"

She breathes a relieved exhale. "Exactly."

"Okay," I say. "I'm in. I will be your fake boyfriend until the wedding. I will be there whenever you need, for whatever performances are required to convince Bennett Barlow that you don't have the hots for her fiancé."

She narrows her eyes, her gaze instantly mistrustful. "That easy? You don't even know me."

I shrug. "I'd like to."

Obviously, this isn't the most ideal situation to get to know the woman I have been pining after, but it's the situation I'm in.

She purses her lips, suspicious, even though her cheeks start to glow with the hint of a pleased blush. "It can't be that simple. You have to get something out of this arrangement, too."

Here is the part that I have been waiting for. The part that I have only hinted at, that has been in the back of my mind since the second I saw her at the engagement party that afternoon.

"There is something I want," I admit. "I wasn't lying about my sister's wedding before. She is getting married in October, and she did get a quote from you a month ago. You're just a little out of her price range."

"A cake?" she asks, blinking in surprise. "That's what you want?"

It's what the doting older brother inside me wants, yes, and it's a good enough excuse. But what I really want is the opportunity to know the woman who has enthralled me for the better part of a year. It seems pathetic to admit I would have done it for free, though.

Instead, I say, "Not just *any* cake. I want Emery to have her dream cake. Whatever she wants, for whatever she can pay you."

She smiles in relief, as if she had worried my price would be much steeper. "I'll do you one better. I'll give it to her at cost. Just pay for the materials, and the labor will be free. It's the least I can do for you bailing me out like this."

I smile widely at her. Emery is going to go nuts about this. Emery is stubborn by nature, prideful. With both our parents gone now, she and her fiancé Charlie are paying for their entire wedding, even though I begged her to let me contribute. While she adamantly refuses to let me outright pay for any part of her wedding, she does, however, love a bargain. She will gladly take whatever discount or connection I can find for her from my friends on the wedding circuit.

I reach my hand out to Palmer. "It's a deal."

She looks at the offered hand for a short, wary second before placing hers in mine, her skin warm and soft.

"It's a deal," she echoes, shaking my hand firmly.

"I guess we should set some ground rules, then?" I ask.

"Ground rules?" she repeats, concern evident in her tone.

"So that we're both comfortable with the arrangement."

"Okay..."

"Ground rule number one," I begin. "We keep the true nature of our relationship between us. We don't tell family or friends it's fake. To help sell the act."

This is very specifically for Emery's sake. I don't want her to think I'm bribing anyone to get her wedding paid for (even though I *would* do just about anything to give her the wedding of her dreams.) I can already see her happily accepting a gift from my new girlfriend, however.

She winces. "About that. I *may* have already told—"

"Your friends?" I ask, chuckling. "I know. Jenna called me 'the fake boyfriend' when I walked in."

The door to the kitchen suddenly swings open a few inches, and a distant voice sings, "Don't worry! Your secret is safe with me!"

"*Jenna Rhodes,*" Palmer scolds, in the authoritative voice of a mom with her teenage daughter. I had heard that tone turned on my sister many times before. Palmer looks at her watch. "The shop is closed. Get your ass home to your husband and stop eavesdropping."

I can hear her distant cackle through the wall, and a few moments later, the tinkling bell over the front door chimes as if she has left.

Palmer sighs. "I'm sorry. Jenna and Evan know, but that'll be the end of it, I swear. I don't have many friends outside of the shop, anyway, and no family in town."

"That sounds lonely," I remark.

She shrugs, her eyes roaming fondly around her kitchen. "I basically live here, but it's my happy place. Jenna and Evan are the two best friends I could ask for, anyway."

I can't judge her for sticking with a few close friends when I do the same.

"We were working on ground rules, right?" she reminds me. "I suppose our second ground rule should be that we keep things strictly professional until the wedding. We put on the act in front of Grant and Bennett, but outside of that, we'll just be friends."

I wonder if she notices the corner of my lips dipping downward into an involuntary frown for the briefest second, because she adds, "Probably shouldn't mix up any real feelings into this, right?"

I straighten my spine, trying to look just as casual and confident as she does when I say, "Right. Of course."

It's for the best, I know. She may have seemed attracted to

me at the party, before this enormous monkey wrench was thrown into the mix, but she is admittedly hung up on her ex. These six months of being her friend will allow me to evaluate just how tangled up her feelings really are for him.

In turn, I'll use this time to grapple with my own feelings, to figure out once and for all if this attraction to her is capable of being something more.

I track the slow sweep of her gaze as it travels up my chest, settling back onto my face. Her tone is light, almost unnaturally casual, when she says, "After the wedding, though... we can reevaluate?"

A little jolt of electricity courses through me at the thought that she might be as attracted to me as I am to her.

"After the wedding, we can reevaluate," I agree.

Her answering smile is hesitant but so unbearably sweet and hopeful that it knocks the breath from my lungs.

The next ground rule comes to me suddenly. I hold up the number three. "Third ground rule. Neither of us can date other people while we're fake dating each other."

Her face scrunches in concern. "I can't ask you to do that. It's not fair to you, to put your life on hold for that long."

"I can go without sex for six months, Palmer," I assure her. Her cheeks turn adorably pink in response.

"God forbid anyone see us out with someone else, and it gets back to Bennett Barlow," I warn. "Both of us would probably be out of a job if she finds out we lied to her.

She nods. "That makes sense."

Besides, just because we've resolved to remain friends for the next six months, doesn't mean I want her dating anyone else in the meantime.

"Any other ground rules to add?" I ask, but she shakes her head.

"Those seem reasonable," she replies, standing from her stool and brushing her hands over her pink apron. For a moment, it seems like she might dismiss me to return to her work. But we're only getting started.

"We have a double date to prepare for, don't we?" I ask, grinning wickedly.

Her eyes widen, as if she is just remembering this detail. "A *double date*. Hell, why did we agree to this? How are we going to convince them we have been dating for a month?"

"We have a week to study," I reassure her. "In fact, why don't we start now? Go for a walk with me?"

She looks over at her cake, seeming initially unwilling to part with it. But she scans my face for a long moment and seems to decide I'm worth it. She carefully brings her cake to the industrial refrigerator and exchanges her pink apron with a sweater off a hook by the door.

She leads me out onto the street, stopping to lock up the shop behind her. We amble past the rows of colorful buildings, the wind wafting the faintest hint of salt and seaweed in our direction.

"So..." she starts, a little awkwardly. She pulls her sweater tightly across her chest, as if shutting herself off, even though we just promised to open up to each other.

"Another ground rule," I say firmly, thinking of it on the spot. "We have to be honest with each other. At least, whenever we're alone. We're going to be doing enough lying to everyone else, might as well be honest with each other."

She nods slowly, chewing on the idea. "Okay. Honesty it is. I'm an open book."

For some reason, I doubt that. Palmer seems less like an open book and more like some sacred ancient text locked in chains, kept in a tower, and guarded by a fire-breathing dragon. Thankfully, I'm not afraid of a challenge.

"Let's start on some easy questions," I say. "Rapid fire. Don't think—just the first thing that comes to mind. Favorite color?"

"Green," she replies, but clarifies, "Soft, pale green. Like in the shop."

She hits me with the full force of her wide, sparkling, emerald green eyes, impossibly bright in the waning light of dusk, and I am suddenly tempted to change my favorite color on the spot. But honesty is what we promised.

"Navy blue," I respond in turn.

"Favorite movie?" she asks.

"The Longest Yard."

"Titanic," she supplies.

"Age and birthday?" I ask.

"Twenty-eight," she answers. "And December twelfth. You?"

"I just turned thirty-one on February seventh," I reply.

She pauses just a half step in her pace at this news. "Happy Belated Birthday!"

"Why, thank you," I reply. "You know, a good fake girl-friend would have made me a cake. I'm partial to chocolate."

The corners of her eyes crinkle with quiet mirth. "I'll make it up to you sometime."

"What's your favorite flavor?" I ask. "What does a baker want on their birthday?"

She puts a hand to her chest, in mock offense. "Asking me to pick a favorite flavor is like asking a mother to pick her favorite child."

"Pick one," I repeat.

"I can't! Besides, I don't expect anyone to bake for me—"

"*Pick one.*"

"Fine!" she throws her hands in the air in defeat, but her smile is wide, her eyes bright with amusement when she admits, "Boxed yellow cake with chocolate frosting!"

I stop in my tracks, leering at her in shock. "Boxed cake?"

She cringes, looking sheepish. "I know. It's blasphemous. But my mom couldn't cook or bake worth a damn, and it's all she could manage when I was a kid. It's my guilty pleasure."

I shake my head, reeling at the idea of a professional baker wanting *boxed* cake. "Your mom clearly didn't teach you what you know, then. Where did you learn?"

"The internet, mostly," she replies. "And baking shows."

I whistle, impressed. "Wow. Self-taught."

She shrugs, downplaying how impressive this is. "How'd you pick up photography?"

"My mom got me my first camera when I was a teenager," I explain. "I loved it, so I took some courses in college. Then I started working for a wedding photography company here for a couple years before I started my own business."

We continue like this, wandering down the street together as we attempt to stuff ourselves with as much knowledge of each other as we can possibly fit. I can almost feel her steadily relaxing beside me with every step we take, every laugh over our likes and dislikes and pet peeves. I realize, when we've been walking for nearly forty-five minutes, how much I'm enjoying myself. How every layer of herself that she reveals is more fascinating than the last. Palmer is witty and interesting and easy to talk to, once she lets her guard down.

We run into Murray Boulevard and cross the street, stopping to admire the expanse of ocean sprawled out ahead of us. Palmer braces her hands against the railing, closing her eyes with delight as the sea air tickles her cheeks. The evening is growing dark, with streaks of orange and pink stretching across the sky. This lighting is perfect. I can't imagine a type of lighting exists that doesn't make her look beautiful, but she looks particularly remarkable right now.

She opens her eyes and sees me staring intently. She flashes a tentative smile.

"This is my favorite time of day," I comment.

"Dusk?" she asks.

I nod. "Golden hour. A bit cliché for a photographer, I know, but it's our favorite for a reason. There's something about the light just before sunset that's so soft. No harsh lines or shadows. You just seem to glow."

I realize only after I have said it that it doesn't sound like I'm using the term "you" to mean "anyone." It sounds like I'm talking very specifically about *her*. And maybe I am.

She breathes in sharply, looking momentarily flustered by my words.

"Do you want to grab something to eat?" she asks. "There's a great Greek place near here—"

"Yia Yia's?" We say at the same time, with equal delight.

"I love Yia Yia's," I reply with a grin. "Honestly, this might be a fantastic idea. Yia Yia herself has been trying to set me up with her last unmarried daughter for years. Maybe meeting my 'girlfriend' will finally get her off my back."

She laughs. "I have good news for you, then. I made her youngest daughter's wedding cake six months ago."

I shrug. "Probably for the best. If I stayed single much longer, I was considering marrying her daughter just for the food."

"I'd marry her daughter for those gyros too," she agrees without judgment.

Not twenty minutes later, we are sitting inhaling those very gyros, pausing between bites to continue our rapid-fire get-to-know-you questions.

"Any siblings?" I ask.

"Two much younger half-brothers, on my dad's side," she says, and I notice she quickly moves past the topic. I take a mental note to follow up on that later. "You just have the one sister?"

I nod, smiling to myself. "Emery. She's six years younger."

"Wow, that's a pretty big age gap. Were you close growing up?" she asks.

"No, not when we were growing up," I say. "We are now though."

I take a deep breath, knowing where this conversation will inevitably lead. I know she *needs* to know, if we're going to act like we're dating. It just feels heavy to talk about, even now. And it feels like a quick transition to go from our favorite colors to my dead parents in the same evening.

"Our mom got sick when I was a teenager. Ovarian cancer. It kind of forced us to be close. Mom died when I was twenty-two, and our dad randomly died less than a year later of a ruptured aortic aneurysm. We were all each other had after that. Emery was seventeen, and I legally took custody of her for a year."

Palmer gasps, and I wince a little. I know it's a sad story—I lived it. But I didn't tell the story to gain sympathy from her, to make her feel anything resembling pity for me. It just feels impossible to explain my relationship with Emery without this history.

She says, "Oh my God, Silas, I'm so sorry—"

"It's really okay," I assure her, "but if you want to make me feel better, you can always tell me whatever your tragic backstory is."

She laughs at my wry tone, my attempt to lighten the mood. "Not nearly so tragic. Both my parents are alive, just very, *very* divorced. Which is for the best. They're both much happier now. My dad lives in Savannah with his new wife and my half-brothers. And my mom is married to a lovely woman —they own an art studio in Myrtle Beach together."

It still feels like there's more to the dynamic than she's letting on, but I'm guessing I'll have to earn that over time.

We continue to talk, trying to find as many details of our lives to share with each other as possible, until Yia Yia merrily shoos us out at closing time.

Even when we've had our fill of dinner, I realize I haven't

had my fill of Palmer. I don't want our evening together to end. But I remember that cake she was working on when I stole her away from her shop, how desperate she looked to complete the work. I offer to walk her home.

When we make it back to the pink building with the green and white awning, she looks inside the dark shop and back to me. "Well, this is me."

I ask, "You're going to work on your cake more tonight?"

She shakes her head. "No, I'll finish the cake in the morning. I actually live here. There's an apartment on the second floor."

"When you said, 'I basically live here,' you weren't kidding."

She shrugs. "Not the most glamorous place in town, but the rent was included with the bakery."

"Makes sense," I say.

She fiddles with her keys for another moment before she starts to turn away. But I'm not ready to say goodbye to her, not just yet. Not ready for this night to end. I clear my throat.

"You know, there is another ground rule we should probably address before Friday," I say, and she pauses in her retreat.

"Oh?" she asks.

"We should probably set some expectations for what's allowed. Physically, I mean," I remark.

She laughs, crossing her arms over her chest and leaning casually against the pink bricks. "I doubt we'll need a safe word. I can't imagine a scenario where we would need to get truly physical to sell the relationship."

If that's the truth, she doesn't have an imagination nearly as good as mine. I can imagine several scenarios, even if they're not particularly realistic. But that isn't what I mean.

"I mean we should probably set some expectations about what we're willing to do to sell the relationship," I explain. "Will we hold hands?"

"Of course," she says quickly.

"Put our arms around each other?" I take a step closer to her, leaning against the wall beside her.

"Naturally," she confirms. "We did that within minutes of meeting each other."

"Kiss?" I ask, grinning down at her.

She hesitates for just a moment, her lips pursing, clearly fighting a smile. "I imagine the circumstance will arise where we might have to kiss, yes."

"And if we *have* to," I emphasize her phrasing, as if it would pain me to be forced to kiss her. As if kissing her isn't all I can think about, looking at her in the moonlight. "Where do we draw the line?"

I catch the slight hitch in her intake of breath. "I guess... we do whatever the circumstance calls for?"

"And don't you think," I begin to ask, reaching up to brush a stray golden strand of hair behind her ear, "that it would be ill-advised to have our first kiss be in front of an audience? To risk looking terribly awkward and unconvincing when it really matters?"

She searches my face, her eyes sparkling and wide.

"I guess," she whispers, "you might be right."

"So, naturally," I continue, "don't you think we should practice before then?"

I'm pretty sure she has stopped breathing, but she manages to say, "I suppose so..."

And while it's not the emphatic yes I may have wanted, I'll take what I can get. I rest my hand against the side of her neck. I lean down until I can feel her breath warm against my lips. Her body freezes, daring me to make the first move.

I am typically the one in a relationship to initiate, and I test the waters as I usually would. I brush my lips against hers, careful and slow, giving her the chance to pull away and end it if she wants to. But she doesn't. She exhales through slightly parted lips like a sigh, and I take that as a good sign.

I want to go further, to deepen the kiss. But this is supposed to be an experiment, a *practice kiss*. Just a moment to test the waters on our physical compatibility before venturing into the public eye. I slow my movement with every intent to pull away.

But the reserved being I had been coaxing to open up to me for the last few hours suddenly flees, leaving behind a woman who knows what she wants. I had expected her to return with a shy, tentative press of her lips to mine.

Oh, how wrong I was.

She suddenly melts into my chest, deepening the kiss. She presses her body against me and angles her mouth more firmly over mine. She moves like she's been waiting for this. Her hands lift to my chest, her fingers curling into the fabric of my shirt. She's kissing me like she has something to prove.

Her kiss is soft and sweet, but with incredible heat beneath it. It's intoxicating. My pulse spikes instantly at her touch. Her fingers flex against my chest, like she's fighting to pull me closer, so I help her. I wrap an arm around her waist and tug her body up to mine, until she's standing on her tiptoes to reach me. She lets out a small, surprised sound at the action, but it only seems to encourage her.

And I feel like I'm coming undone. Like she will be my undoing.

I started this kiss in control, confident, leading—but Palmer doesn't seem like one to just *follow*. She's pushing back, matching my energy, and suddenly I'm the one struggling to keep up with her. I thread my hand into her hair, feeling like I need the anchor in the storm she has unleashed in me.

Time seems to exist in a vacuum for us. It doesn't matter that we are standing on the street for anyone to see—no one else exists.

I truly don't know how long we are there, tangled in each other. But we break away from each other suddenly, almost aggressively, as if an unseen force has torn our bodies apart. Her eyes flutter open, and for a long moment, we just stare at each other, gasping, trying to make sense of what just happened. I stumble backward a step, alarmed by the tumult she has unleashed in me.

I've never felt anything like this. *Ever.*

She straightens, her expression suddenly casual. She smooths her hands down the front of her sweater, like she's trying to brush away whatever just happened.

"Well," she says, her voice steadier than I would have thought possible, "that should be convincing enough, don't you think?"

CHAPTER 3
Palmer

I plop a twelve-inch round of fluffy, pink strawberry cake onto my turntable, followed by a huge dollop of white buttercream. My beveled spatula turns the sloppy mound of frosting into a perfect, thin disc as I rotate the table with my free hand. One after the other, I assemble the layers: cake, frosting, filling, repeat. When the cake is assembled, I stick it in the freezer, fetching the smaller tier from inside. I start to cover the smaller tier in another layer of frosting.

My mind never feels as calm, as quiet, as when I'm decorating cakes. The routine is comforting, smoothing all the rough edges from my thoughts. The world fades away, and it's just me and my work.

"What are you doing?" I look up at the sound of Jenna's voice, momentarily snapping out of my trance.

"What does it look like I'm doing?" I turn back to my cake as I smooth out the lines and imperfections with my bench scraper.

"Not getting ready?" she responds with righteous indignation.

I look at the pink clock mounted on the wall. Friday at five o'clock—closing time. "The date is in three hours."

"And you need every second of those hours, ma'am," she insists, crossing the kitchen to stand beside me. She plants her fists on her hips. "Look at you."

I pause, looking down at myself. I don't know what my jeans and sweater did to offend her.

"What could I possibly spend the next three hours doing? All I need to do is change, throw some makeup on, and do my hair. That takes me an hour, tops."

She impatiently taps her foot. "Yeah, maybe for your typical look. This is not a typical night. How often do you simultaneously need to impress your hot new boyfriend and make your old one jealous in the same evening?"

I put my bench scraper down with a sigh and turn to face her, meeting her steely gray, disapproving stare. "Let us be clear. He is *not* my new boyfriend, as you know. And I'm *not* trying to make Grant jealous! I am only going so that we don't lose a paycheck."

She rolls her eyes, turning and heading for the door. "Fine, then. Don't listen to me. Show up to dinner looking like *that*. It'll be a good reminder to Grant of just how much of an upgrade he has now with Bennett Barlow."

I sigh, smiling to myself as she slows at the kitchen door. She looks as if she might be about to leave, but I know she's not going anywhere. Jenna lives for relationship drama. It's almost a shame that she fell in love with her college sweetheart, her first everything. Contented monogamy is *so* wasted on her. She would have reveled in a messy dating life, had true love not hit her like a bus at the tender age of nineteen.

"Jenna, would you like to help me get ready for my date?" I call.

She is back at my side before I can even finish my sentence, yanking me off my stool.

"I thought you would *never* ask," she gushes.

I pull my arm from her grasp to take my work-in-progress off the turntable and return it to the fridge.

She latches on to me the second I return, pulling me toward the exit.

"Okay, so there's not much time, but I'm thinking we may just be able to fit in a blowout, nails, and a wax before Silas picks you up."

"A *wax*?" I squeak, disbelieving. "Jenna, this isn't even a real—"

"But then what are you going to wear? Shopping, first," she continues, ignoring me.

"I'm sure I have something to wear,"I stress.

"I have seen your entire closet, Palmer Anne Sullivan."

"Not the middle name," I grumble.

"It has barely changed since the day I met you," she carries on as if I said nothing at all. "And nothing you have is good enough for a night like this."

When we walk through the doors of a boutique twenty minutes later, I am surprised to see Evan there, already holding a stack of dresses in his arms as he peruses the racks of clothing.

"Evan?" I ask, not displeased to see him. Evan has been a godsend for the last few years since we hired him. It took me a while before I was able to let go and allow someone else to make my recipes, but now I can't imagine life without him. He has made it possible for me to focus all my time and energy on the decorating. I would trust Evan with my recipes, my life, and definitely my wardrobe.

He offloads his stack into my arms. "We don't have much time. Get started with these. I'll bring more options to the dressing room."

I laugh, trying to peer at him over the mound of clothing in my arms. "How did you even know we were here?"

Jenna explains, "I sent him ahead for reconnaissance. We needed reinforcements."

He turns me by the shoulders and pushes me firmly toward the dressing room.

We spend a comical amount of time in front of the mirror outside the dressing room until we find an outfit that meets my friends' discerning tastes—and more importantly, my budget.

A few hours later, I stand outside the bakery, wearing a form-fitting green dress with sheer fabric over the arms and in wide panels down my sides. I curled my hair in waves to my shoulders. The only other concession I made to Jenna and Evan after the dress was to get my makeup done at a Mac bar. No nails. Definitely no wax.

Silas pulls up in his black truck, parks, and gets out of the car to greet me. He looks incredibly handsome in a navy suit with no tie. He slowly sidles toward me, taking in the whole look with an approving nod.

"Wow," he whispers with a coy smile.

I look down, my cheeks warming.

"*Wow*," he repeats, emphasizing the word even more. "You're telling me I have to *pretend* to be attracted to you to keep my end of the bargain?"

My answering smile is radiant. He looks at me with such genuine, fervent appreciation that it makes me realize that I missed this—having a reason to get dressed up, having someone recognize the effort. As much as I love nights on the couch watching movies with Jenna and Evan in our sweatpants, I'd forgotten how much fun this could be.

"Pretty much, yeah," I reply.

"How will I manage it?" he asks, opening the door for me.

I look back at him with a smile as I take the offered passenger seat.

The warm, pleasant feeling that Silas elicits in me starts to steadily fade the closer we get to the restaurant. By the time we pull into the parking lot, my stomach feels like it has been wrapped in knots several times over. He parks and walks around to open the door for me. He extends his hand to me with a smile, and my stomach lurches uncomfortably.

He makes it easy to picture how good this could be. He is so handsome it's heart-wrenching, kinder than I could hope for. We could be here, just the two of us, enjoying a nice meal together. A normal date.

Instead, I feel like I'm preparing to walk the plank, ready to jump into shark-infested waters with an open wound.

I take Silas's offered hand, though he doesn't drop it once I'm out of the vehicle. He laces his fingers through mine instead.

"Ready for this?" he asks with a grin.

I take a deep breath. "Not even a little bit."

"Relax," he says with a gentle squeeze of my hand. "I'll be right beside you the whole time."

I exhale, and his words manage to settle some of my unease. At least if I'm bound for dangerous waters, it's nice not to do it alone.

Chez Claire is one of those restaurants so upscale that they don't need to pack it with people each night. It's small, intimate, with no more than twenty tables. A pianist plays a soft, flowing melody from the corner of the room. The waiters circulate quietly, wearing starched white shirts and thin black ties.

When we were dating, Grant's salary so egregiously surpassed my own that I never got comfortable with the idea of letting him spend his money on me. He used to beg to take me on dates in places like this.

And, here we are, going on a date. With other people.

Grant sees me across the room, considering there's nowhere to hide. The second he sees me, he stands from his chair abruptly—like he's the prince in the fairytale, and I'm the princess descending the staircase at the ball. It sends a jolt of something hot and painful through my heart.

This was such a terrible idea.

I freeze as his eyes fix on me, and I drop Silas's hand subconsciously. But despite my stricken reaction, Silas doesn't miss a step. He settles his abandoned hand on my lower back, leaning in close.

"Kiss me."

The words don't register in my mind for a long second. I feel like I'm stuck, paralyzed beneath Grant's stare.

"What?" I ask, my voice sounding distant and confused.

"Kiss me," he urges again. He pulls me in by my waist.

I panic, hyper-aware of Grant's eyes fixed on me from across the room. A part of me begs, *don't do it. This will hurt him.* And hurting him isn't what I came here to do. But when I glance at the table where he is waiting, I see that Bennett has stood alongside Grant, likely to be polite. She looks unsurprisingly stunning in a fitted black dress.

And suddenly, the panic clears. *He* broke up with *me.* He is the one who moved on within weeks of our breakup. I shouldn't feel guilty about any of this.

With suddenly concrete resolve, I turn back to Silas, lifting a hand to his face before brushing his lips with mine. It's not nearly as long a kiss as we shared before, but I couldn't imagine stopping in the middle of a restaurant to kiss someone like that. Even so, it is soft and sweet. Not only does it make me smile with delight, but it drives away the panic and the worry and the guilt broiling inside me almost instantly.

Something slightly wicked flashes in Silas's eyes as he draws away. He leans in a second time, his breath brushing against my ear, his voice dripping with amusement as he says, "If he's going to look at you like that, might as well give him a show."

I shake my head at his antics and let him lead me to their table.

Bennett throws her arms around me as soon as I'm within reach, startling me. "Sweet P! You made it. I love your dress!"

I nearly laugh at her insistence on calling me by my moniker, even now. "Thank you, Bennett. Thanks for inviting us."

I force a smile to my lips, even though I could not be any less thankful for the invitation.

Silas and Grant shake hands stiffly, mumbling greetings.

When we settle at the table, I open the menu, more to avoid eye contact with Grant than anything. My stomach drops to the floor at the sight of the prices. *I guess I'll be having a glass of water with a side of air.*

"Oh, don't worry about the bill," Bennett says quickly, as if she saw my eyes go wide at the menu. "My family always has a running tab here. Get anything you want."

A prideful piece of me wants to decline the offer, but that part is instantly stifled by the knowledge that I can't afford to refuse.

"That's very generous," I say quietly. "Thank you, Bennett."

She smiles warmly, asking, "Okay, now that I have you in my clutches, you *must* tell me—how did you come to be such a talented baker?"

I look at her perfect manicure, the pointed and painted tips of her claws, and instantly find the imagery of me being trapped in her clutches to be a little too close to the mark.

I take a sip of water and shrug, muttering lamely, "Lots of practice."

"Incessant amounts of practice," Grant adds under his breath, not looking up from his menu.

I resist the urge to glare at him. I wondered, before coming tonight, what the vibe would be between us. Resentful is what

I should have expected, I suppose. And I know that it's warranted, his resentment. But a part of me had been holding onto a glimmer of hope that a year of distance from our breakup—not to mention his gorgeous, millionaire fiancée sitting beside him—would mellow his bitterness toward me just a little. I suppose that had been a bold assumption to make.

Silas puts one hand over mine on the table, squeezing it. "You can't get to be as good as Palmer without incessant amounts of practice."

"I bet," Bennett says, with complete sincerity. "How did you get started?"

The waiter takes this moment to fill my wine glass, and I take a long sip, grateful for the moment to collect my thoughts.

"I loved baking shows when I was younger, so I started experimenting for myself—cupcakes, cookies, brownies, at first. I found it relaxing, stress-relieving, in a time where it felt like I was always stressed," I explain. "Then I started trying my hand at cake decorating and realized I could make money doing this if I got good enough. I practiced day in and day out. I taught myself everything I know from watching videos online."

"And look at you now!" Bennett enthuses, as if she is genuinely proud of me and how far I've come, as if she has known me since I was that anxious teenager spending every dime she had to spare on flour and sugar.

Look at me now, indeed, I think with dark amusement. *Bonding with my ex's stunning fiancée.*

Bennett leans forward, her eyes wide with interest. "Jenna is your business partner, right? When did you two meet?"

"We were roommates in college," I respond. "We went to USC."

"*Jenna* went to USC," Grant amends, scowling over his wine glass. He looks pointedly in the direction of the pianist.

"We *both* went to USC," I correct.

"But only Jenna finished," he supplies coldly. I narrow my eyes in his direction, though he still adamantly refuses to meet my gaze.

"I didn't finish," I relent. I can feel my chin lift subconsciously, defiantly. I refuse to act embarrassed about this fact. I explain to Bennett, "I didn't see the point in it. I was baking so much just to help pay for school, only to be hopelessly bored in class. I decided I might as well commit myself fully to the thing that truly made me happy."

This is the moment when Grant finally makes eye contact with me, and his stare from across the table feels sharp, accusing, at my choice of words. He doesn't say it out loud, but the look is loud enough—*glad you can commit to something. Glad something makes you happy.*

I don't know if Silas senses the tension steadily building in my shoulders, but he drapes an arm around me in this moment, his thumb brushing my shoulder. I feel just a bit of the strain ease with the motion. Grant tears his eyes from me again at the gesture.

"That's amazing," Bennett says, completely unfazed by the dynamic between her fiancé and me. Maybe she doesn't notice it. "I *wish* I had something I loved like that. I graduated from the University of Alabama as a communications major." She laughs prettily. "I spent a lot more time *communicating* with football players than going to class, though."

"Did you go to a lot of the games?" Silas asks, expertly navigating the conversation into safer territory.

"I went to every game," she says, then adds with a wink, "Never wearing the same number though."

She looks at me with a wicked gleam in her eye, as if I can relate. I don't think I have ever related to anything less.

"Maybe we crossed paths," Silas says with a grin. "I played tight end for Clemson. I'm sure I graduated a few years before you, though."

This launches a full debate between Bennett and Silas regarding the merits of their respective college football teams that mercifully gets us through ordering and awaiting our food's arrival. I suppose that in all her time "supporting football players," Bennett gained a genuine appreciation for the game. She talks strategy, coaching staff, and recruitment with just as much knowledge and appreciation as Silas.

They find a lot to talk about, though I know their college years never overlapped. Silas is thirty-one to Bennett's twenty-six. I know her exact age because I Googled her when the news broke about their relationship. And while two years is hardly older, it certainly felt like I was being traded in for a newer model at the time.

"So how does one go from star tight end to photographer?" Bennett asks.

Silas laughs. "Star is incredibly generous. I was second-string, at my best. But I'm like Palmer, I started taking pictures when I was a teenager. My mom had terminal cancer and put me in charge of preserving as many memories as our family could get together before she passed."

Bennett nearly melts at this admission, and I feel a similar sharp pang of sympathy and admiration in my heart. He told me bits and pieces of the story—his mother's diagnosis, how he started experimenting with a camera in high school. But he hadn't linked the two together for me before this moment.

"Have you ever considered franchising your bakery?" Bennett asks me suddenly over the last bites of her branzino. "I just think your shop is so cute, and obviously the desserts are amazing. I think it would do so well."

I purse my lips. "Jenna has mentioned it before. I'm not so

sure, though—it feels like we just started getting comfortable. I don't want to mess that up, you know?"

Grant remarks, "Palmer isn't a big fan of taking risks."

"I don't know about that," Silas responds coolly, taking a sip from his wine glass. "In my experience, she is well-versed in going outside her comfort zone."

I can practically feel the resentment radiating from Grant at this remark.

"It takes a lot of guts just to start your own business, I bet," Bennett says. "That's a big undertaking."

"You must know a bit about that yourself, Bennett," Silas says kindly. "You're involved in your family's company, right? That's more than a business; that's a whole empire."

Bennett flushes a little. "Dad doesn't really involve me in the important stuff. Mostly just planning parties."

Grant's steely expression softens, and my heart gives an uncomfortable flutter when I see him fix a tender look on Bennett. "Don't sell yourself short, Benny. You're brilliant at what you do."

She flashes him a grateful smile. "Thanks, Babe. But I want to do more. I'd love to do some investing myself."

I expect Grant, an actual investment banker, to have some thoughts on this matter, but he looks away, falling instantly back into that cold and distant trance, where he remains for the rest of the meal.

A part of me is angry with him for acting this way, so childish and petulant. I know it's not fair to expect him to spend time near me and my "new boyfriend," when he's supposed to be reveling in the joy of his upcoming nuptials.

But I'm here, watching him move on. And I can smile. I can be civil. I can talk to his fiancée—who is delightful, I hate to admit. For a woman with the most unrelatable lot in life I can imagine, she makes herself seem admirably relatable, inexplicably down-to-earth, and kind. If she weren't the new love of my ex's life, I could see us being friends.

Grant seems to breathe an audible sigh of relief when we finish dessert and finally leave the restaurant. He takes Bennett by the arm and leads her, just a bit faster than is polite, out the front door, handing his valet ticket to the waiting attendant.

He opens the passenger door of his Porsche for Bennett, and she takes the seat with a smile and a wave in our direction. When he closes the door behind her, he turns to us.

Some of the cold and the distance melt from his expression in Bennett's absence, and a bit of something sharper settles over his features as he takes a good look at Silas.

"Well," Grant says, his tone icy. "This was… something."

Silas smiles brightly, unfazed by the tone. "It was. We should do it again sometime!"

Grant looks at Silas like he has just grown a second head.

"See you at the tasting," I say feebly.

Grant looks alarmed. "The what?"

"The cake tasting," I repeat. "To decide the flavors for the wedding. Bennett set it up for next month."

"Right," Grant replies, in a slightly annoyed tone that I'm certain means he was completely unaware that he had another appointment to see me. He turns back to Silas. "See you at the wedding, I guess."

Silas nods, curling a hand around my waist and drawing me into his side. "See you at the wedding. And who knows? Maybe after that, it'll be our turn."

Grant looks me up and down, unable to hide his true feelings any longer. "Somehow I sincerely doubt that."

He walks to the driver's side and departs into the night. I stand there for a long time, silently fuming. I know I had been a lost cause to Grant, but did he have to go and spoil me for anyone else, too?

"Wow," Silas says, filling the silence. "The guy still seems pretty bitter."

I let out a slow breath. "With good reason. I suppose I should let you in on the secret before too long—I'm unlovable."

"Now, I *highly* doubt it," Silas replies.

"And yet, it's true," I say with a sigh.

"I'm going to need just a bit more explanation if you're going to drop a bomb like that."

"Then, I'm going to need a drink," I say, feeling incredibly worn down from the evening.

"I know a place," he offers.

After a short drive, we walk into a bar not far from my bakery called Full Proof. We stop just inside the doors, and I can't help but admire the high ceilings decorated in oak barrels, the tables and booths filled with patrons, the huge Edison-bulb light fixtures, the shelves above the bar lined with rows and rows of whiskeys. I look over at Silas, only to find him watching me, waiting anxiously for my assessment. Like he's showing me his favorite movie and waiting for my reaction to the best parts.

I break into a wide grin. "Now *this* is a bar."

His shoulders sag with relief at my approval.

We settle on two stools, and immediately one of the bartenders approaches, with more grace than you would expect for a true Goliath of a man. I have to lean backward to see all of him—his copper red hair and full beard, his impressive height, his enormous chest so wide that it looks the size of a small vehicle. I'm too stunned at the sight of him to ask for a drink.

"Dude," the man says, smiling broadly at Silas. "I didn't know you were coming in tonight!"

"It wasn't planned," Silas explains. "We were in the neighborhood. Cal, this... is my girlfriend, Palmer. Palmer, this is my best friend, Cal. He owns the bar."

Silas's best friend. He took me to meet his best friend. That's why he looked so nervous about me approving the place. I grin up at the man warmly.

Cal's eyes light up at the sight of me, and a broad grin stretches across his face when he turns back to Silas. "Dude. Girlfriend? Why didn't you tell me?"

He offers a hand to me, and my hand feels impossibly tiny in his massive palm.

"Callan McLean," he introduces himself. "But everyone just calls me Cal."

"It's so nice to meet you."

"Si and I played at Clemson together," he explains.

Silas adds, "Cal was O-line."

"I mean, I suppose I should have guessed." I gesture to his massive form.

Silas laughs. "Cal was way better than I was. He played for the Carolina Panthers for a few years before he tore his ACL."

"But look where just a little NFL money can get you." Cal gestures widely to the bar, glowing with pride.

"It's a beautiful bar," I agree. He flashes a wide, very pleased smile at me.

"And for *that*, your first drink is on me. What can I get you?"

I gesture to Silas. "I'll take whatever he's having."

Cal doesn't bother asking Silas what he's having, immediately fetching two lowball glasses and preparing our drinks with practiced ease. He slides the two nearly identical amber drinks toward us—the only difference between them is an extra cherry in my glass.

"I should have named this Old Fashioned the Silas Howell with how many I've made your boyfriend over the years," Cal says with a wink. "Enjoy."

When he turns to tend to the rest of the bar, I lean into Silas, whispering conspiratorially, "Does the extra cherry mean he likes me?"

Silas grins, clinking his glass against mine. "The amount Cal likes you is directly proportional to the garnish."

I take a sip and hum in appreciation. Damn, that's a good drink. And I don't typically gravitate toward whiskey beverages, but in a place like this, I figure, *when in Rome.*

"So," Silas prompts. "How many drinks is it going to take to unpack the *unlovable* comment?"

I sigh heavily, lifting my glass. "Just the one emotional support beverage should be enough."

He takes a slow sip from his glass, watching me from the corner of his eye as he waits for me to begin my story.

"You asked for my tragic backstory. And I told you, in simple terms," I begin. "But I probably undersold just how much my parents' divorce really screwed me up. My parents described the beginning of their relationship as a whirlwind. My mom was studying art abroad in Paris. My dad was vacationing there. And after just one week together, she moved back with him to Georgia and immediately started a life with him. They got married and had me all in less than a year. But they couldn't have been more polar opposites. My mom is a free spirit; an artist who suffers doing anything resembling a normal job with a steady paycheck. My dad is a strait-laced, quiet man who sells insurance. And when she had me, it's like she was stuck. She didn't make enough money from her art to provide for us, so when it became abundantly clear that they weren't meant to be together, she had nowhere to go. She was trapped. And she resented my dad. Resented her life. Resented me, I'm sure, though she never said so explicitly."

Silas whistles. "That must have sucked, feeling like that as a kid."

That was an understatement.

"It did," I agree. "And I know she didn't want to make me feel that way. She loved me—*loves* me. But somehow it always felt like it was then *my* job to make *her* feel better. To make her feel less guilty."

Silas shakes his head, "That's a tough job for anyone, much less a little girl."

"And *so*," I say, bringing us back to the thesis, "as my therapist likes to say, I have trouble being emotionally vulnerable with a partner and relying on someone. Knowing it derailed my mom's life to do so."

Silas gestures between us. "Is this not you being vulnerable with me?"

I laugh, leaning forward to whisper, "This isn't a real relationship. Remember?"

He doesn't answer, just grins and takes another sip of his drink.

"Grant was incredibly patient with me, waiting for me to be comfortable with the idea. I finally agreed to move in with him after two years. But it wasn't enough, in the end. *I* wasn't enough to make it work."

Silas doesn't acknowledge this, instead asking, "You said your mom remarried?"

I smile brightly, thinking of my stepmom. "Margot. She's wonderful—the best thing that ever happened to my mom. She takes all my mom's eccentricities in stride; keeps her grounded without bringing her down, you know? She really makes my mom the best version of herself."

Silas looks a little smug, a little triumphant, as he says, "Huh. It's almost like the *right* person makes you feel like you're enough just the way you are."

I sputter a laugh. "Wow. That... That was good. Smooth."

He grins, lifting his glass to mine. "Just something to think about."

I clink my glass against his and take another sip.

CHAPTER 4

Silas

I have been sitting here in our favorite booth at Cal's bar for half an hour, passing the time by scrolling through the Sweet P Bakery Instagram page.

It wasn't a conscious decision, really. My subconscious mind has been unusually attached to my phone for the last two weeks—fueled by the allure of seeing another text message from Palmer Sullivan waiting for me on my screen. But tonight, Palmer is busy finishing a bridal shower cake, so her texts haven't come with the frequency I have grown accustomed to. In the absence of her conversation, I find myself wandering through her social media, as if needing to fill the space with her.

If I'm being honest with myself, what I really want is to see her again in person, but since I have no good excuse to seek her out, pictures will have to do.

Most of her Instagram page contains images of cakes, as one would expect. But interspersed throughout the images are rare glimpses of Palmer, proudly holding one of her creations or smiling at Jenna under the front awning of their shop.

I pause on one particular picture of her and linger there,

unable to scroll past. In the image, she is sitting at the table nestled in the window of her shop, wearing a white and blue floral sundress that looks, in the very best way, like something a German milkmaid would wear; with a low neckline fastened with a little bow nestled between her cleavage. Her hair looks longer than it is now, falling in soft waves over her shoulders. There is a tiered dessert stand of cupcakes in front of her, and she plucked one cake off the stand for the picture, sampling the frosting with her finger. Her green eyes are wide and impossibly bright, looking at the person behind the camera.

I wonder to myself who took the picture; whose idea it was to pose her like this. Whoever it was, that person was a God damn genius. And I can't help it—I admire them. Envy them. Want to be them. I want to be the one who took this picture of her, the one on the other side of that lens who she is looking at so fondly.

"Oh, thank God you're here!"

I drag my eyes reluctantly from her image at the sound of my sister's voice.

Emery zooms across the bar, giant white binder in hand. When she slides into the booth beside me, I quickly hit the power button on my phone to turn the screen dark. Emery's fiancé Charlie greets me with a, "Hey, man," as he slides into the booth across from us.

"I need alcohol," Emery declares as she settles in. She flops her giant wedding planning binder open on the table before us. It is thick with color-coded tabs filled with lists and budgets and inspiration boards for each aspect of her big day.

"Rough day?" I ask her, smirking at the flustered expression on her face. She is subtly shaking her head, her dark brows furrowed, her eyes darting across the laminated pages. She blows a stray curl out of her eyes.

"Wedding planning is ruining my life," she laments, very

dramatically. But Emery doesn't really have a mode that isn't dramatic.

I look to Charlie to explain, since he speaks fluent Emery and can always translate her moods. His lips pull into a grimace. "Just got done talking to the florist about a quote."

"They're far, *far* more expensive than I budgeted for," she says with a huff. "I'm going to have to cut the florals in half compared to what I originally wanted. Maybe just have the bouquets and the centerpieces. And even then, I'm going to have to find somewhere else in the budget that we can cut back, if we even want that."

I think fondly of what's sitting just behind the lock screen on my phone, waiting for me. And I suddenly can't wait to share the good news with her.

"Actually, I can think of the perfect place for you to cut down the budget," I suggest.

She scours my face like she is lost at sea, and I have just offered her the one and only lifesaver in a hundred-mile radius.

"Where?" she asks, looking back down at her binder desperately. That analytical brain of hers crunches the numbers, trying to figure out what crack in the algorithm I could have found of which she would not already be aware.

"The cake," I suggest, purposefully withholding further explanation.

She shakes her head, her curls bouncing, as she insists, "I still haven't narrowed it down between these three bakeries, but there's no way to—"

"You're not using any of those bakeries," I cut her off. "You're getting a three-tiered cake from Sweet P Bakery. Nothing else will do."

I quote an Emery from many months ago, the one who originally recited all her wildest wedding dreams to me before the cruel reality of "the wedding budget" became a factor. She looks at me wide-eyed.

"But I can't afford Sweet P Bakery?" she questions, knowing that I'm dangling the reveal just out of her reach; like when we were little, and I'd play keep away with one of her dolls.

I managed to secure quite a few freebies and discounts for her along the way so far—one of my buddies was doing her photography and videography; I had secured her a big discount on the DJ; Cal was providing a lot of the booze and two of his bartenders. We were scraping together quite the dream wedding from our combined efforts. But there were a few big budget items that we hadn't yet found any loopholes for—the venue, the dress, the florals, the cake. Until now, that is.

"You'll be getting the cake at an incredible discount," I attempt my best impression of a used car salesman. "The baker has offered to give it to you at cost. Just pay for the ingredients, and the cake of your dreams will be yours."

Her whole face suddenly glows with awe at the prospect. A slow, disbelieving smile stretches across her face.

"Silas?" she asks with delight. "How did you—?"

"It's called the sleeping with your brother discount," Cal jokes as he approaches our booth, sliding a gin and tonic in front of Emery and a beer to Charlie, before taking the open seat beside Charlie. Charlie scoots over to make room for Cal's massive form.

Emery and Charlie go completely, deafeningly silent in the wake of this statement. I wince to myself before shooting a disgusted glare at Cal.

"Seriously, dude?" I ask.

Once Cal's words sink in, Charlie and Emery have directly opposing reactions. Charlie breaks into a wide grin, clearly delighted for me. Emery's surprise collapses into a look of devastated betrayal.

"I'm sorry, what?" she directs her question at Cal, bypassing my input.

Cal nods, seemingly unaware of the wrath that he has brought upon himself, even after all these years of knowing my sister. He takes a handful of pretzels and mixed nuts out of the bowl between us and pops them into his mouth, chewing loudly. "Silas's new girlfriend? He's dating that baker you're always going on about."

I narrow my eyes at him as I await the onslaught from my sister.

"You're new *what*?" she murmurs, her tone dangerous.

I set my glare on Cal like daggers. "Cal, why do you do this to me?"

His eyes dart between my face, glaring at him, and Emery's, glaring at me, like a tennis match. "What? I thought she knew!"

"*Now* she knows," I supply dryly.

"You have a girlfriend?" she seethes, "A girlfriend! And you didn't deign to tell me? Your one and only sister. Your flesh and blood. The one living member of our family you have left?"

I sigh. "Okay, that's all a bit dramatic, Em."

"When were you planning on telling me about her? At your wedding? Maybe at the birth of my first niece or nephew?"

Charlie mouths the words *I'm sorry* over his beer at me, knowing there is little he can do to quell my sister's anger at this stage in the process. He can diffuse Emery better than anyone, but the match has been set on the fuse, and I can only pray it fizzles out before it gets to the explosion.

"It's not that big of a deal!" I argue.

"Not that big of a deal?" she repeats, over-enunciating each word. "You haven't had a real girlfriend in years. This is colossal news!"

"What do you mean? I've dated several women over the last few years."

"*Several* being the keyword," Emery insists. "You've become a bit of a fuckboy, if we're being honest."

Cal chuckles an aggravating, knowing little laugh, as if picturing all the women I have brought by his bar over the years. I glare at him again.

"I have not," I protest, but Cal and Emery both shoot me very withering stares. Even Charlie, as gracious as he is, raises one eyebrow in my direction while sipping his beer. That's how I know it's bad, when Charlie can't help but judge me. Charlie is the least judgmental person I've ever met, only after my mother.

Seeing their looks, seeing how very *aware* they have all been of my dating history without ever commenting on it, makes me wonder if maybe she's right. I haven't been trying to be that type of guy, the kind of guy who gets around. I just haven't found anyone who sparked my interest beyond a few dates.

It's not that I don't want something long-term. That initial spark of attraction just fizzles out every time I start dating someone. I meet a woman, flirt, take her on a date or two, sometimes—not every time—sleep with her. And somewhere in that process my interest just seems to die, a quick and unceremonious death.

I'm temporarily stunned as I process this realization. Is something wrong with me? It's not like I have some opposition to monogamy or some inherent desire not to find the woman of my dreams. I want that. I want what my parents had. But why had it all just seemed so inconceivable to me for such a long time now?

I sigh, relenting, "Okay, so maybe I haven't had a steady girlfriend in a while. Sue me. None of those women was the one, okay?"

I say this statement without realizing the implication of my words. I regret them instantly when Emery lets out a stricken gasp, as if I have stabbed her. Her tone is both offended and delighted as she says, "Are you saying she is *the one*?"

I nearly forgot, in all my panicked reflection about my unintentionally sordid dating life, that the subject of this conversation was my supposed serious girlfriend. As far as they are concerned, someone *has* sparked my interest and held it long enough to become my steady girlfriend.

"It's still early," I insist, trying to get my sister off my back.

I idly wonder if maybe this ruse we're trying to pull off, this experiment I'm conducting, might be good for me. Maybe this will prove, once and for all, whether I'm capable of going the distance. Of holding a woman's interest and having her keep mine for more than just a few weeks. I have six months just to get to know her, to enjoy spending time with her. Nothing to muddy the waters. No easy exit routes. *Definitely* no sex.

But just the thought sends my brain into a dangerous line of fantasizing that I instantly fight to reign back in. My brain pulls the image from her Instagram—looking at the camera coyly, the low neckline of her dress... *This is not the time*, I tell that unhelpful part of my brain, the part governed more by my dick than logic or reason.

She is still hung up on her ex, I remind that part of myself sternly. *Do you want to sleep with someone who would be wishing you were Grant Foster the whole time instead? Do you want her just to use you to get over that insufferable J. Crew mannequin come to life? Do you want to be the rebound?*

Yes, that part of my brain replies. *She can use me however she wants.*

Now I'm arguing with myself. I'm going insane.

I turn to Emery, trying to console her. "Look, I wasn't

trying to keep anything from you. I hadn't worked out the details of the cake with her yet, but I wanted to surprise you with both the cake and the girlfriend at the same time."

Somewhere in the back of my mind, I register that this is probably a bad idea; getting Emery all excited and worked up about my new girlfriend. Especially now that this moment of self-reflection has taught me that maybe I'm not the kind of guy that things work out with—not the kind of guy a woman ends up with forever.

Maybe, somewhere along the way, something broke inside of me. Maybe I'm destined to never find *the one*. Palmer is talented and beautiful and easy to talk to, everything I could possibly want that woman to be. But she is still in love with someone else.

Emery presses her lips into a dissatisfied line, not quite mollified. "I can't believe you're dating the person who runs my favorite bakery in town, and I'm the last to know."

I roll my eyes. "You're the second person to know."

"After *him*," she retorts, pointing an accusing finger at Cal, like he hasn't been my best friend for the last ten years.

Cal only grins, clearly wanting to stoke the flames further. He must think that he, in his massive 300-pound frame, is impervious to my tiny sister's particular brand of terror. That he may somehow come out of this unscathed. But my sister is scrappy.

"It's not so much that I wanted her to meet Cal before she met you," I explain. "She lives and works just a few blocks away, so the bar seemed like a logical place to go."

"You wanted her to see this dump before she met me?"

All three of us—Cal, Charlie, and I—roll our eyes, groaning in offense.

"You don't call it *this dump* when I'm giving you free booze," Cal argues, some of his amusement fading with the grave insult to his baby.

But he knows she doesn't mean it. Emery loves the bar. We all do. This is where we have, for the last five years since Cal opened, celebrated all our victories, mourned all our losses, watched every sporting event we cared about, and passed our boring Tuesday nights together. We didn't even drink half the time. It wasn't about the alcohol; it was about the people. This was our home.

Emery redirects her energy back to Cal suddenly, her voice growing high-pitched with her excitement. "What's she like?"

"She's hot and seems nice," he replies through another mouthful of bar mix.

Emery drops her forehead to the hard table with an audible thud that sounds painful. She groans. "This is why I should have met her first. Men suck at details."

"What do you want to know about her?" I ask through laughter.

"What does she look like?"

My mind instantly pulls her image into my mental view, and I break into an involuntary grin at the sight.

"Gorgeous," I begin. "A few inches taller than you. She has this sort of dark blonde hair that falls to her shoulders. She usually has it pulled up though, since she works with food. She's got the most incredibly bright green eyes with little flecks of gold in them. A cute little button nose that she scrunches a little when she's focused on her cakes, and—"

I realize suddenly that the three of them are staring at me wide-eyed as I'm rambling on, with mischievous grins creeping steadily across their faces.

"What?" I ask, taking in each of their wry expressions in turn.

"That was... descriptive," Charlie remarks.

"I was literally just asking to see a picture," Emery says with a far-too-knowing smirk. "But oh my God. She *is* the one."

I look anywhere but directly into her eyes, feeling my cheeks heat. "I told you. It's new."

"When do I get to meet her?" she begs. I roll my eyes, turning my attention to my future brother-in-law.

"Charlie," I say, desperate to change the subject, "how's the new job?"

Charlie opens his mouth to speak but doesn't get a single syllable out.

"Silas," Emery says. "When do I get to meet your girlfriend?"

I sigh heavily. "Soon."

"When is soon?" she probes.

"Soon," I repeat.

"That's not good enough," she complains. "I need to know. Text her. Ask her right now!"

There are times in my life when my relationship with my sister feels mature and adult, befitting two grown siblings. This is not one of those times. She makes me feel like a teenager again, shirking her desperate attempts to hang out with me and my friends after football practice, when she was barely out of braces.

"I'm not texting her right this second," I say.

"Give me her number then. I'll ask her myself."

"Absolutely not," I nip that idea in the bud immediately. Palmer may not have much choice about this relationship at the moment, but the last thing I want is to immediately scare her away with my overbearing little sister.

"Then ask her," she repeats. We stare each other down for a full minute. Her chin juts forward stubbornly.

My shoulders deflate, defeated. There is no winning with my sister. In the end, she always gets her way. And I know I'm going to have to introduce them eventually. I pick my phone up off the table and pull up Palmer's contact. I realize with some concern that Emery is staring over my shoulder, trying to see my message to her. Luckily, our existing conversation seems perfectly appropriate for a new relationship.

I type a message to her, keenly aware of Emery analyzing every letter.

> Hey Babe

"Babe" has become our trigger word, the word that can instantly turn on the charade at a moment's notice.

PALMER
> Hey 🩶

I know it's part of the act. But the sight of that little heart beside her name does something to me. Makes something in my chest ache.

> Cal might have let it slip to my sister that I have a girlfriend...

PALMER
> Oh? How'd she take the news?

> She's holding me hostage until she gets to meet you.

The "..." with her pending reply sits there on the screen for a long time, and I can practically feel Emery holding her breath beside me waiting.

PALMER
> Is she free next Sunday for lunch and hostage handoff?

Emery squeals with delight.

CHAPTER 5

Palmer

"You planning to pay for those?" Jenna asks dryly as she watches me assemble a four-pack of cupcakes from the display case.

"Take it out of my paycheck, Boss," I shoot back, rolling my eyes.

I second-guess the combination of flavors a dozen times, wondering if I should go for the most popular ones, my personal favorite recipes, or the most interesting flavors. I obsess over the choices for several long minutes before I finalize my selections—red velvet, lemon, vanilla, chocolate. The classics.

"I see we're employing the way-to-a-man's-heart-is-his-stomach technique," Evan remarks, swiveling lazily on a barstool behind the counter, carefully scrutinizing my outfit with a discerning eye. "That, and the boobs, of course."

I groan, tugging self-consciously at the neckline of my dress. "The cupcakes aren't for Silas. They're for his sister and her fiancé."

"But the boobs are definitely for Silas," he amends with a nod.

I huff in annoyance. "Evan, you were done with the baking hours ago. What are you still doing here?"

"Are you kidding? I'm here for the show!" he insists with a grin, leaning his elbows on the counter.

There's a fluttering sensation in my stomach as I look out the front door of the shop, waiting for the black truck to appear. "Joke's on you then, because I'm running out the door the second he gets here. I'm not going to let him be harassed by you two."

"Come on!" he protests, pressing a hand earnestly into his chest. "We'll be on our absolute best behavior!"

"That's not saying much," I mumble under my breath. Jenna snorts while counting bills in the register.

"You seem really worked up about meeting the sister," she remarks. "Considering you're *not really dating* and all that."

I fuss unnecessarily with the bow I have tied around the cupcake box. "Silas and Emery are very close, and she believes we are really dating. I want to make a good first impression."

"Close like... *Game of Thrones* close?" Evan asks, his voice dropping into an ominous whisper.

I shoot him a death glare, unable to suppress a reluctant smile. "No. Not like *Game of Thrones* close. Like he took care of her after both their parents died."

"Okay, now I feel like a jerk," he admits, his teasing grin dropping suddenly.

"As you should," Jenna retorts.

Just then, his truck pulls up, and my stomach does another uncomfortable flip at the sight. "He's here."

"Don't worry," Jenna reassures me. "She'll love you. And even if she doesn't, you always have boobs and cupcakes to keep him around."

"No straight man can resist that," Evan adds helpfully.

"Okay, bye!" I call, ducking out the door. My goal is to make it to the truck before Silas can emerge from the driver's side, but my hopes are in vain. Silas parks the truck and walks around.

He looks me up and down, laughing at the sight of my dress.

"What's so funny?" I ask, inspecting my outfit with some dismay. "You don't like the dress?"

He shakes his head but fishes his phone out from the pocket of his jeans. "I love the dress. So much so that I made it my lock screen."

There on his phone is the picture of me in this very same dress from the Sweet P Instagram page. The sight of it makes a flush rise in my cheeks. I can remember taking the picture vividly—I had fought Jenna on it at the time, telling her I didn't want to be in the photo, that the food should be the focus.

Sex sells, she argued.

I let out a shaky laugh. "Wow, you sure know how to do your homework."

He nods with a satisfied grin. "I'm an excellent student."

"But that leaves us with an awkward conundrum," I muse. "I don't have a picture of you for my lock screen."

He grimaces, his hand drifting upward to clench over his heart. "You mean to tell me you didn't spend hours stalking my social media for the perfect one? I'm hurt."

I imagine Silas scrolling through pictures of me for hours, deciding on his favorite, and there is a fluttering sensation in my stomach.

I admit to it before I can bother to be embarrassed, "I *did,* but your Instagram is all pictures of other people!"

He grins. "I'm meant to stay behind the camera."

I'm wondering how someone with his face—his molten caramel eyes and model-worthy jawline—can possibly be unphotogenic when he takes a purposeful step toward me.

My whole body freezes when he leans in. His hand lifts my

chin, steadying it as he closes the distance between us. At the last moment, he turns my face to the side, planting a kiss squarely on my cheek. I look up in surprise to see his phone poised in front of us to catch the picture.

He draws away, showing me the photo he just took. It's a perfect, adorable picture, of course. Is he capable of taking a bad shot, even a dumb selfie?

He airdrops the image to me. "There. Now you have a picture for your lock screen. Not to mention, we gave your friends a nice little show."

I look up with alarm at the door of the bakery, seeing Jenna and Evan nearly pressed against the window, watching us intently. Silas waves at them in greeting, shooting them a friendly smile as he opens the door of his truck for me. I shake my head and flip them the bird as I settle into the passenger seat. As he pulls away from the curb, I set the picture he took as the lock screen on my phone.

When we walk into the restaurant ten minutes later, I spot Emery immediately. She's hard to miss. Seeing her makes me want to see pictures of their parents, to see where they got such favorable genes. Emery jumps up from her chair the second she sees us approaching, her brown curls bouncing as she nearly vibrates from excitement. She pulls me into a hug the second I am within arm's reach.

"You don't know how excited I am to finally meet you." She beams at me with those same toffee-brown eyes. "You're so pretty. Si, you didn't tell me how pretty she was!"

"I'm certain I did, actually," he says warmly, and I flush with embarrassment and just a little delight. A very silly, girlish part of me dwells on the idea of Silas telling his sister that I'm *pretty*. The idea of him telling his sister—the most important person in his life—anything about me makes me unexpectedly giddy.

And just as suddenly, I feel guilty. Silas warned me about

his sister, how emotionally invested she gets in everything she does, especially matters involving her brother. It leaves an uncomfortable feeling in my belly, knowing that there is an edge of deceit behind this meeting. But I slap a huge smile on my face, wanting to share in her delight.

"I'm so happy to meet you too," I tell her.

Her fiancé stands to greet us as well. He's tall, just a few inches shy of Silas, and lean, with a fringe of jet-black hair. He wraps an arm around Emery's shoulders and extends a hand to me, which I gladly shake.

"Charlie Zhang," he says. "Emery's fiancé."

"So glad to meet you, Charlie," I reply. "I'm excited for your wedding!"

"We are so grateful to you for offering to make the cake," he says earnestly.

"It's my pleasure. Really."

At least, if I must deceive kind people, they're getting something out of the deal.

We settle in for lunch, and it only takes a few minutes to realize that all my worry and anxiety over meeting Silas's sister was for nothing. She and Charlie are funny and warm and kind. I worried that, like our disastrous double-date, it would feel like a test. Like Emery would grill us over every detail of our relationship, to prove our worth as a couple. But Emery takes us completely at face value, demanding nothing of us except conversation. Even better, Emery practically tries to sell her brother to me.

"You don't know how glad I am to see my brother find someone," she says, rolling pasta with her fork. "I thought he was a lost cause."

"Wow, thanks, Em," Silas says dryly.

"Why is that?" I ask her with a grin.

"He is *thirty-one*," she emphasizes, as if this should be enough explanation.

Silas rolls his eyes.

"These days, I think getting married at our age is the exception," Charlie says sagely. I learned that he and Emery are twenty-six and twenty-five respectively, just a couple years younger.

"That's getting married," Emery replies. "Which requires a real relationship. Something Silas hasn't had in *years*."

I try to hide my surprise at this revelation, taking an opportunistic bite of gnocchi.

"We can't all find *the one* in college," Silas retorts.

Charlie and Emery look at each other sidelong, in that fleeting way couples who are in love do, and it sends a painful jolt through my chest. I envy that look. There's so much love and trust and understanding in just that one look.

I have never experienced a look like that, not once, and I dated a few people seriously, even before Grant. But Grant never looked at me that way either. I had seen looks of interest, of attraction, of fondness. But never once had anyone looked at me like I was the center of their whole universe.

I suppress a sigh, not wanting to reveal the depth of my jealousy, and ask, "How did the two of you meet?"

Charlie grins like it's his favorite question, and that grin sends another sharp jolt through my heart.

"We were at Duke—I was a sophomore; she was a freshman. I was crossing the campus one afternoon, and it was raining. And there's this girl walking in the rain—walking, mind you, not running to get out of it—completely unbothered that her hair and her clothes were getting soaked. I had a big umbrella, so I went to see if she wanted to share. But she got mad at me—"

"I did not get mad at you," Emery insists with a playful nudge of her shoulder against his.

"She got mad at me for offering my umbrella, protecting

her from the rain," Charlie goes on, unfazed by the interruption. "Then I did the only logical thing."

I laugh. "You left the crazy girl alone in the rain?"

Emery shoots me a playful glare.

Charlie continues, "I folded up my umbrella and walked with her in the rain. Had to see what all the fuss was about."

Emery picks up the story, "And he walked me all the way back to my dorm room, which is where we realized that my roommate was his sister."

"Annie was horrified when her brother and roommate showed up at her door, soaking wet, making goo-goo eyes at each other," Charlie says, seeming delighted at the idea, even in hindsight.

"She came around eventually," Emery adds with a wink. "She's my maid of honor."

When the server brings us two bills—one per couple—Silas snatches the leather bill fold out of my hands, handing it back to the server with his credit card inside before I can protest. And I can't really protest, not with any gusto, because paying for my lunch is a normal thing for my boyfriend to do. I can't make a scene about it in front of his sister, so I resolve to address it with him later. Or, if he refuses, sneak the money into his pocket when he's not paying attention.

On our way out of the restaurant, I hand Emery her box of cupcakes, saying, "This is just a few of the flavors to try. We can do a formal tasting whenever you want."

Emery takes the box and pulls me in for a hug.

"It has been so wonderful getting to know you," she says, squeezing me tight. "I'm so happy you and my brother are together. I'm not sure what it is, it just... it feels like I've known you for years, you know?"

Oddly enough, I do know what she means, which isn't typical for me. I usually warm up to people slowly, taking time to get to know them for months, sometimes years before letting them in. Jenna, Evan, Grant—all of them claim to have pulled me out of my shell. But something about the Howells is just so disarming.

Silas gently puts a hand on my lower back, as if to guide me out of the restaurant, and my entire focus is suddenly pulled to the warmth of his skin seeping through my dress, the press of his palm against my spine. The casual touch, while new and foreign, doesn't feel uncomfortable. He acts like touching me is second nature.

My focus is abruptly brought back to Emery when she suddenly settles a firm grasp around my arm.

"Oh my God," she says, her eyes locked on me. "I have a brilliant idea! You should come look at wedding dresses with me. I'm going to that bougie bridal boutique a few blocks away. How fun would that be?"

Silas attempts to interject, "Now, Emery, she doesn't want—"

"It does sound kind of fun, actually," I say quickly, not wanting to disappoint her, and because I relish the idea of spending more time with her.

"Really?" Emery says with an eager squeal. "You'll come? It won't be long, just an hour or two."

"Sure," I agree. "Are your bridesmaids going?"

She shakes her head. "Nah, they stopped coming after the first eight trips."

I sputter a laugh. "*Eight*?"

She grins wickedly, taking me by the hand, wrenching me from Silas's side to drag me toward the door. She pointedly does not address the *first eight trips* thing.

Which is how I find myself sitting on a cushy white couch with a glass of champagne in hand as Emery tries on one beautiful white gown after another, assessing each option in front of three floor-length mirrors.

After nearly two hours, she steps onto the platform

wearing one of the most beautiful wedding gowns I have ever seen in my life (and I've seen a lot of wedding dresses.) She looks like an ancient sculpture plucked straight from the Louvre. The structured, strapless corset is more detailed than anything I've ever seen before in fabric, with tiny, impossibly intricate patterns woven into the lace. A sliver of golden skin is visible over one hip before the fabric of the skirt begins, draping over the curve of her hip and falling to an elegant pool of satin beneath her. She is breathtaking.

"Wow, Emery," I say with an amazed, breathy laugh. "That has to be the one, right? It was made for you."

"Isn't it incredible? It's a Livie Laurent," she says with a wistful sigh. She turns this way and that, admiring every angle of the dress in the mirrors. "It's too bad I couldn't afford it in my dizziest daydreams."

I shake my head at her. "Why do you torture yourself, coming to a place like this? Trying on dresses that are out of your price range?"

She smiles at me over her shoulder. "I came here just for fun, originally. My plan was to find the style I like, then find a more affordable designer. I started looking months ago. But time is running out, and I just can't find anything that makes me feel the way this dress does. I keep coming back to her. I've tried it on at least half a dozen times now."

"It is an amazing dress," I agree. "I mean this in the most respectful way possible—your boobs look amazing."

"Don't they?" She adjusts the neckline, pushing her breasts upward into an even rounder, more pronounced shape. "Sometimes it feels like a sick joke that God gave me great breasts, only to be forced into a boob job when I'm thirty-five anyway."

I blink in surprise. "I'm sorry?"

She turns, steps off the platform, and approaches me, a river of satin trailing behind her. Her brows furrow. "Silas didn't tell you. I'm shocked he didn't warn you. He accuses me of making it my whole personality."

I shake my head, but I'm too nervous to respond, worried I might reveal an ignorance of something that Silas's real girl-friend should know.

"You know that our mom died of cancer, right?" she asks. I nod emphatically, relieved that I don't have to feign knowl-edge of this detail.

She continues, "She had ovarian cancer; got diagnosed when I was eleven. Silas was in his senior year of high school. Our mom was adopted, so she didn't know much about her family history. But when they were doing her treatment, they tested her for all kinds of genetic disorders for cancer. They found out she had the BRCA mutation, so Si and I were tested too. Silas doesn't have it, but I do. So that means, I have to have everything removed—breasts, ovaries, uterus, the whole enchilada—when I'm thirty-five. If I don't, I have like an eighty percent chance of getting cancer."

The words sink uncomfortably into my heart. I shake my head, stunned. "Emery, I am so sorry. Silas told me about your mom but never told me about this."

She flashes me another grin. "It's okay, really. I've had a long time to come to terms with it. That's why I'm so deter-mined to live life to the fullest, you know? Only so much time any of us has anyway. When you have that added pressure, that clock ticking in your head counting down the seconds you have left with your body as you know it, it changes everything."

I stare at her, dumbstruck, unable to come up with a good response. The moment calls for something reassuring and profound, but the words don't come to me.

Emery takes another long, wistful look at her reflection before she sighs. "I'll go change, and we can get out of here, okay?"

Emery pointedly tries to steer our conversation to lighter topics after that. I stand outside her dressing room, listening through the curtain as she recalls stories from her and Silas's childhood. I'm nearly bent over laughing at a tale about teenage Silas wearing a tutu, when a sharp voice cuts through our laughter.

"That just won't do. Look at how hippy it makes you look! Maybe in college when you were a double-zero, but not now. It just doesn't work."

Emery emerges from behind the curtain at that moment, meeting my eyes with concern.

A middle-aged woman appears from the adjacent dressing room. She is all sharp features—sharp cheekbones, pointed chin, perfectly angled eyebrows. She has clearly attempted to reverse her aging with Botox, but otherwise, her face looks incredibly familiar.

I know instantly whose mother this is by looks alone. A flustered shop attendant peels the curtain back, revealing Bennett Barlow in a beautiful, fitted wedding gown.

"I'm going to pull a couple gowns myself. I don't think this salesgirl knows what kind of gowns are appropriate for *fuller* figures," the woman announces, strutting away suddenly, her stilettos clacking loudly.

Bennett is inspecting her reflection in the mirror, running her hands down the curves of her hips, when she catches sight of me behind her. She startles, her hand flying to her chest like she has seen a ghost in the glass. For a moment, it looks like she genuinely thinks I am one. She whirls to face me, the lace and tulle of her skirt swishing against the floor.

"Sweet P?" she asks, disbelieving. She wipes at her face, and I realize, with a sharp twinge of sympathy, that her eyes are glassy with tears.

I wave a little sheepishly. "Hi, Bennett."

I hear Emery take a sharp intake of breath. "Oh my God. You're—"

Bennett collects herself suddenly at the recognition and smiles weakly at Emery, whose eyes have gone wide and starstruck. She reaches out to shake Emery's hand. "Bennett Barlow. Nice to meet you."

Emery takes the offered hand, looking a little dazed at the thought of Bennett Barlow needing to introduce herself.

I gesture to Emery. "Bennett, this is Emery Howell—"

"Soon to be Emery Howell-Zhang," she corrects.

I grin. "Soon to be Emery Howell-Zhang. She is—"

"Silas's sister!" Bennett enthuses. "The one who is getting married in October. It's so nice to meet you."

I can't help but admire Bennett's incredible memory.

"We were just looking at some dresses for Emery's wedding," I explain. My eyes follow the lines of Bennett's gown, unable to deny how truly spectacular she looks in it. That woman—Bennett's mother—had to have been hallucinating to think the dress made her look anything less than angelic.

"I think that dress looks beautiful on you, Bennett," I say softly.

"Thank you," she says, smiling feebly, the gesture not quite reaching her eyes. "It was one of my favorites online. I asked them to pull it for me. I think it's a beautiful dress."

"I do too," I agree, not lying in the least. I look around in dismay, noticing the decided lack of people Bennett has brought with her.

"Your bridesmaids didn't come with you?" I ask.

She breathes out sharply. "No, I—No. They couldn't make it."

My brows furrow. She looks so resigned, as if she had never expected them to come at all.

At this moment, Bennett's terrible mother returns,

holding a few heavy, clear garment bags in her hands. She pushes them into Bennett's arms, ignoring Emery and I completely. "Now *these* dresses look like they would be more flattering."

I shoot Bennett an apologetic look, backing away from her and her mother slowly. "Well, it was good to see you, Bennett. Good luck with the dress hunt!"

Her face looks pained as she turns away, back to her mother and the dresses she clearly doesn't want to try on.

We leave the boutique, and Emery drives me back to the bakery. She stops to hug me across her center console before she lets me get out of the car.

"Thank you for coming with me today," she says. "I know it's new and all, but for the record, I think my brother *really* likes you."

An involuntary smile tugs at my lips—one of those wide, stupid grins that makes my cheeks ache. I can feel my eyes crinkling with the force of it, betraying how much I want to hear that. Knowing how much I *shouldn't* want to hear that. It's foolish of me to get excited.

"You think so?" I ask, feigning casual interest.

She nods. "I know he always takes beautiful pictures, but I saw that picture he took of you in his apartment."

My breath catches. *His apartment?*

"There's just something about it." She tilts her head, studying me, like she's seeing pieces of a puzzle come together. "It's like you can see the love in it, you know?"

My stomach does a violent flip, and it takes everything in me to school my face, to hide my surprise. *This is a detail I should already know*, I remind myself. *Silas is doing me a favor, putting details into his life to reinforce the act.*

I nod, my throat thick as I say, "Silas does take beautiful pictures."

We say our goodbyes, and I head straight up to my apartment, my mind reeling. I flop backward onto my bed, staring up at the ceiling in a daze.

I can feel my phone like a hot iron burning a hole in my pocket. I want to talk to him, desperately.

But really, what's stopping me? We're friends now. Friends can talk whenever they want.

I take out my phone, only to be temporarily distracted by my new lock screen—the strong line of Silas's jaw, the press of his lips on my cheek, the surprise and delight in my wide, green eyes.

To text or to call? Calling feels riskier. Calling means there is tone and impulse involved—the potential to say something I can't take back. I can consider a text for minutes before sending it, edit it a dozen times if I want to. A phone call feels more serious, more concrete.

But I want to hear his voice, especially when I ask him about the picture.

I click the call button before I can overthink it any longer. It rings once before he answers.

"Hey," he says, his tone warm but concerned. "Please tell me you didn't just get home."

I grin. The tension in my body instantly unravels at the sound of his voice. "I did."

He groans. "I'm so sorry. My sister can be—"

"You don't have to apologize," I assure him. "I had a *great* time."

It's not a lie, either. Despite the uncomfortable run-in with Bennett and the heavy revelation Emery dropped on me at the end, it really was a wonderful afternoon. Emery's infectious joy and sharp humor were irresistible. Truly, I don't think anyone could resist Emery Howell once she decided to befriend them.

He hesitates for just a second, like he is caught off guard, before asking, "You did?"

I nod, then laugh when I remember he can't see me. "I did. Emery's great. I really like her."

"She is great," he agrees, and I swear I can hear the smile in his voice.

"She told me something interesting just now. She told me you have a picture of me in your apartment?"

He pauses even longer this time. "I do."

"Interesting," I comment, trying to sound bored by the idea, even though it thrills me. "I appreciate the commitment to the bit."

He exhales with a soft laugh, but there's something almost nervous about it. "Right. I mean... I'm nothing if not committed to this."

I let the pause stretch just a moment too long before adding, "When she said that, it made me realize something."

"What's that?"

"I've never actually *seen* your apartment."

"That can be easily remedied." His voice drops into that deep place—that tantalizingly smooth inflection that I wish I could preserve in a jar. Calling was the right move.

CHAPTER 6

Silas

"**Y**ou put me right in the middle," Palmer says, her eyes roving across the collage that covers my living room wall.

These photos are my favorites, all some iteration of artists basking in their art. Some are more literal than others—a painter and her brush, a sculptor and her clay, a street artist and his can of spray paint. But I've also included a mother looking lovingly down at her child; a street performer spinning on a broken-down cardboard box; a quarterback clutching the ball to his chest, eyes scanning the distance for his receiver. Every picture is organic; not one is posed, like the subjects are frozen in a single, brief, and beautiful moment, forever.

And at the very center of the collage is Palmer, taken the minute we first met, brows furrowed and lips parted as she inspected her cake.

I have a clear favorite among them.

"I did," I reply.

We are only standing beside each other, looking up at the pictures, but having her in my apartment in such proximity proves to be far more difficult than I could have anticipated.

We stand inches apart, and I can feel her hand next to mine like a magnetic pole, beckoning my hand to cross that space and hold hers.

"I've never seen pictures that make me feel like yours do," she whispers so quietly I almost can't hear the words. But I do. And I wonder if she knows the effect they have on me. My chest grows suddenly tight. I hold my breath, involuntarily. Of all the things she could have possibly said about my work, this feels like the very best—the highest compliment she can pay me. And hearing those words come from her makes me feel suddenly weightless. Like something inside me is glowing.

"You said this was *the real stuff*," she muses. "I see what you mean. Your wedding pictures are beautiful, of course, but this is... different, somehow."

She meets my eyes, and I note with curiosity how the color of her irises has darkened to a forest green. I look at the photo on the wall and back to her again, studying her features in contrast. She decided to keep her hair down today, and it falls in a straight glossy curtain to her collarbones. She wears a little more makeup than when I first met her. Her white top shows just the smallest sliver of skin over her stomach peeking over the hem of her light blue jeans. I wonder idly if she thought about the outfit, thought about how she would look tonight when we saw each other. Even though we aren't calling this a "date," it all feels very date-like.

Seeing her in person, looking even more incredible than the moment I met her, I suddenly feel like the picture isn't good enough. It was a good photo, but it didn't do her justice. I want to fix that, no matter how many pictures it takes.

But how do you ask a woman that? *Please, let me take endless pictures of you until I'm satisfied.* I have never been so obsessed with capturing someone's image before. Is it even possible; to take a photo that might satisfy this feeling?

I realize I must be staring at her rather intensely, because she asks, "What's that look about?"

I tear my eyes from her face, but only to settle my sight on the picture of her. I don't bother lying, don't bother hiding my true thoughts from her.

"I was thinking it's not good enough," I reply. "The picture doesn't do you justice."

She lets out a disbelieving laugh, gesturing to it. "That's the best picture anyone has ever taken of me. You're clearly not a good judge of your work."

I grin. "Maybe. But I was also thinking that I'd really like it if you would let me keep trying. Until it's perfect, that is."

She shakes her head, and her eyes have gone bright again with the force of her smile. "I think you're chasing perfection that doesn't exist."

It does, I think. *I'm looking at it.*

But I think that's enough honesty for one day.

"Let me show you the rest of the place," I say, and I lead her along with me as I show her my apartment. It's a loft-style home, with high ceilings, brick walls, and nearly floor-to-ceiling industrial windows that provide excellent lighting. I have a pull-down backdrop in the corner for shoots with a variety of neutral tones to choose from.

"I've only lived here for about a year," I tell her as we walk through the space. "I lived in my parents' house for several years, until Charlie and Emery got engaged. Now they live there, so I started renting."

"You kept the house?" she asks, as if surprised that a kid straight out of college, doing a gig-based job could afford it. She's not wrong.

I explain, "My mom was a lawyer, so she thought of just about everything. Left us well taken care of. She made it possible to keep the house in the family, and Emery and I didn't want to lose it. I stayed there while she was in college, but I knew she would want it someday. And it's the kind of house you should raise a family in, and she wants one."

"And do you?" she asks. "Want a family, that is."

I shrug nonchalantly, but the question immediately draws to mind the image of kids with my curls and big green eyes that I attempt to stifle immediately. "With the right person, I think I would."

Our last stop is the bedroom, and Palmer's eyes wander over the low bed frame and charcoal bedding. I have purposefully put about four feet of space between us, feeling that having her within arm's reach in this moment would be inadvisable.

"When Emery and I were wedding dress shopping," Palmer says, her tone somber, "she told me about her genetic testing."

I let out a sigh. "It's tough, you know? It's hard not to feel guilty that I don't have the gene. We suffered through everything together. It feels like I'm somehow hurting her by not sharing in this too."

"Sounds like survivor's guilt," she remarks gently. "You know her better than I do, obviously, but it doesn't seem like Emery resents you for it."

"She doesn't," I agree quickly.

Emery went through a *very* resentful stage after Mom and Dad died, justifiably so, but never once was that resentment ever directed toward me. I don't know if I would have been so gracious to her if the roles were reversed.

I realize my thoughtful silence stretches just a little too long. I clear my throat painfully, trying to relax my face, to smooth the worry lines that I know have appeared on my forehead.

"Hungry?" I ask. "I thought I'd make us some dinner."

She looks concerned, her lips parting as if she wants to say something more on the subject, but after a pause, she says, "Yeah, that sounds great."

I lead her to the kitchen, where I start to assemble the ingredients for shrimp linguini. She leans against the counter beside me, filling the time and the space with her voice and her laughter as I chop vegetables and whisk the sauce. We settle into a rhythm that feels natural, easy—wonderfully yet painfully domestic—in a way I've never consciously longed for.

But I realize with some fear and excitement that this feels good, how easily two people can orbit one another. Existing near Palmer feels as natural as breathing.

I bring a spoonful of the sauce over for her to try, admitting, "Now I may not be as good a chef as you are, but give it a try."

She leans in, looking up at me from beneath her lashes, as she whispers, "Can I tell you a secret?"

I fight to keep my hand steady. The warm light through the windows is catching her hair at just the right angle, turning it into molten gold, her green eyes sparkling. The steam from the hot pasta sauce curls in a tendril past her lips, and they part as if to taste the air.

I curse my dumb luck that my camera is out of reach, because if I could capture this moment right now, I would blow the picture up to fit my entire living room wall. Maybe my bedroom wall.

"Of course," I reply.

"I'm a *terrible* cook," she admits.

She lets her lips settle around the wooden spoon, eyes closing with delight as the lemon and garlic hit her tongue. A feral whimper comes from her lips at the taste, and I have to step away or lose all my composure.

I laugh, my response to her words delayed. "Wait, *what*? You can't cook?"

She shakes her head, her eyes crinkling with amusement. "I'm not a good cook. I feed myself the most disgusting combinations of girl dinner you've ever seen. This, however," she points approvingly at the pan, "is delicious."

"How is that possible?" I breathe with a laugh. "You create culinary masterpieces daily."

"Cooking and baking are *not* the same thing," she explains, her shoulder nudging me playfully. "Baking is chemistry— sugar, butter, and flour, and what comes out of those ingredients just depends on the ratios and preparation. It's precise, predictable. By the time I get done with baking for the day and get around to thinking of what to do for dinner, the thought of cooking a real meal is..."

"Unpleasant?" I offer.

"Unbearable," she finishes. "It's not so much that I *can't* cook. I can follow a recipe, obviously. I simply have no interest in it. I usually can't be bothered with anything more elaborate than rotisserie chicken and bagged salad. Or boxed mac and cheese, if I'm feeling fancy."

"Fancy boxed mac and cheese?" I tease. "Glad I can provide some variety in your life."

I start to load a bowl with pasta for her, ladling the sauce over it.

"Be careful," she warns. "I might start expecting this kind of treatment regularly."

"That sounds dangerously close to an invitation," I say softly, my heart thrumming at the way her gaze lingers on me.

Her lips curve into a slow smile. "Maybe it is."

We settle in at my kitchen table, and she goes relatively silent except for the occasional soft—and may I add, entirely indecent—hums and moans of appreciation. I force myself to eat, even though I'd rather watch her consume the plate in rapt attention.

After she has finished her meal and used a piece of bread

to gather every drop of sauce from the bottom, she leans back in her chair.

"Your place is really beautiful," she remarks. "Business must be good."

I shrug, grinning. Mom taught me to be humble, but I won't lie to her. "It is good. I have a steady gig with *Ever After*, the bridal magazine. And I've become popular enough with the wedding scene around here that I'm usually booked out at least six months in advance. I can choose the work that I want to do. And it's nice, not having to pick up bartending shifts at Cal's to make ends meet, you know?"

"What about you?" I ask. "Sweet P must certainly be doing well. I swear I must have seen you at a dozen weddings in the last year."

Her brows shoot up with surprise. I realize, only after processing the shock in her expression, that this wasn't information I ever intended to divulge.

"We have worked the same weddings before?" she asks.

I awkwardly try to backtrack. "Yeah, um, a few times at least—"

"You said a dozen," she corrects, her tone suspicious.

"I may have been exaggerating—"

"You noticed me at a dozen different weddings," she muses, fighting a wry smile, "and you never once came up to me?"

"Not because I didn't want to," I clarify, though I realize this doesn't help at all in making me sound less pathetic.

Her eyes are incredibly bright with amusement. "Then why didn't you? You don't strike me as the shy type."

I sigh, running a hand through my hair. "I'm usually not. You were just so incredibly beautiful... and obviously so focused on your work that you never noticed even once that we were in the same room."

She shakes her head as she inspects me, her cheeks glowing

with a blush. "It's probably for the best that you didn't meet me sooner, anyway."

"Why's that?"

A shadow of sadness crosses her features. "The reason why you saw me at so many weddings is because I was trying to distract myself. If I stayed so busy that I only had time to work and to sleep, then I didn't have time to feel sad about the breakup."

Silence settles over us for a long minute at this admission. An uncomfortable ache weighs on me, knowing it still hurts for her to talk about it; hating the idea of her loving anyone else so desperately that it could affect her this much, even after all this time.

Her tone lightens as she adds, "If nothing else, working like a dog over the last year finally got us financially stable. Jenna wants us to start planning the next steps for the shop."

"What do you want your next steps to be?" I ask.

"Jenna wants us to explore franchising. She's so business-minded, you know."

I take note of how she doesn't answer my question. There is no spark of excitement in her eyes at the idea. No sign in her expression that this is a goal she shares with Jenna. It piques my curiosity. "What do *you* want?"

She hesitates for a moment before she says, "I can explain it better at my bakery. You want some dessert?"

In more ways than one, I think, but I'm assuming she means food. "Always."

When we're walking through her kitchen a little while later, she starts to explain, "When Jen and I were getting started, we got pretty much everything second-hand. We hit the foreclosure sales from restaurants, the online marketplace, whatever we could do to save money on this place."

She gestures to her tools one by one. "That mixer squeaks relentlessly whenever it gets above a level two. My worktable has a rusty leg that I swear threatens to give under the weight of some of my bigger cakes. My whisks have all seen better days. And now that we're doing well, Jenna has started making plans to replace all the hand-me-downs."

"That's a good thing, right?" I ask.

She sighs. "It is. But we always said, once we got to this point, that we'd start discussing the future."

"And what do you want for your future?" I ask again, recalling how pained she looked at the idea of franchising.

A shy smile crosses her lips. She steps in close, whispering like she's letting me in on a secret, "You really want to know?"

I nod emphatically. At the moment, I can't think of any topic that interests me more than this woman's future.

She walks away suddenly, and the part of my personal space she once occupied suddenly feels hollow and cold in her absence. She opens the industrial fridge in the corner, pushing aside several large, covered bowls before fishing something out of a back corner. When she returns, she is holding a small plate with an opaque plastic cover. She sets it in front of me and removes the cover, revealing a tiny, dome-shaped red dessert. The color is so vibrant and glossy that it looks impossible to achieve in something edible. It is decorated beautifully with delicate chocolate curls, white pearls, and a single raspberry.

I smile at her but feel a little confused. "You want... to eat this tiny dessert?"

She laughs, shaking her head. The sound of her laughter is so melodic, so rich. Just the sound of it seems to shoot a surge of dopamine straight into my brain.

"You asked when we met if I wanted to see the wedding stuff or *the real stuff,*" she says.

I nod along, remembering the moment vividly.

"This is the real stuff," she concludes, gesturing once more to the tiny, immaculately prepared dessert. "I taught myself how to do this."

I know already that she is entirely self-taught, but clearly this is different.

She explains, "It's called an entremet. It's French."

She fetches a knife from a block. I almost stop her when she moves to cut the beautiful little piece of art, but I don't, wanting to see where she is going with this. She cuts the dome perfectly in half, pushing it open to reveal many tiny, perfectly formed layers within. It's just as beautiful inside as it was out.

I look at her again, expectant.

She takes a deep breath, as if bracing herself for her next words. "I feel like I'm at my limit. There is only so much I can teach myself from the internet. I want real training."

"Like culinary school?" I ask.

She nods, but amends, "Pastry school. But I don't want just any pastry school. I want the best."

My brows furrow as I process what she's trying to say. "And the best is—?"

"In France," she finishes. She watches my face with so much concern in her eyes, as if afraid that I am going to scold her or tell her she is being silly.

I whistle long and low. "France. Wow."

A part of my brain, one that I cannot entertain in this moment, adds unhelpfully, *there are lots of things to take pictures of in France.*

"I know. It's a ridiculous dream," she adds, admonishing herself.

I immediately start to say, "It's not—"

"I finally get the bakery to be somewhat profitable, and after all that work, a part of me just wants to leave it behind. But... I couldn't just leave it all behind."

"You could," I retort, but I know she isn't listening anymore. A slow grin spreads across my face as she rambles on.

"It's so impractical."

I shrug. "Practical is overrated."

"Can you imagine what Jenna and Evan would say? They'd be crushed."

"They would survive."

"I probably don't have what it takes, anyway."

"You never know unless you try."

She starts flapping her hands in front of her like she's getting frantic, reaching for the plate in front of me. "It's silly. I can't believe I showed you this—"

I reach out and grab her wrist, stopping her from taking the plate.

"Palmer," I whisper firmly. "Don't you dare take that plate. Let me try the damn entre-nay."

"Entre*met*," she corrects quietly, but she puts the plate back down in front of me obediently. She hands me a spoon.

I take it and grab a spoonful of the dessert, carefully getting a piece of each individual layer. I hold her intense gaze as I put the spoon into my mouth.

And then I lose all track of time and space, of who I am and where I have been. My eyelids flutter closed.

Sweet Jesus, that's good.

There's so much going on that my brain can't fully comprehend what I'm tasting. There is raspberry and vanilla, the faintest taste of lemon. Maybe mint? I don't even know. I imagine there are people out there with palates far more refined than mine who could name each individual flavor she has managed to capture in this single bite. There is so much going on, and yet, all the flavors blend together perfectly into one cohesive moment. It's like the flavors are individual instruments from which she has created an orchestra, and the concert that is going on in my mouth is powerful and cohesive and grand.

God, she is talented.

I point my spoon at Palmer, accusing, "You should not go to French pastry school."

Her eyes go wide, looking so sad and surprised that I almost give up on the bit instantly.

"I shouldn't?" she asks, her lips quivering into the smallest frown.

I shake my head, resolutely. "It would be unfair to the rest of the world. To be this talented and to seek more. You really have to leave some for the rest of the bakers out there."

She smiles, breathing a small sigh of relief. "You like it?"

"Palmer," I murmur, holding her gaze, "I think it's the single best thing I've ever had in my mouth."

Her cheeks go pink. She drops her gaze for a second before her eyes flick back up to mine, almost as if she is afraid of what she might find in my expression but can't look away either.

I take another bite of the dessert, slower this time, savoring it. She watches me intently, gauging my reaction, waiting for my next words. But the words never come to me, because my brain is hyper-fixated on the way she's staring at me, staring at my mouth.

She tilts her head curiously.

"Hold still," she whispers.

Before I can ask why, she steps closer, nearly between my legs, her hand lifting to my face. The soft pad of her thumb grazes the corner of my lips. Her touch sends my heart racing. It feels like she has set every nerve in my body on fire. When she draws her thumb away, now smudged with the bit of mousse that she rubbed off my lip, my brain goes temporarily numb and quiet, absent of all thought. I lock my fingers around her wrist before she can pull away.

"What if I was saving that?" I ask her, teasing. My tone sounds cool, confident, but inside my brain feels like mush. Having her body so close has set off some chemical reaction in my mind that has driven away all rational thought. When I lean forward and put my lips around the pad of her thumb, licking away the bit of dessert, the action is done completely on instinct with no conscious intent behind it.

Her chest rises and falls rapidly, and the motion is terribly distracting. I have to wrench my eyes away, back up to her face. But forcing myself to look at her face is no better. Her eyes are wide, the pupils dilated. And I suddenly can't look away from her full, pink lips, parted with surprise.

I have to get my act together. I force my lips to form coherent, sensible words, even though my entire consciousness seems incoherent and insensible.

"What do we have to do to make this happen?" I whisper.

She blinks in surprise. "W-what?"

"Pastry school," I reply, forcing my voice into something resembling a casual tone. "How do we make it happen?"

She takes a sudden half step away from me, and I let her hand fall from my grasp. She smooths her hands over her shirt, rubbing away the last trace of my lips on her.

"Oh, um…" she mumbles, sounding like she's coming out of a daze. "I'd have to put together a portfolio of my best work. Cakes and desserts. Things like this that prove my technique. But I haven't even started, and the deadline is the first of May to be considered for next year. That would only give me a few weeks to get it all together."

"Pictures?" I ask with a wide grin. "You need pictures of your work?"

Her smile wavers. "Yes, but I'd have to make the desserts too. Probably a dozen different desserts that show the same level of technical skills as this—"

"Let's do it," I say firmly.

A nervous laugh bubbles up in her throat. "I wouldn't want Jenna or Evan to see. I'm not ready for them to know—"

"Don't tell them," I insist. "You make the desserts after the shop closes every night, and I'll come take the pictures for you.

We'll stay up as late as we need to get the work done. We'll make a portfolio they can't look away from."

Her lips purse as she considers my offer.

"Okay," she says finally, a hesitant smile tugging at her lips.

"Okay?" I ask to confirm, breaking into a wide smile of my own. "You're going to do it?"

She nods. "I'll do it."

"You just let me know what days you plan to make the desserts, and I'll be here. If I have an event to shoot, I'll come by as soon as I'm done. And afterward—" I lean over, grab the spoon, and take another bite of the entremet, suppressing a groan at the reminder of how delicious her work is. "It'll be my job to get rid of the evidence so that Jenna and Evan don't get suspicious, of course."

"Of course," she agrees, her eyes crinkling with amusement.

CHAPTER 7

Palmer

I carefully slide a tiny slice of salted caramel cake off my knife onto the long rectangular tasting plate, finishing the row of samples. Somewhere in the back of my mind, a very unwelcome voice reminds me that caramel is Grant's favorite.

"Palmer, your boyfriend is here," Evan croons from across the kitchen, impish and suggestive, like we're in kindergarten. I whirl at my station, my face breaking into a wide grin when I see Silas at the door of my kitchen.

Suddenly, that voice, the part of me that knew the ins and outs of what Grant Foster liked or didn't like, is smothered.

Silas's form seems to take up the whole width of my kitchen door. He's wearing a navy button-down today over dark jeans, looking unbearably handsome. The sight of him momentarily drives all the breath from my lungs, all thoughts from my mind, and eases the tension from my body.

"You're early," I say in place of a greeting, unable to shield the delight from my voice.

"It couldn't wait," he responds with a huge grin, crossing

my kitchen in what feels like three strides. He hands me a wrapped package. "I've got a present for you."

"Ooh, is it something dirty?" Evan sings. I shoot him a dark look.

I take the package from Silas, and as soon as I have it in my hands, I know what it is instantly by the shape and the weight. I glance furtively at Evan where he is carefully removing rounds of red velvet from the pans. He may *appear* busy at work, but I know he is paying close attention to us from across the room. I take Silas by the hand, dragging him into the office at the back of the kitchen.

As we retreat, I hear Evan call after us, "Definitely something dirty, then."

Once Silas closes the door behind us, I pull the book from its packaging. I run my hand lovingly along the black spine, tracing the letters of my name across the front in silver script.

"It's beautiful," I whisper.

"Open it," he urges. "You have to see the pictures."

I open the portfolio, and I need to go no further than the first picture for his work to take my breath away. It should feel shallow and self-indulgent to be captivated by a headshot of myself, but somehow it doesn't. It's not my face that is so impressive, but the way his angles—his appreciation for light and shadow—have combined to create something so beautiful. We decided to go with something simple—just me, in my apron, standing in my kitchen. But somehow, he made it look anything but simple.

I exhale slowly. "Silas, this is incredible."

"I agree. Your face is incredible," he remarks.

I shoot him a playful glare. "Not what I meant."

"You haven't even made it to the food yet. Keep going."

I skim briefly over the cover letter that I agonized over up until the moment Silas sent the final draft to the printer, before turning to the desserts that we spent two weeks capturing together. Nearly a dozen late nights in my bakery together, immortalized in paper and ink. I turn through the vivid images, each one bringing another equally tender memory to mind.

The honey and lavender croquembouche, a towering pyramid of cream puffs decorated with delicate wisps of spun sugar. I told Silas that he didn't need to come the first day, that it would be all prep work and baking with no photographable results until the following day. But he came anyway. He sat beside me, regaling me with stories of his and Cal's college antics that made me laugh so hard that I fumbled piping more than a few balls of puff pastry. I didn't care though—it was worth the sacrifice.

When it came time to assemble and decorate the pastries the following day, Silas tried to help, pinning puffs of pastry to the cone one by one beside me. His attempt to help was admirable, if a little sloppy.

He laughed at the obvious differences in our work, saying, "It's like a Christmas tree. We'll just put the ugly side toward the back."

I turn the page again, seeing the raspberry vanilla entremet followed by a rosewater panna cotta.

When he tried this dessert, he looked at me like I was some kind of wizard, like I possessed dark magic.

"This shouldn't taste good," he commented.

I laughed. "It shouldn't?"

"It's mush made out of flower water," he replied dryly, taking another heaping spoonful. In response to the taste, he made that contented humming sound that came from some-where deep in his chest, the one that always made a fluttering sensation erupt in my belly.

"A lot of things are flower water, if you really think about it," I retorted. "Pretty much any tea: Chai, Earl Grey, Laven-der, Chamomile. All excellent flavors."

I flip to the next page, a neat stack of macarons, their colorful shells impressively reflecting the spotlights that Silas carefully hauled into and out of my bakery each night. The night we took those pictures, he had already shot a wedding that day. He arrived after midnight, wearing an almost identical uniform to what I had first seen him in—the black slacks, black button-down, brown suspenders. He looked worn, exhausted from work. I felt terrible.

"This is too much, Silas," I told him, when he slumped heavily into a stool beside me as I finished assembling the sandwich cookies. "It's unfair to expect you to do hours of work, only to turn around and do more work for me. For free, I might add."

He shot me a tired but genuine smile, reaching out to rest a hand against the back of my arm, his thumb brushing over my skin. "This has been the highlight of my week. Besides, you are paying me."

He grabbed a green pistachio macaron from the reject pile and popped it into his mouth.

I turn the page again, past the lemon layer cake, onto the chocolate opera cake.

This one, without a doubt, was Silas's favorite. He regularly stole spoonfuls from the bowls of chocolate ganache and French buttercream when he thought I wasn't looking.

Eventually, while I was assembling the layers, I saw him stealing yet another sample out of the corner of my eye and said, without looking up from my work, "If you keep eating my ingredients, I'm not going to have enough to make the dessert."

He grinned at me like a sheepish child caught with his hand in the cookie jar. "It's just so damn good, I couldn't wait."

I sighed but felt my cheeks heating as I finished the cake's assembly.

Once he tried the actual dessert, it seemed to be a nearly transformative experience. He closed his eyes, his tongue brushing across his lip as the flavors washed over him. The sounds that he uttered made something warm and pleasant pool inside my belly.

Once he opened his eyes, the look he shot me was something dark and simmering, the look of someone who had far more just happen inside his body than mere taste.

"I could marry you right now," he said, his tone low and agonized, "for this cake alone."

I had been half-heartedly cleaning my supplies, trying and failing not to watch him, and I paused completely in what I was doing at these words. I looked at him, wide-eyed, a soapy sponge aloft in one hand. My heart thrummed a little painfully against my ribs, like a hummingbird trying to escape its cage.

"Don't worry," he said through laughter, the dark look in his eyes cooling into something lighter, more amused. "That wasn't a real proposal. You would know if it was."

I resumed my washing, my cheeks as hot as if I were leaning directly over my oven, and said nothing.

I flip through the remaining pages, a pressure building beneath my chest as it settles in that we're done. Two weeks of spending nearly every night together, laughing and arranging desserts until we were delirious, is over. And while my sleep will improve as a result, I know my quality of life is about to take a dramatic turn downward. The disappointment of it is a sinking weight in my stomach.

"It's pretty great, right?" Silas asks, and I look up into his face. Though he's smiling, I can see it there—my same feelings reflected at me. The smallest wince puckering the corners of his eyes, a crease between his dark brows. He's happy with the work, but just as sad as I am that it must end.

And why does it have to? I can tell him how I'm feeling

right now, ask him if he'd be willing to break the rules. I don't want to wait four more months to see what this could be.

It's not completely clear in his eyes, but I think he feels this way too. He's leaning in so close—not that we can be very apart in this tiny office. But over these last two weeks, he has seemingly tried to occupy the same space as me every opportunity he could get. Two weeks of quiet moments, little inadvertent touches, close calls that we refused to acknowledge.

What if I just did it? What if I just leaned in and kissed him, right now? What's the worst that could happen?

I'm seriously considering it when Evan bangs on the office door, startling us both. We jump away from each other as if caught in the act.

Evan calls, "Hey, put your pants back on. The happy couple just pulled up."

A stark reminder of why we're waiting, driving up to my bakery in his Porsche.

I hurriedly put the portfolio back into its packaging and hide it in a far corner of the desk drawer. Jenna rarely comes into this office, even though it technically belongs to her, so I'm certain she won't find it before I can ship it to Paris tomorrow.

Once the portfolio is safely tucked away, Silas winks and opens the door to the kitchen for me. "I'll sneak out the back and return to make my grand entrance in a little while."

I shoot him a small, grateful smile. I'm suddenly glad he didn't wait until after the tasting to show me the portfolio, relieved that he managed to distract me from the unpleasantness that this afternoon promised.

Silas managed in just a few minutes to resolve the dread and unease I felt at the prospect of this afternoon, leaving only the pleasant memories of the effort we poured into the pages of that portfolio; the moments we shared while creating it— not even one which felt anything like pretend.

Silas slips out the back exit to the alleyway behind the kitchen. I have about thirty seconds to collect myself before I hear the distant ring of the bell chime over the front door.

"They're here," Evan sings ominously. "You ready for this?"

The answer about ten minutes ago was a resounding *no*, but now, shockingly, I feel ready. It's just a cake tasting—something I've done hundreds of times. It doesn't matter who it's for. Not when I feel like I'm floating, like my feet don't touch the ground as I approach the door to the shop.

Not even the sight of Grant standing there, his hand resting on Bennett's lower back, is enough to bring me back down to Earth. Jenna welcomes them, her back turned to me.

"Welcome to Sweet P!" I enthuse. "You two excited to try some cake?"

I greet them with such a brilliant smile and such a cheery tone that Jenna looks at me over her shoulder, alarmed.

Bennett looks equally stunned by my demeanor, but her face soon settles into a wide and brilliant smile. She wraps me in her arms. "So excited!"

I catch Grant's eyes for the briefest second over Bennett's shoulder. My smile doesn't falter at the look on his face; that same, somewhat pained expression with which he always seems to look at me these days, like I'm about to give him a root canal instead of a table full of cake.

Bennett pulls away and scrutinizes my face with a curious pucker of her lips. "You seem... different."

"Different? I don't feel different." I look down at my little green dress and my apron, as if it might be the clothes. Not this splendid, bubbly sensation bursting in my chest.

It's a lie, of course. I feel like a whole new human compared to two months ago, even compared to two weeks ago.

Bennett's head tilts as she inspects me. "I don't know what it is. You just seem... I don't know. Like you're glowing."

I smile brilliantly at her. "Well thanks, Bennett, that's so kind."

Grant, I register absently, is looking at me a little stricken, as if he notices it too. But I don't linger on his expression for long.

Jenna settles Bennett and Grant at the table by the window as I disappear back into the kitchen to fetch the tasting trays. Evan helps deliver two long tasting plates filled with cake, and I bring out an additional tray with artfully arranged tasting cups filled with buttercream.

Once all the samples are arranged in front of Bennett and Grant and I take the seat across from them, I start walking them through the options, giving suggestions for combinations of cake and buttercream.

Grant immediately goes for the salted caramel. I know that there isn't a flavor on this plate that he hasn't tried before. I'm certain he didn't need this tasting to decide which flavor he wanted. He dips his fork into the sponge and lifts it to his lips, as if he has been waiting for me to stop talking so that he could taste it again. His shoulders sink with relief at the taste. He catches my eye over his fork, a warm, knowing gleam in his eyes. And for the briefest second, he's *my* Grant again—the man who walked into the new bakery in town to get his mom a birthday cake and wouldn't leave until he got my number.

I inhale sharply, bracing myself for the flood of emotions to come in response to that look—the longing, the grief, the hurt. But the place in my belly that those emotions once occupied, that I could pull forth in an instant at the thought of Grant, seems somehow empty now, a hollow pit with barely a trace of those feelings left behind. I nearly laugh, I'm so giddy with relief.

I arch an eyebrow at him. "Salted caramel, huh?"

He swallows hard, his Adam's apple bobbing dramatically with the action.

"It's my favorite," he murmurs, as if this isn't a detail I already know. As if I didn't make a salted caramel cake with cream cheese frosting every year on May eighth for three years.

"Ooh, let me try!" Bennett says, sinking her fork into the cake beside the piece Grant just took. His eyes narrow at her fork, as if he hadn't been planning to share.

"Oh my God," Bennett gushes around the bite. "This is otherworldly. I want to marry this cake. I want to marry *you*."

Never thought I'd get marriage offers from the bride and the groom, but here we are.

I chuckle half-heartedly. "Save room, you two. There's still a lot of cake to get through."

After sampling each of the options, Bennett starts to play with combinations of sponge and frosting, having difficulty eliminating choices. She is deciding whether the pink champagne goes better with vanilla or cream cheese frosting when the bell chimes over the door.

I look up, my face breaking instantly into a huge, radiant smile. Even though we orchestrated this little drop-in, even though we planned his arrival to reinforce the act, nothing about my smile feels forced.

Our plan was simple—Jenna texted Silas when we were getting close to the end of the tasting, and he would show up early for our "date." What we didn't discuss, what he did completely of his own volition, was to show up with an enormous bouquet of white and pink flowers. He crosses the shop, not even glancing at Bennett and Grant as he approaches me.

He looks at me with so much delight, as if he didn't see me just forty-five minutes ago. As if he hasn't seen me in days and needs to drink in the sight while he has the chance. When he makes it to my side, he palms my cheek and immediately leans down to kiss me. Firmly. On the lips. Like he has been waiting for the opportunity. Like we are the only two people in the room.

God, I wish we were the only two people in the room.

Even when he pulls away, he doesn't spare a glance for the couple across the table.

"Hi," he whispers. That single word sounds so sweet in his voice; it's like he injected it with honey.

"Hi," I reply, my voice tight with the force of my smile. "You're early for our date."

"I know," he says. "I couldn't wait any longer."

And while all of this—the flowers, his words, the way he is looking at me like my face is the best part of his day—should all be part of the scheme, it doesn't feel like it. My heart seems to swell until it's painful to take a deep breath.

He hands me the flowers, which I take slowly, feeling like I'm in a daze.

"Thank you," I whisper. "What's the occasion?"

The glimmer of something genuine and heartbreaking flashes in his eyes at the question. "Just to tell you how proud I am of you for following your dreams."

My stomach flutters with panic at the reminder of our secret, until he straightens and acknowledges Grant and Bennett. He gestures around to the shop. "I mean, can you believe how incredible this place is? Jenna and Palmer built this all when they were only twenty-four. Amazing, right?"

Bennett smiles at Silas fondly. "It is. You have an amazing girlfriend, Silas."

He directs his gaze back at me. "I do, don't I?"

My eyes search his face for some trace of deceit, for some hint of the ruse—like I'm searching for the edge of a mask that he must be wearing that makes him look at me so adoring and proud. Is he really such a good actor? I just can't tell what's behind those warm toffee eyes, if he's drawing these feelings from some true and genuine place in his heart.

He settles his gaze on Grant and Bennett once more, and I suddenly remember that Grant is still here, watching this exchange. I notice, with some dismay, the faintest trace of hurt in his expression. His lips are pressed into a line, his cheeks barely flushed, as if he is embarrassed.

Silas didn't know the whole story of our breakup; didn't know the nerve that he must have struck in Grant with his words.

But I can sense it, like it's a real, physical presence between us.

My smile falters just a bit.

"Well, I didn't mean to interrupt," Silas lies smoothly. "I'll just wait for you in the kitchen, Babe. Come get me when you're done."

"Good to see you, Silas!" Bennett calls after him. Her fiancé does not appear to share the sentiment.

"And always a pleasure to see you, Bennett." He shoots her a wink before disappearing through the kitchen door, like he does this all the time, like the bakery is his second home. For the last two weeks, at least, it has felt that way. And the thought of my home being his home makes me nearly silly with joy.

I shake my head, my brain suddenly hazy. Maybe it's the smell of the flowers. I put them aside, trying to focus back on the task at hand.

"Right," I say. "You still have some time to finalize your choices. I just need to know your final selections six weeks before the wedding, so I can prepare."

I stand, a clear invitation for them to stand and walk with me toward the door. Bennett and Grant follow, but before Bennett ducks out the door, she fixes a knowing smile on me.

"Mystery solved," she declares.

I hold the door for her and Grant as they exit, saying with mild interest, "What mystery?"

"Why you seem different," she responds.

"Oh?"

"You're in *loooove*," she sings.

I swear I see a muscle in Grant's jaw twitch.

I shake my head, the gesture almost involuntary. I don't know what to say to that, because it's *crazy*. She doesn't even know how crazy it is.

A nervous laugh hiccups out of me. "I—well. See you soon, Bennett. Call me if you have any questions about the choices."

I lock the door behind them and flip the sign from "open" to "closed," before leaning heavily against it. I steady myself with a long, deep breath when I hear Jenna and Evan's muffled laughter coming from my kitchen.

I grab my flowers and follow the sound. Inside the door, I find Silas perched on a barstool, arms crossed easily over his chest, as he listens to one of Evan's exaggerated stories. Jenna leans against the counter beside Evan, watching Silas with a thoughtful, calculating look. She catches my eye, her brows lifting in silent question at the flowers in my arms.

"Oh good, you're here!" Evan exclaims when he sees me. "Palmer, you never told me that your fake boyfriend is hilarious."

Silas smirks in my direction. "You hear that, Palmer? I'm hilarious."

"Don't encourage him," I reply dryly, fighting a grin as I take the place beside Silas. My arm brushes gently against his, and the brief contact instantly sets my pulse racing. But instead of shying away, Silas leans into the contact, prolonging it, increasing the surface area of his skin that is touching mine. He lowers his voice, his tone suddenly serious as he asks, "Everything go okay with the tasting?"

"It went great, actually," I reply, surprised by the truth of it. A huge weight has been lifted off my shoulders after getting through this hour with Bennett and Grant. I didn't feel once like a clumsy idiot, or a pitiful, pining ex. I felt confident. I felt like myself again—at least, a version of myself that hadn't existed for several years. A version that I once worried I may never be again.

"Thanks, in large part, to you," I tell Silas, looking into his eyes. He looks a little taken aback at first by the earnestness in my voice, but his lips start to curve into a smile.

Before he can reply, Evan groans, "Oh *God*, you two are disgusting."

I roll my eyes, ignoring the heat creeping up into my cheeks. I can practically feel Jenna's eyes boring a hole into the side of my skull. Her silence is deafening. But when I risk a glance in her direction, her expression has softened into something warm and knowing. The look unnerves me.

Silas straightens suddenly, clearly sensing a shift in the atmosphere. He addresses all of us, "Actually, while I have your business partners here, I wanted to ask you something. Mostly because I don't want you to say no, and I'm hoping they'll pressure you into it. "

"Oh, how exciting," Evan says. "Proceed."

"You're not a business partner," Jenna reminds him, elbowing him in the side.

Silas chuckles but grows more serious as he turns back to me. "I'm doing a big shoot for *Ever After* magazine in a few weeks, and they mentioned wanting wedding cakes for it."

My heart stutters in my chest. "Oh?"

"I recommended you for the job, obviously," he says, his voice gentle but steady. "They loved the idea, so I'm officially asking—will you do it? I know it's a bit short notice, but—"

"She'll do it," Jenna responds, and I shoot her a glare. I was going to say yes anyway, but still.

"I'd love to," I respond.

His entire face glows with his smile. "It's a date, then."

I grin. "It's a date."

CHAPTER 8

Silas

I am spending my Saturday afternoon in Wonderland.

I take a test shot of the scene, firing my camera several times in rapid succession to test the angles. The picnic blanket before me is ornately arranged with red roses, playing cards, golden pocket watches, and teapots in various haphazard states. There are several cake stands and vintage tiered dessert stands interspersed throughout the décor. The only thing missing is the desserts.

Palmer isn't late, of course. She's never late. The models are still in the tent finishing up hair and makeup. I suppose I'm just feeling impatient.

It's alarming how desperately I want to see her. My brain is constantly thinking up excuses, good reasons why she needs to be in my proximity.

Did the magazine's creative director Tara specifically say the photoshoot needed cakes? No. Did I suggest that the addition of an amazing local baker's work would add another personal layer to the shoot? Absolutely. Tara ate that shit up. And I managed to talk my way into another afternoon with Palmer.

I look around the park for the tenth time in ten minutes, when I see it—the white refrigerated van with Sweet P written in script along the side, parking close to the tent.

Palmer exits the driver's side, and I immediately head in her direction. She opens the sliding door of the van, and I pick up the pace until I'm practically jogging. She looks up over her shoulder at the sound of my approach, then smiles when she realizes it's me. Her back straightens, and she brushes her hair behind her ear. She's wearing a blue dress with buttons down the front and a tie cinching it in at her waist.

God, she's gorgeous. I resist the urge to put my camera to my eye and capture her in this moment, looking at me like she can't imagine another person in this world she'd rather see more.

I feel my entire face light up with my smile.

"Hey," I greet her. "You made it. Need help?"

She looks into the van, back to me, and then back into the van once more, as if she momentarily forgot what she was doing. A startled laugh escapes her.

"Yeah, that would be great!" she says. She picks up a mint green box from inside the van and opens it toward me. "Want to sample the goods first?"

I peer inside the box at the rows of tiny cupcakes in a variety of colors. I pick up one treat with green frosting on top. I raise an eyebrow at the phrase written on it, in perfectly neat buttercream letters: *Eat Me.*

"I thought you'd never ask," I say, grinning at her over the cake before sinking my teeth into it. She rolls her eyes at my joke, but I note the faintest hint of a blush color her cheeks deliciously.

And she's done it again. I let out an agonized groan at the taste flooding all my senses.

"Jesus Christ," I swear. "That's good. You do know this is a photoshoot, right? You could have brought decorated cardboard. Why would you waste your best work on something that no one is going to taste?"

Her pleased smile widens. She picks up two more boxes and balances them against her chest. "Doesn't matter if it's for looks or not, it must taste good when it comes from my shop. And if you think that's my best work, just you wait, Howell."

I suppress another groan. This woman is going to kill me, I'm certain of it—if not from longing, then probably diabetes, at the very least.

I wonder idly who the dumbass was that agreed to wait to make things real between us for six months. That couldn't have been me. That was some other man who had never seen this woman up close—who had never taken a bite out of one of her creations while she watched for his approval. I'm certain that if she fed me cardboard, I would act like it was the finest thing my taste buds had ever encountered, if only to make her happy. But everything she makes is the best thing I have ever tasted, so there is no pretense here.

I stack three boxes of sweets in my arms and lead Palmer to the shoot. She assesses the picnic blanket and the arrangement of dessert stands carefully before she begins to fill the scene with cupcakes and cookies. She places two beautiful, white, one-tier cakes with extravagant buttercream piping work on the cake stands. She leaves the center cake stand empty, and I follow her back to the van to fetch a whimsical three-tier white and cream cake, with each layer tilted on its side, defying gravity—perfect for the Alice in Wonderland theme.

I carry the cake for her and help her set it onto the cake stand. The whole setup looks amazing—decadent and expensive and fantastical. Palmer grins at me when the work is in its proper place.

"Looks good, right?" she asks.

"It does," I agree, rushing to add, "You'll stay for the shoot? Do you have anywhere you need to be?"

She shakes her head. "No, I'd love to stay and watch you work."

"Silas. Wow." I hear Tara's voice from behind us, and Palmer and I both turn to greet her. "You were so right about the cakes! They make the whole scene!"

Tara spots Palmer beside me and reaches her hand out to greet her. "Tara Corbitt, artistic director for *Ever After* Magazine. Your boyfriend has told me so much about you, Palmer."

Palmer shakes her hand, but shoots me a furtive, questioning glance. I'm not certain which part she's questioning—introducing her to Tara as my girlfriend, telling Tara *so much about her*, or the fact that I was the one who suggested we include cakes in the shoot. I flash her a grin, very unembarrassed about any of the three possibilities.

"It's so nice to meet you," Palmer responds.

"Your work is incredible," Tara gushes. "I'll be sure to include information about your bakery in the spread. Do you have a business card?"

Palmer reaches into the pocket of her dress and fishes a green and pink business card out, handing it to her. Tara pockets it, then turns to me.

"We have a bit of a hiccup with our models. Karina woke up this morning throwing up her guts. Thinks she had some bad sushi last night. Which means we are without our Alice. The Mad Hatter and March Hare will have to suffice."

I shrug, saying, "We'll make it work."

Tara turns as if to head back to the tent before her eyes catch on Palmer's form. She surveys her slowly from head to toe, inspecting her dark blonde hair in its updo, her blue dress, stopping at her white tennis shoes. She blinks, processing what she is seeing.

"Unless..." She makes a thoughtful humming noise, and I can see the gears in her mind turning.

Palmer, I think. *Palmer should be our Alice. She would be perfect.*

"What if Palmer steps in?" I ask.

"My exact thought," Tara confirms with a slow, mischievous grin.

Palmer looks back and forth from Tara to me, her eyes going wide.

"I'm sorry?" she asks. The picture jumps instantly into my mind at the look—the wide, innocent eyes, the button nose. If she only took down her hair, she would be the spitting image.

"You would be perfect to play Alice for our shoot," Tara clarifies.

Palmer laughs dubiously. "I am not a model. I'm not model size—"

"Karina is a size eight. You can't be far off," Tara says with another expert scan of her form. "Besides, it's a corset. We can adjust the dress to fit."

Palmer sputters, "No, I couldn't. I'm telling you, I am not a model. I am not good in front of a camera—"

"I beg to differ," I interrupt. She shoots me a small, panicked glare.

"That's your camera," she amends, like my camera has some magic properties that other cameras do not. "I mean, in general, I'm not good in front of a camera. I'll ruin the shoot."

"Who else's camera will you be in front of but mine?" I argue, in a tone that's far more possessive than I intend it to be. But the thought of anyone taking pictures of Palmer is almost as unpleasant as the thought of someone else looking at her, kissing her, touching her. It's incredibly, viscerally unappealing. I want exclusive rights to capture her image, even if I have no right to demand exclusivity.

Palmer insists, "Really, I couldn't—"

"You could," I disagree.

"You should," Tara urges. "How often do you get to be

fully made up by a professional hair and makeup team and wear a beautiful Livie Laurent wedding gown? I'll compensate you for the work, of course."

Palmer pauses, her look of panic fading. I wonder for a second if it's the money that intrigues her, but then she asks, "Livie Laurent?"

Tara seems thrilled at the recognition. "Yes, she designed all the gowns. She's a close friend, in fact."

Palmer's tone is suddenly resolved when she says, "I'll do it."

Tara sports a wide, triumphant smile as she directs Palmer to the glam tent. I settle into a folding chair by the set, passing the time by fiddling with my camera settings.

A little over half an hour passes before I hear a nervous clearing of the throat behind me.

"So, what do you think?" she asks.

When I turn to see her, I immediately stand, feeling like sitting in her presence would be an insult.

God damn. This was a brilliant idea. I've never had a better idea in my life, I'm certain of it. I would have taken the job for free if I had known I would get to see her like this. I would have paid for the honor of taking her picture.

I swallow hard.

"Well?" she demands, her hands lifting in question. She does an experimental twirl, her full skirt fanning around her. "Aren't you going to say anything?"

But I've gone mute. I have no words. She looks so God damn beautiful that there aren't enough words in the English language to describe it. And even if the words exist, I could never be good enough at stringing them together to do it justice.

It's an ivory wedding gown; the corset covered in floral lace. The sweetheart neckline fades into see-through lace over her ribs and stomach, revealing white boning and her creamy skin beneath. The full skirt fans out to her ankles, with some fluffy material peeking out beneath the hem. Her arms are covered in elbow-length, see-through gloves speckled with ivory pearls. Her naturally straight hair has been coaxed into holding voluminous curls, held back from her face with an ivory satin ribbon dotted with pearls.

The hair, the makeup, the styling are all a little dramatized for the fantasy-themed photoshoot, but I can see it so clearly —how breathtakingly beautiful she would be as a bride. Some inane part of me wonders if this is somehow bad luck to see her in a wedding dress. I have to remind myself that, not only is she not my bride, but she's not even my real girlfriend.

"If you're trying to make me more comfortable with this whole deal, you're doing a terrible job," she complains. "I look ridiculous—"

"No," I manage to say. I clear my throat, trying to form more intelligent words. "You don't look ridiculous. I can't seem to find words adequate to describe how unbelievably beautiful you look. But ridiculous is the last one I would use."

Her cheeks turn decidedly rosy, and it somehow makes her look even more appealing.

"Okay, ladies!" Tara joins us, trailed by the two other models. "Let's get started!"

The model playing the part of the Mad Hatter is in a high-neck gown with a white, wide-brimmed hat atop her curls. The other model, the March Hare, is wearing an impossibly ruffled dress with a pair of white, fluffy ears pinned into her hair that somehow manage not to look silly with the whole ensemble.

The two models wander forward into the scene, settling into the space with practiced ease. Palmer doesn't budge, watching them with wide, fearful eyes.

I slip one hand over her lower back, leaning down to whisper, "Hey. Relax. You're going to be great."

Her breath seems to catch. She whispers, so quietly that I can barely hear her, "You'll tell me what to do?"

God help me.

"I'll tell you what to do," I confirm. "Go sit on the picnic blanket. Right in the center."

Tara moves through the scene, tweaking little details as she does—a stray curl, a tilted teacup. She fluffs and fans Palmer's skirt around her until she seems to be emerging directly from a cloud.

Tara poses her at first, from one stiff posture to the next, but it's not good enough.

I clear my throat, suggesting, "Ladies, have you tried one of the cupcakes yet?"

The model playing the March Hare grins, leaning forward to pluck a red velvet cake with blue frosting off one of the dessert tiers. She takes a bite and moans in delight.

"Oh my God," she gushes. "This is *amazing.*"

The Mad Hatter immediately grabs one for herself—all the while, maintaining her angles, keeping her best self forward, as she is trained to do.

"This may be the best cupcake I've ever had in my life," she agrees.

And Palmer's awkward, stiff posture immediately melts away beneath the compliments. Her shoulders relax. The tension in her face releases. A soft, natural smile pulls at her lips.

Click. Click. Click.

"That's perfect," I encourage her. "Eyes up. Lift your chin just a bit—*there.* Good girl."

Her eyes flit to me, her cheeks going pink. The way she's looking at me, the way she's dressed, it's all meant to look so angelic and soft. And it does something to me. It clashes violently in my head, because all I can think of is how badly I want to do terrible, filthy things to her.

Click.

I hide behind my camera, forcing that desperately unhealthy thought to the back of my mind. This is a professional atmosphere, I remind myself. But she looks so damn stunning. And she seems to be enjoying herself now. All the stiffness in her posture has faded away, leaving this lithe, relaxed, gorgeous creature behind.

It is with great difficulty, but I manage to power through the rest of the shoot with some semblance of composure. By the end, she and the models seem like the best of friends, exchanging numbers with their goodbyes. They each walk away from the shoot with a box of leftover cake and cookies in hand.

I help disassemble the scene while Palmer changes back into her normal clothes.

When she returns, I ask, "What are you doing this evening? Want to get some dinner?"

I need this not to be the end. I'm not ready to be without her, not when I worked so hard to get this time with her.

She smiles. "I'd love to. Come back to the bakery with me? I need to take about a gallon of this makeup off before I go out in public."

When we make it to her bakery a few minutes later, it has already closed for the afternoon. She unlocks the door and leads me inside, flipping the lights on. She puts her tote bag of supplies behind the counter and leans against it, looking at me. I rest my arms on the side opposite hers. My body naturally leans forward, desperate to cross the distance between us.

"Today was..." she laughs, shaking her head. "Crazy. I've never done anything like that before."

From the previews alone, I know it's going to be an incredible spread. Palmer may not be a seasoned model, but she shined today. Once she allowed herself to relax and enjoy herself, she carried the shoot.

"You were a natural. The camera loves you," I remark.

She hits me with the full force of her sparkling emerald eyes. "Maybe *your* camera."

Her saying it, confirming what my mind has been repeating all day long, does little to quell that possessive animal inside me. My mind has been going wild all afternoon, imagining more opportunities to take her picture—in normal, wholesome scenarios, sure, but in very *unwholesome* ways as well. The thought takes root in my brain and lingers, conjuring fantasies of taking more intimate pictures of her— in lingerie. In nothing at all.

With that thought, I'm suddenly thankful the counter is covering everything below my waist.

"My camera *does* love you," I say softly. Her lips part with surprise but don't immediately form a response.

We gravitate across the counter toward each other, almost subconsciously. There is no audience, no camera to put on the show for, but I realize that I *want* the show. I want to have a reason to kiss her. And from the way she's looking at me, I know she wants it too. I'm trying and failing to remember why we agreed to keep things friendly until after the wedding, when the bell chimes over the door.

"Sweetie Pie, there you are!" The high-pitched squeal breaks us violently out of our spell.

"Oh, shit," I hear Palmer whisper under her breath. She recoils, a touch of fear in her eyes.

A blonde-and-rainbow-colored blur approaches, darting behind the counter to scoop Palmer into a hug. Palmer catches my eye over the woman's shoulder, and she mouths the words, *I'm sorry.*

"Mom!" she says, pulling out of the woman's embrace. "What are you doing here?"

Palmer's mother. I could have guessed—the resemblance is obvious enough. Her mother's hair is just a shade lighter with some gray in it. They are of similar height and stature. They have the same button nose. But her mother is wearing something I couldn't imagine Palmer wearing—some gauzy dress-shawl-combination thing in splotches of every color imaginable.

"Does a mother need an excuse to see her only daughter?" she asks.

"When it's a two-hour drive, she does," Palmer replies warily.

She takes note of Palmer's makeup and curls suddenly, and she coils one curl around her finger. "Well, aren't you done up today! What's the occasion?"

"Long story," she says, avoiding the question. "What are you doing here, Mom?"

Palmer's mother suddenly seems to realize that she and Palmer are not alone, and she looks at me across the counter, her expression delighted.

"And who is this *fine* young man?" she asks.

I smile, pleased to draw the woman's attention so suddenly and with such appreciation. I note, with some amusement, the look of horror plastered on Palmer's face at this interaction.

I reach my hand out, introducing myself.

"Silas Howell," I say, and I look to Palmer, searching for permission to say the words, *Palmer's boyfriend.* Palmer seems to understand my meaning, because she immediately shakes her head, her eyes still wide and panicked.

Palmer's mother takes my hand in both of hers, running a finger along my palm like she is about to read my future. "Aren't you a beautiful man?"

"*Mom,*" Palmer groans.

"I'm Celeste Kincaid-Sullivan-Dupree," she says, quickly adding, "but that's a mouthful, so you can just call me Celeste."

"It's very nice to meet you, Celeste," I reply. I know, from the pure misery radiating from her, that Palmer is not enjoying this interaction. But I'm enjoying it greatly, even though Celeste has not yet let go of my hand.

"Sweetie Pie, what is this beautiful man doing in your shop after hours, looking at you like he wants to have you for supper?" she asks.

I let out a surprised guffaw. "I wasn't—"

"It's okay, Dear," Celeste assures me. "You don't have to be embarrassed. Palmer is a beautiful girl. Takes after her Mama, doesn't she?"

She winks at me, and I think Palmer may just melt into an embarrassed puddle on the floor at the gesture, but I can't stop grinning.

"Palmer *is* a beautiful woman," I agree. Palmer inhales and seems to hold it, but her cheeks flush at the compliment.

Celeste finally lets go of my hand, turning to her daughter. "Palmer, Sweetie, you must bring him to Margot's birthday party next weekend."

"What party?" she asks feebly.

"Margot's party. Next Saturday. I just decided to throw it together last minute!" she declares brightly. "You simply must come. That's why I'm here, to invite you... *and* your handsome man."

She shoots me another appreciative look, and I stifle a laugh for Palmer's sake.

Palmer's lips curl into a cringe. "I have a wedding that day, Mom."

"It's your stepmother's birthday," Celeste insists. A little unfair, I feel, considering Palmer was only just informed of the party's existence. "I was hoping you could bring a cake."

Palmer sighs, and I can see the fight dying out of her before my eyes.

"Okay," she relents.

Celeste throws her hands up in glee, curtains of gauzy rainbow fabric flowing around her like the wings of some exotic bird. She embraces Palmer, kissing her on the cheek.

"Wonderful!" she says. "You know Margot—she likes florals. Tulips are her favorite. I trust your creative vision. The party starts at six o'clock. I have to head out—I'm meeting an artist to get a piece for the studio. But I'll see you both on Saturday!"

Celeste flows out of the shop just as quickly as she appeared, like a burst of rainbow lightning. I stare at the door long after her retreat, reeling in the wake of her appearance.

Palmer pinches the bridge of her nose and closes her eyes, as if she has suddenly developed a tension headache.

"So, that's my mother," she explains unnecessarily.

"I never would have guessed," I say wryly. "She seems—"

"Like a lot?" She sighs deeply.

I laugh. "You said it, not me."

She lets out a rueful chuckle. "Just you wait. I'm sure you'll get the full Celeste show when we go to Myrtle Beach on Saturday."

I thank my lucky stars that I don't have a job planned that day, knowing I would cancel all my plans to be with her. And to see exactly what the "Celeste show" might entail.

CHAPTER 9

Palmer

"You seem tense."

Silas glances sideways at me from the driver's seat, one hand on the wheel, the other casually draped across the center console between us. He looks incredibly at ease, in stark contrast to the anxiety buzzing inside me. He also looks unbearably handsome in a fitted white button-down, the sleeves rolled up to his elbows. I find myself momentarily distracted, watching the steady rise and fall of his chest against the fabric.

"Do I?" I reply, feigning ignorance, dragging my gaze back out the window, fixing my eyes on the glistening gray water.

He chuckles softly, as if he knows that I had to force myself to look away from him, as if he caught me staring. If not then, he might have caught me any of the other fifty times I was distracted by him in the first hour of this drive.

"Worried about the wedding cake?" he asks.

While I genuinely wasn't dwelling on this source of anxiety, I am now that he brought it up.

"No, Jenna and Evan can handle the delivery," I say, trying to sound earnest.

I know they can handle it. I really do. But I don't typically delegate cake deliveries. In some ways, it's the most important part of the process—it doesn't matter how a cake looks in my kitchen if it doesn't get to the event unscathed. Jenna is a good driver, but she can't fix any mistakes once she arrives. Evan can decorate a cake almost as well as I can, but he drives like a damn maniac. I know that together, they make a great team. But it's still driving me crazy that I'm not there.

"Are you worried about your moms believing the act?" Silas asks, a gentle note of concern in his voice.

I turn back to him, surprised. "What? No! Not worried about that at all. I can't imagine there will be anyone at my stepmom's fifty-second birthday party who travels in the same circles as Bennett Barlow."

"Then what is it that's causing that little crease between your brows?" He asks with a wry turn of his lips. "It's been there since I picked you up."

Self-conscious, I purposefully relax my face, trying to smooth away the traitorous crease.

"Being around my mom is always just a little stressful," I admit, though it feels like an understatement.

My mind conjures memories of Grant before I can suppress them.

I don't know why being around your mom stresses you out so much, he would say. *She's so much fun.*

I shake my head, as if I can clear the memory like an Etch-A-Sketch.

When we arrive at my mom's beachside cottage, the silence is unsettling. Balancing Margot's cakebox—a one-tier confection within decorated with vibrant tulips—against my body with one hand, I knock with the other. No answer. My lips pull into a frown.

I test the door handle and find it unlocked. Inside, the

quiet deepens, the silence stretching ominously through the small, empty rooms. Not a single sign of life.

Silas trails behind me as I wander the halls, peering inside the living room and the kitchen, with no evidence of my parents. I put the cake down on the kitchen counter, noting the two lonely bottles of wine and untouched bags of chips. I inhale deeply, but the breath burns painfully as it courses through my lungs.

"Are you sure they're having the party here?" Silas asks, as if hopeful that I misunderstood the instructions. But I know I haven't.

I sigh, resigned. "Positive."

I head for the stairs, in my heart knowing exactly where I'll find my mother. Silas and I climb to the loft, the space bathed in natural light and filled from wall to wall with my mother's works in progress. And, as I expected, she's there on the floor, cross-legged in paint-splattered overalls, a paintbrush in one hand as she brushes streaks of powder blue onto her canvas. My heart sinks.

"Mom," I say sharply.

She startles at my voice, as if I'm pulling her out of a deep trance. A wide, delighted smile breaks across her face at the sight of Silas and me standing at the landing of the stairs.

"Sweetie Pie! What a wonderful surprise!" she calls, pulling herself off the floor as she runs to draw me into her embrace. I feel my body go stiff in her arms.

"Surprise?" I say, my voice falling flat with disapproval. "Mom, *you* invited *us*. Margot's party is in an *hour*."

Her eyes widen in shock. "Oh, my goodness, is it Saturday already? I lost all track of my days. I have this new painting I'm working on, and I—"

"Mom," I cut her off sternly, unable to swallow my frustration. "Are you telling me forty people will be here in an hour, and you haven't prepared anything?"

She gives a sheepish grin. "You know how I get when inspiration strikes, Sweetie..."

I shoot Silas an apologetic look, asking, "Do you think you could bring me to the store?"

Without hesitation, he nods. "Of course. Tell me how I can help."

It takes us forty frantic minutes to sprint through the grocery store and return to my mother's cottage. We unload trays of sandwiches, chips, veggies, and dip. Silas works on drinks—filling several Styrofoam ice chests with water, seltzers, beer, and sodas.

He locates a punch bowl and fills it with ice. He starts to slice fruit with precise, practiced movements, settling into the muscle memory of a former bartender as he prepares some kind of punch.

I busy myself decorating the back porch, stretching up on tiptoe to tack colorful streamers to the wooden beams.

After a few minutes, I hear Silas call my name, and I nearly lose my balance as I strain to reach a high corner.

When I don't immediately respond, I feel his warm presence behind me. His hand reaches up to take the streamer from my hand and effortlessly attaches it to the post.

"Let me help you," he insists. He towers over me, peering down at me with those toffee-brown eyes.

I protest weakly, "No, you're a guest, I can handle—"

"You were supposed to be a guest too, if you remember," he counters. "Let me help."

I sigh, relenting, handing him another package of streamers. "Fine. I *could* use your height."

A mischievous gleam lights his eyes. "Please, use me as much as you want."

I roll my eyes, but I don't even have time to acknowledge his joke before I turn to my next task. Before I take two steps away from him, he forces a red solo cup into my hands that I didn't notice he was holding. "Here. You look like you could use a cup of my sangria."

I take an experimental sip, and it is delicious— the right amount of sweetness, just a bit tangy, the faintest bite telling you that there is alcohol in it.

I nod gratefully. "This is exactly what I needed."

He grins before returning to the decorations.

The best thing about my mom and stepmom's friends is that they're all artists—all very go-with-the-flow types. Therefore, not one of them shows up even close to the advertised six p.m. start time. Fashionably late, some might call it. But I showed up an hour early, somehow knowing, deep in my heart, that this would happen. That it would be up to me, once more, to make up for my mom's shortcomings in the planning department.

My mom emerges from her bedroom, freshened up and wearing one of her many colorful, flowing dresses, just in time for my stepmom to walk through the door.

Margot has a severe bob, barely cheek-bone length, curled in at the edges with wispy bangs that don't quite reach her eyebrows. Her brown eyes are so dark they're nearly black. Her skin has an olive tone to it.

"Happy birthday, Dearest," my mom says, kissing her wife sweetly. Margot looks delighted that my mom remembered. She looks even more delighted when she sees me.

"Palmer," she coos. "I'm so happy you're here."

"Happy birthday, Margot," I say, accepting her embrace.

She must see the decorated porch over my shoulder, because she gushes, "Oh, how beautiful! You didn't have to do all this for me, Sweetheart."

"It was mom's idea," I say, but Margot immediately hits me with a knowing smile. And it's not like I can hide the truth from the woman who is married to my mother, who knows about her eccentricities just as well as I do. Maybe better, since she has graciously taken on most of the Celeste-tending duties these last ten years.

I turn to Silas. "Silas, this is Margot Dupree, my stepmom. Margot, this is Silas, my—"

"Incredibly handsome new beau," my mom supplies with a devilish grin. I don't bother correcting her. Or slapping the self-satisfied smirk off Silas's face.

It isn't until an hour later that the majority of my parents' friends arrive, and the party gets going. I finally start to relax, knowing we pulled it off, even last minute. Everyone is having a great time. Silas has had to replenish the supply of his sangria multiple times to meet the demand.

After we sing Happy Birthday and cut the cake, we wander out onto the beach. One of the partygoers starts a beachside fire, and people fall onto the benches or sand surrounding the fire pit. Someone summons a guitar from who knows where and starts to play. Mom perches on the sand, her arms wrapped around Margot as they sway to the rhythm. *The only thing missing is a set of bongos, and the hippy circle will be complete*, I think with amusement.

I'm standing at the periphery of the circle, not quite a part of the group, when Silas joins me. He hands me another cup of sangria.

I arch an eyebrow at him. "If I didn't know better, I would think you were trying to get me drunk, Howell."

Despite my disapproving tone, I immediately take a sip. If he is trying to get me drunk, he's certainly on his way to succeeding.

He grins, sipping at a bottle of water. He, notably, hasn't been partaking. "Just trying to offset some of the mom-related stress, if I can. Besides, I'm your designated driver for the evening. Take advantage of it."

I marvel at how someone can manage to be so casually considerate, so effortlessly dependable.

"You're asking me to take advantage of you?" I tease.

He steps closer, brushing a strand of my hair back behind my ear. His voice is soft when he says, "Take advantage of someone taking care of *you* for once."

I inhale sharply and hold the breath. Another memory of Grant forces its way into the forefront of my mind—his voice strained and angry, desperately asking, *why won't you let someone take care of you for once?*

The words are basically the same, yet this offer feels so drastically different.

"Want to go for a walk down the beach?" Silas asks, pulling me violently back to the present.

A moonlit walk alone down the beach feels anything but casual and friendly, like we promised when we first started this thing, but I relish the thought of escaping the gentle chaos of my mother and her friends. We leave our shoes behind and head in the direction of the waves crashing against the shore, the white caps stark in the moonlight.

We walk in silence, side by side, and while it's a comfortable silence, it also feels expectant. I can sense Silas waiting for me to acknowledge the elephant in the room. For bailing me out today, I suppose he deserves an explanation.

"I'm sorry about earlier," I say softly, watching my toes as they sink into the sand with each step. "About my mom. Thank you for helping me scramble to fix everything."

"You don't have to apologize," he reassures, but there's still that lingering edge to his voice, the expectation that I'll continue to talk, to lay my feelings out for him to inspect and scrutinize. It's a gentle, kind expectation, but it terrifies me, nonetheless.

I inhale deeply, the cool, salty sea air feeling good coursing through my lungs. "It's always been like this with my mom."

"You didn't seem surprised," he remarks.

"My mother is a good person. She is," I start, feeling the

distinctive urge to defend her, but I stop myself. I'm almost thirty years old. I've been to therapy, worked through a lot of this stuff with a professional. I don't need to hash it out with Silas to be okay. Why do I feel myself naturally tumbling toward the confession anyway?

"My mom was just never a great parent," I admit. "My dad seems like a great parent, now that he has my brothers. But when my parents divorced, he only made a cursory attempt to get custody of me. In the end, he didn't want to fight with her over anything. Didn't want to fight for me. He just wanted to get away. Move on with his life to bigger and better things. And I'm not even sure if she really wanted to be a parent. But she wanted to win. And she did."

He nods thoughtfully, not interrupting, giving me the space to share the things I've rarely spoken out loud.

"I learned how to manage. How to take care of myself. Take care of both of us," I explain.

He stops walking, turning to face me. His eyes are warm and attentive as they hold mine. "That's a heavy burden to carry alone, Palmer. I'm sorry you had to go through that."

I blink against the sensation of tears in my eyes and force a smile. "It's ancient history. We have a good relationship now. She loves me."

His silence in response to this statement gapes between us, heavy and demanding. But I refuse to fill it with anything more, at least, not on this subject.

"Tell me about your parents," I say, a little too quickly.

He puts his hands in his pockets, looking thoughtfully up at the moon where it hovers over the water.

"They were the best," he says, just loud enough to be heard over the waves. "I wonder every day if they were just too good for this world. Maybe that's why they didn't get enough time in it."

His words are so heartbroken and earnest, so vulnerable, the emotion temporarily takes my breath away.

"When my dad died a little under a year after my mom lost the battle, they said he died of *a broken heart,*" he recalls with a rueful smile. "I guess they weren't wrong, technically. His heart just... burst. It probably wasn't related at all to my mom's death, but they were just so in love with each other, you know? Losing her left him hollow. He put on an impressive show of strength for Emery and me, even though we knew he was hurting. Sometimes, I wonder if keeping those feelings bottled up is what did it. You don't just get over a loss like that. Theirs was the kind of love you never see nowadays."

"Not even with Emery and Charlie?" I ask, recalling just how adoring they looked at each other.

"They come pretty darn close, if anyone ever could," Silas says, a smile in his voice.

I realize suddenly how desperately I want to go to Emery's wedding, to see the joining of two people who love each other so truly and impressively. To prove to myself once and for all that a love like that exists. But asking for that begs questions I don't feel we're ready yet to answer—what does the future hold for us? Will we continue to see each other after the Barlow wedding?

Sometimes, after I have delivered a wedding cake, I'll find a nondescript place to look on during the ceremony, to watch the bride as she walks down the aisle toward the one person she has committed to for all her days. But I know deep in my heart that I don't want to attend Emery's wedding as the baker, as someone who's meant to slip away into the shadows. I want to be there because I'm *wanted* there. And it's an odd feeling—I've never longed so badly to be a part of someone's world like I want to be part of the Howell family.

The contemplative silence stretches between us for a long

time, until Silas glances down at his watch. "We probably ought to head back, huh? We have a long drive ahead."

I nod and turn to head back in the direction of the cottage. By the time we return, the circle of people around the fire has dwindled to less than half, and before long, those stragglers begin to pack up as well.

We follow along as Mom and Margot usher the last few guests to the front door to say goodbye. When we're the only ones left inside their home, I turn to my mom.

"Okay, Mom," I say, linking one arm through Silas's and starting to inch slowly toward the door. "It's been a great night, but Silas and I really should get back home. It's a long drive, and—"

"Sweetie, no!" Mom cries, outraged. "I couldn't possibly let you drive home at this hour! You'll stay here with us!"

"No, Mom, really—"

"I insist," she says, leaving no room for argument. I press my lips together, displeased. But, as it always seems to do in my mother's presence, my resolve crumbles. I feel small and helpless, like I'm eight years old again.

I look to Silas for assistance. He doesn't look at all panicked, like I feel. He looks completely unbothered. He wraps an arm around my waist, saying in a reassuring tone, "It's just one night. We'll leave first thing in the morning."

He clearly isn't going to help at all, I guess. I direct my protests once more to my mother. "Mom, we didn't bring anything with us. No toiletries or pajamas—"

"We have spare toiletries," Margot offers, very sweetly, though it only makes the panic rise in my gut. "And you can of course borrow pajamas from either of us."

"You on the other hand," my mom looks Silas up and down appreciatively, and that look makes me want to die. "I don't think we have anything that will fit you, Dear."

Silas flashes her a smile, saying, "That's not a problem. I don't normally sleep in pajamas anyway."

I try with every fiber of my being not to dwell on the thought of Silas sleeping *au naturale*. I cannot let this happen.

But Margot disappears into their bedroom and returns with pajamas and toothbrushes. My mom bids us goodnight, and Silas merrily returns the sentiment.

This is happening. And there's nothing I can do to stop it.

This is how I find myself standing next to Silas in my mother's tiny spare room, clutching the pile of silky pajamas and spare toothbrushes, very conscious of how close we are. How close we must be, in such a tiny room. I scan the bed with alarm, wondering if it truly is queen-size. It looks impossibly small at the moment.

"What do we do?" I whisper, so quiet I'm certain Silas must be barely able to hear me.

He chuckles softly. "What do you mean?"

"We have to share a bed, Silas," I explain slowly, like I'm speaking to a young and slightly dim child.

He looks endlessly amused at my discomfort, and I don't appreciate it. "It's not a big deal."

"For you, maybe," I retort.

He tilts his head, his tone dropping into some sultry place that I don't appreciate in this moment. "I promise not to bite."

"This is *not* funny," I hiss.

He laughs anyway. "Relax. It's just one night. I'll stay on my side. You'll stay on yours."

My eyes flicker to the bed again in dismay. Did it shrink another few inches? I look back at Silas's form, wondering if his shoulders are suddenly and impossibly broader than I remember.

"Easier said than done," I argue. "You're six foot three. I don't think taking sides is a possibility."

He grins like I have just paid him a compliment instead of a complaint. "I can't really control that.

"You're not helping," I reply.

He draws so close I can feel his body heat against my skin. I tense at the proximity.

His voice is insufferably low and smooth and far too amused when he asks, "How can I help, then? Do you want me to sleep on the floor, Sullivan?"

There's barely enough floor to fit him, if we're being honest, but my sense of decency doesn't allow me to consider the offer for more than a few panicked seconds.

"No," I mutter bitterly.

He smirks, victorious. "Good."

He plucks one of the toothbrushes and the toothpaste from the pile in my arms and heads for the bathroom. As he walks away, he says over his shoulder, "Don't worry. I'll keep my hands to myself... For now."

When the bathroom door closes behind him, I fall onto the bed with a groan. When he emerges, I look up to see him in all his tall, muscular, nearly naked glory. He shed everything except for his navy-blue boxers. Lines of black ink circle his left bicep, and I'm tempted for a moment to inspect it closer, to learn what he has tattooed there. But his infuriating grin is growing slowly wider the longer I look at him.

I stand with a huff, holding my hand in front of my eyes to block my view.

There's a smirk in his voice as he says, "Something wrong?"

"Silas," I say, clear that he is testing my patience. "While I'm in the bathroom, you're going to get under the covers. I better not be able to see an inch of your perfect body when I get back."

"Very demanding," he croons. "Didn't know I'd like

getting bossed around by you so much, but I guess, new kink unlocked."

"*Silas*," I mutter through gritted teeth.

"Okay, okay!" he says with laughter. "Yes, ma'am."

I stay in the bathroom far longer than I need to, trying to shake this restless, uneasy feeling. I take a shower to pass the time, letting cool water run over my flushed skin. I put on the pajamas Margot lent me, realizing with dismay that it's a set of little satin shorts and a matching camisole—not exactly lingerie, but definitely not the baggy sweatpants and t-shirt I was hoping for.

I brush my teeth and towel dry my hair, but no matter how long I stall, he'll still be out there. In the bed. Waiting for me.

I finally tiptoe into the bedroom. I'm cautiously optimistic when I realize that Silas has done as I asked. His form is completely covered up to his neck with the blankets, and he is facing the wall. He seems to be feigning sleep, his breathing unnaturally steady, likely for my comfort. My unease softens.

I turn off the lights and climb into bed, turning so that my back is facing his. After only a few moments in the silence and the dark, he whispers, "I had a good time today. Thanks for letting me come."

I didn't have much choice in that matter when my mom demanded his presence. But I can't deny how grateful I am for what he did for me today.

"I'm glad you came," I admit, my voice barely a whisper.

Silence stretches between us once more, and I think for a second that maybe now he is going to sleep. But instead, he says, hesitantly, "I know what I went through doesn't really make me a parent, or anything like that. I know I'm not qualified to pass judgment. But I had two great parents. And I pride myself on the fact that, since they passed, I've shown up for

Emery... whenever she needed me, I was there. And I'll always be there, for whatever she needs."

I realize his meaning instantly. And after all the teasing, the anxiety about having to share a bed with him, it's the last thing I expect him to say. The shock of his words—so earnest, so sympathetic—renders me stricken and reeling. My eyes prickle with the sensation of tears. My throat grows uncomfortably thick.

"I'm sorry you didn't have that, Palmer," he says, his voice unbearably quiet and sincere.

And I'm horrified and embarrassed when the tears come, completely beyond my control. They're quiet, but my body shakes with the force of trying to keep them inside. I reach up to clap my hand over my mouth.

Why couldn't he have just taken my mom at face value, like everyone else? Celeste, the life of the party. The misunderstood artist. The vibrant, infectious personality.

Not the Celeste who would leave me at school waiting to be picked up so often that the principal knew my home address by heart. Not the Celeste who would disappear for days, without a word, following inspiration when it struck. Not the Celeste who would go into months-long artist block, sulking in a deep depression, leaving us destitute aside from Dad's child support.

That's the Celeste that I knew, that no one else ever acknowledged. Until now.

I hear the rustle of the sheets, feel the mattress shift beneath me as he turns over. Hesitantly, as if afraid I might pull away, his hand finds my waist. He pulls me slowly into his chest, his warmth wrapping around me.

I don't tense or push him away. I put my hand over his and lace my fingers through his, firmly anchoring him to me. He takes the approval for what it is and settles me closer.

"I've got you," he whispers against my neck.

A fresh new wave of emotion surges in my chest—terrifying and devastating and perfect. I have spent my whole life learning how to hold my own, knowing I can only rely on myself, at the end of the day. But in this moment, with his arms around me, his voice warm and steady in my ear, it feels good to rely on someone. Like a relief, instead of a risk.

I don't know when I fall asleep in his arms. At some point, my tears stop, and a warm, heavy exhaustion settles over me. And all the while, he's there, holding me. His breathing steady, his hand still holding mine, his body curved around mine.

It feels natural. Easy. Dangerous.

But I don't dwell on that part of the equation. I let myself sink into his warmth, letting myself believe that maybe I can have this. Maybe I can learn to trust someone like this. Maybe nothing can ruin this.

Nothing except my subconscious, that is.

I realize that I'm dreaming almost instantly.

Silas and I are talking in my bakery, as we have on multiple occasions. I'm sitting at my worktable, with a cake and bowls of ganache and whipped cream in front of me. Silas leans against the table beside me, talking animatedly.

I can't make out what we're saying—our voices sound hazy and far-off, like listening through water. But before I know what's happening, we're both laughing. Until he stifles my laughter with a kiss. Then we start shedding clothes, pulling them off each other like we're well practiced in it, like this is something we've done a thousand times before.

But I know we've never done this before.

I wonder idly if I should try to wake up. But the resistance is fleeting and feeble and instantly quelled when Silas lifts me onto my metal workbench.

If I didn't know I was dreaming before, this solidifies it. For one, I think my weight would send that old table crumbling down beneath that rusty leg. And second, I would *never* let my bare ass hit my table—a clean space I use to prepare people's food. But that logical thought is instantly squashed by the desperate longing to see where my imagination plans to take us.

I am not disappointed.

He grabs the bowl of chocolate ganache and pours it down my body, watching it slide between my breasts, down my stomach, between my legs. He takes a handful of the whipped cream and lathers it over my chest. Satisfied with his plate, he starts to lick me clean. His tongue creates trails in the whipped cream until it finds my now hardened nipple. Dream me arches her back in delight, her head falling back with a groan.

I'm so jealous that she can *feel* this, angry that I'm only getting a dull echo of the pleasure he is providing her.

Once he's done with the whipped cream, he follows the trail of chocolate downward until he buries his face between my legs.

"Silas," I pant, and the sigh of his name feels so real on my lips.

This is unbearable. Torture.

I need to wake up. I need to stop this. But I can't seem to tear myself away from it. Away from him.

Dream me is reaching heights that I'm not sure if I have ever truly reached. She appears to be greatly enjoying herself as his tongue works at her. She is coming undone. I grind my hips, wanting so desperately to feel him, begging for just a glimpse of what my subconscious mind wants me to experience.

And for just a second, I swear I do feel the faintest pressure between my legs, but then he pulls away. He looks up at me from between my thighs.

"Palmer?" he asks with concern.

"No, please," I beg. "Don't stop."

"Palmer?" he says again, and I can feel it. I can feel myself getting pulled away from the dream.

"*Please*," I plead.

Why won't my brain just let me see this through?

"Wake up, sweetheart."

CHAPTER 10

Silas

I wake up in the best and worst possible way I can imagine.

Palmer is still curled into my chest, the way we fell asleep. The moment I realize she's still here, that she didn't pull away from me in the night, an incredible, warm feeling floods over me. The light of the morning is dim through the curtains, but I'm in no rush to wake her. I snuggle her in closer and shut my eyes again, inhaling the faint vanilla and caramel scent that always clings to her skin, savoring the moments until she wakes.

But then she whispers my name.

And while that is not alarming, it's *how* she says my name that's the problem. It's unmistakable—a breathy, pleading whisper filled with need. My pulse races instantly, my heart pounding when she does it again.

"*Silas.*"

"Palmer?" I whisper, checking to see if she's awake, knowing that she is not.

"No, please," she gasps, her voice a dreamy, desperate sigh. "Don't stop."

Fuck.

She's dreaming. Not just dreaming—having a sex dream. About me.

My body instantly betrays me, every nerve ending firing painfully, wonderfully taut in response. Between it being the morning and having her pressed against my body all night, I was halfway there already. But now, after hearing her sweet, pleading voice, there's no halfway about it anymore. I go immediately and unbearably hard.

I start to loosen my grip from around her, but I hear her voice again, begging, "Please."

She really is going to be the death of me.

My back is nearly touching the wall, so it's not like I can escape. Not that I really want to. But for the sake of self-preservation, I feel like I must.

Then, I know I have to escape. Because she arches her back, pressing her ass more firmly into me. Her hips rock backward in a very slow, deliberate rhythm, putting friction against my throbbing cock. My breath hitches at the contact.

I reach down to brace one hand against her hip, intending to halt her motions, but my hand meets bare, impossibly soft skin where her silky little shorts have ridden up during the night. Her body heat against my hand sends another unbearable surge of electricity through me, and for a second, I forget why I would ever want to stop this. Her body feels perfect against mine, every gentle motion of her hips making me lose all rational thought.

But I force myself to focus on reality. She's asleep. This isn't what she wants. She made her intentions not to touch me incredibly clear the night before. I know what I have to do, even if it's agonizingly tempting not to do it.

Summoning every ounce of willpower I possess, I shake her gently by the shoulder and say, "Wake up, sweetheart."

My voice sounds rough, resigned. But it works. I feel it in

her body when she tumbles out of whatever beautiful dream her mind has created for her. She freezes, a wakeful sort of tension settling over her as she comes to grips with reality. Her head turns, as if to check that I'm awake, then she pauses. She does an experimental shift of her body weight, freezing, I imagine, when she encounters my dick.

I wince when she launches herself out of bed with a horrified squeak, stumbling as she spins to face me, her eyes wide and accusing.

"What the hell are you doing?" she demands, breathless and flushed.

A startled laugh escapes me. "What am *I* doing? Trying to wake you up!"

She points an accusing finger toward my waist. "With *that*?"

I grab a pillow to cover myself, my own embarrassment mixing with amusement. "No, that was entirely your doing. You were, uh... pretty insistent, grinding against me in your sleep."

Her face turns an impossible shade of pink. I can't help it —my grin widens at the sight. She's so God damn cute when she's flustered.

"I didn't—I wasn't—" she sputters helplessly.

"Relax," I try to soothe her, chuckling despite myself. "It's okay. You were dreaming. Totally involuntary. Just like my situation here."

"How do you know I was—" She stops abruptly, eyes widening in horror. "Oh God. Did I say something in my sleep?"

I rub the back of my neck sheepishly. "You were pretty vocal, yeah."

She claps both her hands over her face, groaning in mortification.

"Please, tell me I didn't say anything about whipped cream?" she pleads weakly through her fingers.

My jaw drops as laughter bursts from me. "You didn't. Was there whipped cream involved?"

Palmer squeals in horror and runs away, slamming the bathroom door behind her. I can't stop grinning for several minutes after she disappears. My brain keeps coming up with new, tantalizing images of Palmer and whipped cream, making it nearly impossible to reset my body's physiology.

By the time Palmer emerges from the bathroom fifteen minutes later, wearing the same pretty floral dress she wore the day before, the heat and the tension in my body have finally started to fade. I sit up in bed, planning to say something, but she promptly ignores me, heading out into the hall and closing the door behind her with force, just short of a slam. I fall back against the pillow, chuckling to myself.

I guess we're not talking about it.

I shower and dress before heading out into the living area. I follow the sound of Palmer's moms' voices until I see them sitting at the breakfast table. They face Palmer, who has her back to me. They smile when they notice me, and I sense Palmer's shoulders tense.

"Good morning," I say, taking the empty seat beside Palmer and grabbing the coffee pitcher to pour myself a mug.

"I hope you slept well?" Margot asks, pushing the containers with cream and sugar in my direction. I flash her a brilliant smile, accepting the cream.

"Oh yes," I agree. "I don't know if I have *ever* slept so well."

A little stab of pain shoots up my foot as Palmer's heel slams down onto my toe. I move it away from her, resisting a laugh. It's like she barely even tried to hurt me.

"That's wonderful," Celeste says, her pleased grin a bit too knowing. She has the look of a woman calculating how many grandchildren she wants and how quickly she can manage to acquire them. It's a look I've gotten before, but I can't say it bothers me this time.

"You guys know how to throw a party," I remark.

"And you know how to make damn good sangria," Celeste retorts.

Palmer clears her throat, standing suddenly. "Silas and I really should get going. I've got a lot to do today, and Evan was expecting me to be there this morning to help with—"

"Sit down and have breakfast with us," Celeste chides. "Silas has barely had a sip of his coffee."

Palmer's expression falls into dismay, and that pained look in her eyes physically hurts me to look at. I know, even if she might be irritated with me, that I want to help her. I want to wipe that desperate expression from her features, to do whatever I have to do to bring back her smile.

She starts to lower herself slowly back into her seat, but I place my hand on hers, halting her progress. I take a long sip from my mug before placing it back down on the table.

"Palmer's being kind, making excuses for me," I explain. "I have an event to shoot this afternoon. We really should be getting home. We've had a really nice time, though."

This seems to finally convince Celeste that we are serious about leaving, and I'm relieved. I'm trying to keep that little worried crease from plaguing Palmer's brow, if I can help it.

Celeste and Margot walk us out to my truck, and we say our goodbyes.

When we're on the road, Palmer asks, without prompting, "Do you actually have an event to shoot this afternoon?"

I grin. "No. But you looked like you wanted an escape route. And I wanted to give you one, if you needed it."

Her expression softens. "Oh. Thank you."

"You're welcome," I respond, but before I can help myself,

I add, "If you want to thank me for my help, you could always tell me about that whipped cream—"

She leans forward and cranks up the volume on the radio, drowning me out. I laugh, but don't push her. I let her spend the drive looking out at the ocean stretching alongside us. I'm not worried—we will get back to that topic eventually. I plan to make sure of that.

Once we arrive at her bakery, she practically launches herself from my truck before I come to a full stop. The action alarms me. Having her run away from me without saying goodbye feels wrong. Before the events of this morning, it felt like I had made huge strides in getting Palmer to open up to me, to trust me, to confide in me. And I don't want to lose the progress we have made with just one stupid dream.

I can't let her walk away from me like this, feeling so irritated with me. I slam my truck quickly into park and leap out after her.

"Palmer," I call, quickening my pace to catch up with her. "Palmer, wait up."

She turns so abruptly I nearly crash into her, stopping just inches away.

"What?" she demands.

I lower my voice, my eyes scanning her features for some sign of what she's feeling. I know there must be more going through her mind than just annoyance. "Can we please talk about last night—"

"I'd actually prefer we never talk about last night," she snaps, turning to head toward her apartment.

But I can't leave it there. I refuse to let this go so easily. I stay close to her, following right behind her as she ducks inside the door. We barely fit in the tiny stairwell leading to her apartment. The proximity is nearly unbearable, knowing I have to resist the urge to reach out and pull her into my arms.

She fumbles clumsily with her keys, deliberately ignoring me to yank open the mailbox on her door.

"We're just going to ignore it, then?" I press, stepping even closer to her. "Pretend it never happened?"

She glares at me from beneath her lashes, irritation and embarrassment flashing across her features. As she takes a stack of envelopes from her mailbox, she insists, "It didn't happen. It was just a dream. Can we please just let it go?"

Her tone is dismissive, but nothing in me wants to let this go. Sure, the dream was intriguing—more than intriguing. It was all I had been thinking about for the entire morning, the entire two-hour drive home. But even before that, I held her in my arms while she cried. That meant something, and I couldn't just move past it without acknowledging it.

"You're telling me it meant nothing to you?" I challenge.

She sighs heavily, flipping through the envelopes one by one. "What do you want me to say, Silas? Do you just need to hear it out loud, that I'm attracted to you? Fine. I'm attracted to you, okay? Are you happy?"

My heart skips a beat, warmth surging through my chest.

"Ecstatic," I say, but beneath the joy, there is a bitter, desperate double edge to this feeling. I certainly want Palmer to be attracted to me, but I realize that I want so much more than that. I want her to crave my presence, the way I crave hers. I want her to remember last night—incorporating me into her world, confiding in me, falling asleep in my arms— and I want her to realize how perfect it felt.

But it's no use. Despite my proximity, despite my desperation for her to acknowledge me, to acknowledge last night, I've lost her attention completely. She scans the letter in her hand, her eyes darting back and forth across the page as she reads.

She gasps. "I got it."

"What?" I ask.

"The interview," she breathes. "I got an interview for École Deschamps."

"The pastry school?" I ask, straightening instantly.

She looks up at me, her eyes wide with excitement. She nods slowly. "They want me to come for an interview."

I forget for a moment that she was in the process of running away from me, and I pull her into my arms, lifting her off the ground in delight. "That's amazing! You're going to Paris!"

When I let her back down to Earth, she palms either side of her forehead, reveling in the words. She whispers, disbelieving, "I'm going to Paris."

When she looks into my eyes, there is something unexpected in her expression. She looks thrilled, maybe a little nervous, but there is also a glow of something warm and buttery and incredibly affectionate. For me. The force of it makes my grin falter, makes my breath lodge painfully in my lungs.

"You made this happen," she says in wonder. "You didn't have to, but you made this happen for me."

I let out a startled laugh, though it is half-hearted. Nothing about this moment truly seems funny. "I really didn't do much... just took some pictures."

But she takes a purposeful step toward me, dropping her mail in a pile between our feet. And her eyes fix me with a burning expression, one that makes every cell in my body feel like it's melting beneath her gaze.

And if this small thing is enough to make her look at me like that, I suddenly want to lose the modesty, lose the humility. If taking credit for this small favor makes her look at me like that, I want to grab her and tell her, *you're right, I did help you. I did make this happen.* If only to claim my reward.

I would never say something so silly and self-indulgent.

But I consider it for the smallest, most tantalizing breath of a second.

In the end, it doesn't matter what I say, because in that single span of a breath, she presses her body to mine and kisses me.

Her soft hands curl around my neck and pull me into her. My whole body instantly reacts with triumph at the feel of her lips on mine. Every muscle fiber seems to jolt with an electric current at her touch.

But that incredible, tingling sensation is zapped just as suddenly as it appeared when she pulls away from me. I let her go, but only with great reluctance.

"I'm sorry," she gasps between panting breaths. "I'm sorry."

I shake my head, an incredulous laugh sputtering out. I can't imagine anything I'm *less* sorry about than the fact that she just kissed me. I'm feeling a lot of things right now—thrilled, excited, confused, a little (okay, maybe a lot) turned on—but sorry isn't one of them.

"Sorry? For what?" I ask.

She gestures to me. "I attacked you. I didn't mean to. I got caught up in the moment. But we set ground rules for a reason."

I bridge the space between us again, reaching up to cup her face in my hands, thrilled when she makes no motion to pull away.

"What was the reason, again?" I ask, stroking the curve of her cheekbone with my thumb, her lips parting at the touch.

"No clue," she whispers.

I lock my eyes with hers, not letting her look away when I say, "Fuck the ground rules."

I'll admit, I have found every excuse over these last few months to kiss her. It has felt like a loophole, somehow, to the rules we set. A kiss to test the waters. To make her ex jealous.

To show off how adoring a couple we are for Bennett Barlow. But it has always been part of the act, part of this game we have been playing. This feels like the first real kiss we've had together. Maybe the first real kiss I've ever had in my life, I don't know. The touch of her lips against mine drowns out thirty-one years of life and memory. I didn't exist before.

How in that first kiss, the best kiss of my life up until *this* moment, had she possibly been holding back? But that kiss was nothing compared to this. In that kiss, it felt like she was proving something, challenging me. Saying, *I can play this game just as well as you can.*

This kiss is real. Genuine. A declaration that she wants *me*. Not because of some arrangement. Not because of anyone else. Just her and me, in this stairwell, needing each other so desperately it can't wait any longer.

Her hands are all over me, all at once. But there are moments of warmth, of pressure, where her touch lingers on my neck, my shoulders, my chest, my abs. Every new location that she wanders is one that I didn't know could feel this good, that I didn't know was so sensitive to touch. And this is *over* my shirt. God, what would it be like for her to touch me without it? I've never longed for anything so much.

In the back of my mind, I register that her apartment—and her bed—are just one flight of stairs away. It would be so *easy* to give in, to forget every rule we set for ourselves; far easier than resisting, that's for damn sure. The thought alone nearly drives me insane.

I crush my mouth harder against hers, the desperation and urgency of my thoughts seeping into every movement. I press her back into the wall, sliding a knee between her thighs. She grinds against it, hungry for the friction—and fuck, do I want to give it to her.

However, in another example of the universe conspiring to keep me from what I want, my phone rings. I promptly reach down to my pocket and silence it, reaching back with the same hand to tangle my fingers in her hair. But before another second passes, my phone rings again. I let out a frustrated groan as I step away from her, reaching back to yank my phone from my pocket.

"I am so sorry, let me just—" My words halt when I see Charlie's name on my screen. Many things pass through my head in this moment. My initial instinct is to hang up again, but I already did that once, and he immediately called back. That can't be good.

My brain pulls a memory forward, one that is entirely unwelcome, especially in this otherwise perfect moment—the memory of Emery calling to say Dad was in the hospital. The memory of pushing mute on my phone, only for her to immediately call back to say that I needed to come home. That Dad collapsed. That he was rushed to the hospital. The memory of not getting to the hospital in time to say goodbye.

I look up into Palmer's eyes, feeling desperate as I say, "I'm so sorry. I have to take this."

She waves a hand, smiling feebly and mouthing, *it's fine,* as I answer.

"Hello?" I say, my voice hesitant, expecting the worst. Because the worst always seems to happen to the Howells.

CHAPTER 11
Palmer

I lean heavily against the wall, my breath shallow and uneven as I watch Silas take a half-step away to answer his phone. The sudden absence of his warmth is disorienting.

What just happened?

My eyelids flutter closed, and I can practically see the black words against the white paper imprinted there.

Congratulations. We are pleased to offer you an interview at the esteemed École Deschamps.

Paris. My dream, the one I've secretly harbored for all these years, might just come true.

After reading those words on the page, knowing what Silas did to help me, it was like some chemical reaction erupted in my brain, into something huge and explosive and warm as I looked into his eyes.

He believed in me. He believed in me so much, he got me my dream.

And that was all it took. I couldn't wait any longer. I had to kiss him.

The moment I did, it was like something wild and unstoppable was unleashed between us. If his phone hadn't interrupted us, who knows how far we would have gone? Then again, judging by the molten ache of longing practically pulsing between my legs, I know *exactly* where we were headed.

But now, in this pause as he answers the phone, the heat in my body cools abruptly, and the doubts start to creep into my mind.

"Hello?" Silas answers, his voice concerned. "Charlie? What's wrong?"

I'm going to Paris.

I grab the letter from the ground and read the words again, to confirm for myself once and for all that it isn't a dream.

Silas looks at me pensively for a moment, saying, "I am, why?"

Your presence is requested on the sixteenth of August for your interview.

The week after the Barlow wedding. The week that Silas and I were meant to reevaluate our arrangement.

Silas turns from me, and I watch the tense lines of his back as he looks out the window, his knuckles blanching with the force of clenching his phone tightly in his fist.

"Is she okay? No, it's fine, I'll be right there—what?"

Silas whirls, a mystified look on his face—his gorgeous, perfect face. Those sensitive, toffee-colored eyes, the strong jawline that Clark Kent would envy. What was I thinking, kissing that perfect face when I might be moving to France?

"She wants Palmer?" Silas says, and my musings are brought to an abrupt halt when I realize I'm involved in this conversation. "Did she say why?"

Silas mutes the microphone and says, "It's my sister. She won't stop crying. Charlie isn't sure why she's so upset. But she's asking for you."

"For me?" I clarify.

"I don't know why she wants you, specifically. But will you—?"

His eyes search my face with such desperation, I know I can't deny him. Nor do I want to—not if there's something I can do to help Emery.

"Let's go," I reply immediately, and his shoulders sink with relief at the promise.

He returns his attention to the call. "Charlie, we'll be there in twenty minutes. See if you can figure out what's going on."

Silas drives us to his childhood home, now Emery and Charlie's home. If we weren't arriving with a purpose, I would stop to take it in longer. It's a beautiful, one-story house with walls of stone and stucco that's the color of shortbread cookies. The yard is small but well-tended and surrounded by a white picket fence.

I can picture it—the beautiful childhood Silas and Emery must have had here. The beautiful future Charlie and Emery would have here. There's a jealous pang in my heart, but I'm not sure what I envy more—their idyllic childhood or their bright future.

We tread briskly up the front walk, but Emery flings the door open before we're halfway there. She launches herself at me, engulfing me in a hug.

As advertised, she is crying. Not in a subtle, demure way. This is full ugly crying, with thick tracks running down her face and snot coming out of her nose. I settle my arms around her, feebly patting her back as I ask, "Emery? What's wrong?"

But she is inconsolable. She blubbers something completely unintelligible. At this moment, though, I see Charlie emerge from the house over Emery's shoulder. His hands are tucked in his pockets, looking very casual and calm, unlike his bride-to-be.

"Em?" I hear Silas ask.

She pulls momentarily out of the hug, wiping at her eyes and her nose with her sleeve. She tries to collect herself, but she is nearly hyperventilating.

"Emery," I press. "What is the matter?"

"I got... a call," she works out between tears. "A phone call."

She holds up her cell and points to it, as if the phone might give us an explanation for her hysterics.

"From?" Silas asks.

Emery works through another round of high-pitched sobs before she finds her voice again.

"Livie... Laurent," she squeaks.

"Oh," I say simply, finally understanding. A soft smile pulls at my lips.

"You... got... Livie... Laurent... for... me..." Emery gasps between sobs, drawing me in for another hug and burying her face into my shoulder. I rub soothing circles in her back, grinning widely now that I know for certain that she is okay—more than okay, in fact. I know that these are happy tears.

"She's going to help you with a dress?" I ask.

"Not *a* dress," Emery corrects. "*The* dress. She's lending me the dress for my wedding. She just called to ask for my size."

"I'm so happy for you, Em," I say.

"Anyone going to clue me in here?" Silas asks, irritable at being kept in the dark.

Emery pulls from my arms, setting her watery eyes on Silas. She takes several steadying breaths, finally able to work out comprehensible speech. "The designer of my dream wedding dress just called to say that she is gifting me the dress for our wedding. And I was so grateful, of course, but I asked her how she even knew who I was."

She turns her gaze on me as if I'm an angel who has just descended from heaven in front of her eyes. I squirm a little uncomfortably beneath that look. "She said one of the models from her last shoot contacted her. I asked for the name, because I don't know any models. And she told me it was Palmer Sullivan who contacted her. Palmer got me my dress."

She squeezes me back into her arms for a third time, and I laugh in her embrace.

I crane my neck until I can see Silas behind me, explaining, "I asked Tara to introduce me to Livie Laurent in lieu of payment for my 'modeling' work."

I really hadn't been expecting much from the call, to be honest. What reason did a big-shot designer have to give a discount on one of her spectacular gowns? I simply told her that my friend was on a budget for her wedding. That both her parents had died when she was a teenager, and that she had her heart set on this one design. That I had never seen someone look so spectacular in a wedding dress before. And Livie proved to be unexpectedly kind and gracious and so incredibly generous. It was luck, really.

"You got Emery a free wedding dress?" Silas whispers, his tone disbelieving. Emery releases me, and I'm suddenly caught beneath Silas's intense stare.

I look back and forth between the adoring expressions of both Silas and his sister, and a bubble of nervous laughter wells up in my throat.

"You guys," I retort. "It's really not a big deal—"

"It's a huge deal."

They say the words in unison, his deep baritone mixing with her higher pitch, but their tone is the same—disbelieving and impressed and adoring. I look between their faces, the way they're looking at me with so much fondness and... And I don't know what to do with looks like that. I don't know how to respond.

"I just made a call," I whisper feebly.

"We're very grateful," Charlie says while wrapping an arm

around Emery's shoulders, breaking the Howell siblings from their trance.

"So grateful," Emery agrees, her voice still shaky with tears. "Please, let us do something for you, to show you how grateful we are. Make you lunch? Name our first child after you?"

I take a step backward. This all just feels like a little too much. "I really should get back to the bakery—"

"Come to Cal's with us tonight, after the bakery closes?" she begs. "Let us at least buy you a drink."

Emery Howell will not be denied, I guess. I nod, relenting, "Okay. I can meet y'all tonight."

"I'll get you home," Silas promises.

He is notably quiet and pensive on the way back to my bakery.

"Want me to pick you up later?" he asks when he drops me off.

I shake my head. "I'll walk, thanks. Meet you there."

I half expect him to argue, but he doesn't—simply waves and drives away.

I take a moment to run up to my apartment to change out of my clothes from the day prior before heading down to the bakery.

When I step into my shop, all I want to do is talk to Jenna, to tell her everything that happened in Myrtle Beach, but I'm disappointed to find her nineteen-year-old cousin, Sloan, sitting behind the register in her place. Sloan's hair is an unnatural jet black with streaks of bright purple framing her face. She wears a black nose ring, thick black eyeliner, and all black clothing. It's not exactly the look we were going for in our store, but Jenna gave up trying to get Sloan to dampen the goth for work a long time ago. Our need for cheap labor behind the register has taken precedence over that losing battle.

"Sloan?" I ask. "What are you doing here? I thought you only worked Fridays and Saturdays."

She shrugs, not looking up at me from whatever she's scrolling through on her phone. "Jen wasn't feeling well."

I frown. Jenna didn't tell me she wasn't feeling well. I resolve to text her later, but duck behind the counter and into the kitchen.

Evan looks up from a bowl of batter to watch me put on my apron.

"You're getting in rather late today, Boss," he remarks coyly. "Late night with your not-so-fake boyfriend?"

I roll my eyes. I open a binder on my workstation, like I do at the beginning of every week. I check the calendar, planning to make a list of all the flavors and sizes of cake, the types and colors of buttercream I'll need for each day.

"You could say that," I mutter. "We got trapped in Myrtle Beach by my mother. Just got back an hour ago."

I trust Evan, but if Jenna ever discovered I gave him intimate details of my life before telling her, she would murder me. The full story will have to wait until we're together.

"Did he get along well with your mom?" he asks. "Did she entrance him, as she does us all?"

I smirk to myself. "They got along swimmingly."

"Ooh, getting on with the in-laws," he teases. "Should I start your wedding cake now?"

I glare at him. "You're burning that batch of cupcakes."

He checks his oven, alarmed, but glares at me over his shoulder when he realizes I was only trying to distract him. Evan has never burned anything, not since the day he started working here.

Throughout my afternoon, as I organize my work for the week and start to assemble the first cakes, my brain keeps drawing forward memories from that morning. The look in Silas's eyes when he demanded we talk about the events of last night. The feel of his lips on mine when we kissed. His devoted expression when he realized what I did for his sister.

There is a weight in my chest that builds steadily as I run through these moments obsessively.

By the time I walk to Full Proof that evening, this weight has become unbearably heavy and uncomfortable. It's some foreign emotion, one that I don't know how to articulate.

Somehow, when I see Cal, Charlie, Emery, and Silas sitting in a booth together and they look up at me and cheer at my mere presence, it only gets worse. They each have a drink in their hands, and they dedicate this first round to me.

I settle in beside Silas in the booth, and he rests his arm across the seat behind me, not quite touching me, but centering his body around me at the same time. He watches his friends fondly as they fight over who gets the honor of buying my drink.

"If Palmer Sullivan has to pay for a drink in this bar, then I'm dead," Emery insists. "She's on my tab, for as long as I live."

Cal's booming laughter responds. "That's not saying much. When was the last time you actually paid for a drink?"

"I'm certain I've paid for a couple drinks recently."

"Show me the receipts," he retorts.

"Who keeps bar receipts?" she argues.

Silas is uncharacteristically quiet throughout the evening, seeming just to enjoy the easy banter and camaraderie between his friends. But there is something unbearably warm in his expression when he catches my eye that elicits a fluttering sensation inside me.

Eventually, Charlie convinces Emery to head home for the evening, reminding her they both have work the following morning. We leave Cal behind in the bar, and Silas turns to me, his hands in his pockets.

"Let me drive you home," he requests, and I accept the offer.

But when we get to the bakery, he gets out and walks me to the door, and I can tell that he wants to say something. He's had something brewing in his mind the entire evening. And I suspect I know what he wants to say.

A cowardly pit in my heart gapes wide, beckoning me to hide within its walls. To not acknowledge any of it—the night at my mother's house, the kiss, what I did for Emery, Paris. A part of me doesn't want to come to grips with what I'm feeling —what we are both clearly feeling—knowing that the future is so uncertain. But his eyes are intense and demanding as they search my face.

"Why'd you do it?" he asks, his voice low and earnest, almost challenging.

I know we promised each other honesty. And I'm tempted to tell him the truth. To tell him how desperately I wanted to do something kind and beautiful for his sister, because I know how much she means to him. To tell him how I want to make his sister love me, because something deep inside me desperately wants him to love me. But I can't make either of them love me. Because I might be moving to Paris. And it's cruel to make good people love you, only to leave them promptly behind.

Instead, I tell him something else. Not quite a lie, but not the truth. "Your sister has been so kind to me. So welcoming. And a part of me dreads the idea of her finding out we lied to her. If things don't work out, I want her to have good memories of me, you know? I don't want her to remember only how I deceived her."

I know instantly that he doesn't like this response, and I don't blame him. I don't like it either. But I don't think he believes me.

He pulls me into his body by my waist. I brace my hands

against his chest, and I can feel the pounding of his heart beneath my fingertips.

"Look at me, Palmer," he demands. "Does this feel like deceit to you?"

Nothing feels deceitful about this. There's no denying the way my pulse quickens at his touch, the way being surrounded by his warmth feels natural and right. I can't deny how good it feels to be folded into Silas's life, to be welcomed by his family. How novel it feels to be supported by someone so profoundly and effortlessly. If this is pretend, I don't know what's real anymore.

But as he leans toward me and my entire body prepares for his kiss, I can't fight away the doubts.

"You agreed that we should be friends," I insist, my voice barely above a whisper. "That we should wait until after the wedding."

"I was wrong," he retorts, pausing with his lips just a breath away from mine. "I don't want to wait. I think it might just kill me to wait any longer."

"Silas, I—" I'm horrified when my voice cracks painfully around his name. "What about Paris?

"What *about* Paris?" he demands, his tone almost angry.

"I might be going to Paris next year, if I get into École Deschamps," I insist, as if I need to remind him. "Is that what you want? To start something between us, knowing I might move to another country?"

"We don't know what the future holds yet," he whispers. "All I know is that we are here now. And I... I care for you. I look for every excuse to spend time with you. I *want* you. Even if you're holding back, for whatever reason—because of Paris, because of your past. I don't care. Even if you can't give all of yourself to me. I don't *care*. I'll take whatever pieces I can get."

The offer is tempting. But I've already hurt someone who I couldn't give all of myself to. I can't do that to someone again. And while I've wanted this, wanted him, for months now, I've wanted Paris for *so* much longer. I'm not going to give that up.

I take a deep breath and pull myself from his arms. May in South Carolina has never felt as cold as it does in this moment, in the abrupt absence of him.

I turn and open the door to my apartment.

"I'm sorry," I whisper, watching his hopeful expression fall into one of defeat. It kills me to be the one to make him look this way. "I can't. I need to see this through. I won't make you any promises until after the interview."

He sighs. "Okay. But I hope you'll think about it. You might not know exactly what you want yet... but I do, whether you go to Paris or not."

CHAPTER 12

Silas

I've scared her off.

Emery has always tended to come on too strong. It was something I had been concerned about from the very beginning, her natural enthusiasm clashing with Palmer's inherent mistrust of people. But I can't blame Emery for this, not when Palmer seems perfectly comfortable with my sister's typical exuberance. This is all on me.

Because, unlike Emery, I usually have the exact opposite problem. I tend to keep my feelings locked behind a carefully neutral facade, remaining aloof, even when I want to share my feelings.

But with Palmer, I dropped my defenses entirely, laid it all out on the table for her. And she retreated. Practically ran away from me. Hid in her bakery.

She manages to hide for an entire month before I can find a reason to draw her out again. She makes good excuses; I'll give her that. *It's June. The busy season.* I can't exactly deny that we're both incredibly, genuinely busy. My calendar is packed, every weekend of the summer booked solid, even weekdays crowded with rehearsal dinners, spreads for *Ever After,* and bridal sessions.

Suddenly, weddings are the only time I get to see her, as we are often hired for the same gigs. But we pass like ships in the night, a fleeting glimpse of her assembling another one of her beautiful creations before the bride pulls me away to take pictures of her bridal party in matching pajamas. It's like I'm back to square one, wondering obsessively if the next wedding will be another opportunity to see her face again.

Deep down, I know it's more than scheduling conflicts keeping us apart. It's deliberate avoidance, carefully dancing around the conversation she's not ready to have. I know I have to give her that space, but it almost physically hurts to spend so much time away from her.

When I receive a text message from Bennett Barlow, I can honestly say I've never been so thrilled to see her name come across my screen. She offers me a lifeline without even knowing it.

BENNETT

Hey, you free this Friday afternoon to come to the hotel around two o'clock? Was wondering if you might want to come scope out shooting locations for the wedding?

It just so happens to be the first Friday I've had free in eight weeks, due to an unexpected cancellation of a wedding. Bennett immediately follows her first text with another.

BENNETT

Bring Sweet P! It'll be fun!

She'll never know how great a service she's done me.

I send a screenshot of the conversation to Palmer and sit watching the screen, waiting for the reply. I swear I see the "..."

of her pending reply start and stop several times, as if she carefully types and retypes her response.

The response is short when it comes, but I inwardly cheer, nonetheless.

PALMER

I'll be there

A wave of relief washes over me. I don't know how long we'll have together at the Barlow Hotel, but I'll take every minute with her I can find.

Pick you up at 1:30

The rest of my week goes painfully slow while waiting for the opportunity to see Palmer again. And I know I shouldn't get my hopes up, but I can't help it. I want to see her again. I want to be with her, be around her, more than I've ever wanted anything.

I already knew how attracted I was to her; how much I enjoyed spending time with her. But seeing how seamlessly she blended into my world was the final piece that solidified it for me. The way she showed such kindness to my sister. The way she fit with my friends like she had been sitting in our booth at Cal's bar for years. It showed me how *easy* this could be if she would only let it happen.

I know she wants this too. Stalling until after the wedding is a defense mechanism, I'm sure of it. Hiding behind her cakes is easier than confronting her feelings.

But in the wake of her weeks of giving me the cold shoulder, I feel at war with myself. A part of me is irritated that she has hardly acknowledged me, barely spoken to me. I think—I know—that she has talked to Emery more often than she has talked to me. Emery can't stop bragging about her *new best friend, Palmer*. How well they are getting along, how they text and call all the time. Emery even convinced Palmer to go out to lunch with her one day. I only found out about it from Emery in hindsight and had to cover for my ignorance at the time.

But far greater than the jealousy, the angst, is a singular desperation to break down those walls she has steadfastly reconstructed around herself. To win her over, without scaring her away.

I have one opportunity, one more display for Bennett Barlow, likely the last one before the wedding. And I can't waste it. It may be my last chance to show Palmer how good we could be together.

When Friday afternoon arrives, I pull up in front of her bakery ten minutes early, unable to wait any longer at home. I sit in the truck with the engine idling, my palms sweating against the steering wheel. I try to convince myself I'm not truly nervous. Just hopeful, I think. Cautiously, stupidly hopeful.

She steps out of the bakery promptly at 1:30, wearing a light purple dress that hits just above her knee, her hair swept up in a loose bun. The sight of her casually knocks the air from my lungs.

When her eyes catch mine through the passenger window, there's a moment of hesitation in her step, a flicker of uncertainty in her expression. She walks toward my truck slowly, like she may just turn around and run.

I lean across the seat and push the door open before she can change her mind.

"Hey," I greet her, offering what I hope looks like a reassuring smile.

"Hey," she echoes, sliding in and pulling the door shut. Her voice is quiet, cautious. There is an awkward beat of silence as she settles in beside me. She fiddles with the hem of her dress.

"I'm glad you came," I say eventually, keeping my tone even.

She shrugs. "Bennett expects me there."

"Still," I respond. "I've missed seeing you."

She takes a deep breath before whispering, "I've missed you, too."

That soft admission is enough to set my heart racing. So much for not getting my hopes up.

We spend the drive in silence aside from the quiet music playing on the radio. Even so, by the time we arrive at the hotel, the tension between us feels electric—fragile, like a single touch could shatter it.

We park and head toward the grand entrance of the hotel —a towering facade of sandy gray stone, huge arching windows, and an old-fashioned awning bearing the name, The Barlow Hotel.

I stop in front of the doors, offering a hand to Palmer. She looks at it and meets my eyes again, hesitating.

I arch an eyebrow at her, grinning. "Have to put on a good show, don't we?"

She nods slowly, reaching out to put her hand in mine. I give it a reassuring squeeze as I lead her inside.

Bennett is waiting for us in the lobby. She smiles widely at us both but draws Palmer in for a hug as soon as she is in reach.

"I'm so glad you could come!" she says, explaining, "The Barlow Annual Charity Gala is tonight in the ballroom, and the setup will be very similar to the wedding. I thought it would be the perfect opportunity to scope out shooting locations for you and your second shooter."

Bennett starts to lead us through the lobby, but Palmer

leans over to whisper, "You have a second shooter? I didn't know you worked with anyone else."

"Second and third shooter," I correct. "Big wedding."

We walk into the grand ballroom, and it feels the size of a small football stadium, with impossibly high ceilings, one wall occupied by towering floor-to-ceiling windows topped with draped velvet curtains of powder blue, and the other wall lined with curved wooden balconies.

"Big wedding, indeed," Palmer remarks. "I forgot how enormous this place is."

In anticipation of the gala, there are round tables evenly spaced throughout the room with black tablecloths. A small army of staff is assembling and decorating the space, and Bennett weaves through them with practiced ease as she explains how the layout of the wedding will compare.

After the ballroom, she shows us the open-air courtyard where cocktail hour will be held, followed by the gardens where they will host the ceremony. The smell of honeysuckle and jasmine and roses envelops us as we emerge into the garden.

There is a half-circle clearing surrounded by a thick border of oak trees with draping curtains of Spanish moss. It's a gorgeous venue—I've shot weddings here before, and it may just be my favorite. Except for the peak of midday, the lighting is always ideal, the backdrop naturally soft and romantic.

"I can picture it," Palmer says softly from beside me. "It's going to be an absolutely beautiful wedding, Bennett."

Bennett looks at her, and for just the briefest moment, I catch a hint of alarm in her features.

I know exactly what draws Bennett's attention, too. It's something about Palmer's tone—something sad and wistful and... longing? She sounds so regretful, almost agonized. I don't even know if Palmer realizes it, as she stands entranced by the venue.

Why does she sound like that? Is it sinking in that this is the place where Grant will be married in just a few short weeks? Is she finally realizing that she's losing him?

The thought practically sickens me.

But I can't focus on how I'm feeling in this moment, not when I know Bennett heard it too. Bennett's dark brows knit together with concern, watching Palmer. Maybe she sees what I see—the beautiful, entrancing woman who Grant let get away. She looks incredible in this light, with the sun flickering through the thick canopy of trees.

I give Palmer's hand a firm squeeze, abruptly demanding her attention. "Keep looking at the venue like that, Babe, and I might just have to reserve us a date."

Palmer looks at me, her eyes wide and a little startled, before she schools her face. "What? Don't be silly. We could never afford it."

I lean down to kiss her cheek, and the brief touch of my lips on her skin is agonizing. "Maybe Bennett will give us a discount."

Bennett's smile returns. "That can *definitely* be arranged."

She is mollified, I think—convinced once again of our unwavering love. Crisis averted.

But the crisis happening in my heart has only just begun. Because now I'm picturing it. Standing in the clearing ahead, with Palmer walking down this pathway in a white gown, her eyes locked on me. My heart gives a painful squeeze.

Bennett guides us back to the lobby. But just when it seems like she'll part ways with us, she asks, "Hey, y'all busy tonight?"

Palmer tenses. "I, uh—"

"You should come to the gala!" Bennett says before waiting to hear the response. "One of our sponsors paid $10,000 for a table, but they aren't coming. I have an empty table to fill, if you're interested. You could bring some friends too, up to ten people. Open bar, killer band..."

I peer at Palmer, grinning. She looks back at me, wary.

"Come on," I urge. "We can't deny our friends an excuse to get dressed up and drink free booze, can we?"

She hesitates for just a moment before smiling. "Evan would certainly kill me if he ever heard that I deprived him of such an opportunity."

Bennett claps with delight. "Starts at seven! I'll leave your names on the guest list."

Another evening with her acquired.

It takes exactly zero convincing to get our friends on board. I text Cal, Emery, and Charlie, receiving immediate and resounding confirmations. Palmer asks Evan, Jenna, and her husband, Jonathan.

When Cal, Charlie, Emery, and I enter the lobby of the Barlow hotel that evening, I see her immediately, standing beside her friends with her back to me. Jenna notices us and nods in our direction. Palmer turns, and I stop in my tracks at the sight of her. The black dress she chose for the evening sinks low across her back, leaving a long expanse of smooth skin visible. It clings to her curves in the most enticing ways. My mouth suddenly goes incredibly dry. My tie feels tight around my throat.

"You're staring," Emery whispers from beside me, her voice tight from fighting a laugh.

"I'm aware," I reply, my voice thick. I don't acknowledge my friends. I can't tear my eyes away from *her*. But the rest of them aren't afflicted by the same paralysis that I am. Palmer and her friends cross the remaining distance, and she—far more polite than I am being in this moment—introduces everyone.

When the rest of the group is distracted with each other, I lean down, my lip grazing the curve of her ear as I say, "You look absolutely incredible."

She seems to stop breathing. I pull away, catching the glow of her blush in her cheeks. "Thank you."

I raise my voice, addressing the group. "Y'all head inside without us. I need just a second alone with my girlfriend."

I catch Jenna's suspicious look, but I pay her no mind. They head into the ballroom.

Palmer's eyes are wide and expectant, waiting for me to say what I kept her behind to tell her.

"The wedding is just a few weeks away," I say. "This might be the last time we have to pretend we're a couple."

Pretend being the keyword. I can only hope that this isn't the end of us, just the end of the pretense.

She inhales slowly.

"It probably will be," she agrees.

"Can I make a request?" I ask, my voice soft and pleading, far less smooth than I would like it to be. "In case it truly is our last night together."

She tilts her head, her soft pink lips pursing, but doesn't voice a response.

"Can we pretend the possibility of Paris doesn't exist tonight? That we're not on borrowed time?" I request. "Let me make believe this is real, just for tonight. Not for Bennett Barlow or our friends. For *us*."

She studies my expression, her green eyes glassy and uncertain. She considers my request for an endless minute, but finally, she nods—just the smallest motion—and it sends a sharp bolt of relief through my chest.

"Okay," she agrees. "Just for tonight."

She extends her hand to me, and I take it in mine. As we walk toward the ballroom, I resolve to memorize every second of her tonight—the way she looks, the feel of her hand in mine.

By the time we are escorted to our assigned table beside the dance floor, I'm delighted to find that our friends have blended seamlessly. Charlie, Emery, and Jenna are deep in conversation. Cal is regaling John with escapades from his short-lived but bright NFL career. They hardly look up to greet us as we take our seats among them. Palmer beams at our friends with profound affection, and I know she can feel it too —how easily our lives could combine. Not her friends or my friends, but *our* friends.

The evening is everything I would expect of a Barlow event. The food is decadent, the drinks expensive, the band incredible. And the best part is that Palmer keeps her promise, in abundance. It's like she needed an excuse to let herself experience this, experience us.

Her hand rests on my thigh where it's pressed against hers, and the touch ignites something low and hot in my chest. She flashes me soft, adoring smiles over her drink. When Cal makes her laugh with his never-ending jokes, she leans her body into mine with the force of her laughter.

And God, it feels good. And right. And so incredibly *real* that it might just kill me to find out it's all pretend.

The band, which has been playing soft jazz music throughout dinner, picks up the tempo, the rhythm beckoning people to the floor. Palmer grins at me.

"Dance with me?" she asks, like I could possibly deny her anything.

I follow her onto the dance floor, surrounded by couples twirling under the soft glow of the crystal chandeliers. Through fast songs and slow, I can't get her off the dance floor, nor do I want to. I've never seen her enjoy herself so freely, letting her body sway to the music—sink into my touch without reservation.

Finally, she tilts her head back, eyes sparkling, and asks, "Want to get some air?"

I nod, not trusting my voice. She pulls me through the crowd by my hand, eventually slipping out through the back doors of the hotel into the secluded gardens.

The humid air engulfs us when we step outside. The sound of the party fades into the distance as we walk into the depths of the garden, the moss-draped oaks casting shadows across the stone path.

She reaches out to stroke one fingertip over the petals of a flower blossoming from the vines climbing up the wall beside us.

"Earlier today, when you saw this place. You looked like you might cry. I thought..." I hesitate, feeling vulnerable and a little embarrassed to admit it. "I thought, maybe, it finally sunk in. That Grant was getting married. That it should have been your wedding."

Her jaw slackens, her expression alarmed. "Do you think Bennett suspected that, too?"

I shrug, unable to care less about Bennett Barlow in this moment. "Maybe. I don't know."

Her head shakes frantically, her blonde curls bouncing with the motion. "That wasn't it at all. It never even crossed my mind."

I curl my hand around her waist, my fingers brushing her skin where her dress gapes open in the back. I feel her exhale, unsteady.

"Did I?" I ask, my voice barely louder than a sigh. "Cross your mind?"

She searches my face, her lower lip quivering. But she doesn't speak. Doesn't reveal what she was truly thinking in that moment.

But her kiss feels like answer enough.

Her hands grip my lapels, needing the leverage to pull

herself up to me, her lips desperately crushing against mine. I slide my hand up her spine and kiss her without hesitation. I respond like I've been starving for her kiss, for her touch—probably because I have. I've spent a month feeling like I'm fading to nothing, longing so deeply for her.

No wonder she has been avoiding me all this time, because we *both* know that this thing between us is inevitable—that the only way to stop this train is to keep us miles apart. Maybe oceans apart. And now that we're together, there's no stopping it. No denying what we feel.

She gasps into my mouth and clutches me tighter.

The smell of the flowers mixes with her scent, her perfume, and it practically makes me dizzy. The world is spinning around us.

She presses her body flush with mine, and I let myself fall into the sensation of her—the curve of her waist, the warmth of her breath, the soft sound she makes when I drag my mouth down her neck. I kiss the spot just above her collarbone, and her knees seem to buckle beneath me. I hold her tight to me, though.

I've never wanted anyone like this. Never wanted so desperately to know every complicated inch of someone before. To memorize her reactions, her rhythms, the taste of her sighs.

I press her back against the ivy-covered wall, one arm braced beside her head, the other wrapped around her waist, my lips never leaving her for more than a fraction of a second. Her hands roam over me—my neck, my shoulders, my chest—urgent, but reverent. Like she can't decide if she wants to devour me or worship me. Or maybe some equal mix of both.

My hand slides down the curve of her hip, and when I reach her thigh, she hooks it over my leg. The smooth material of her dress parts, the bare skin of her leg peeking out through the slit. I run my hand up her thigh, feeling the muscles growing taut beneath my touch. Her tongue battles with mine, unclear who is in control. We both seem to be deeply out of control in this moment.

Her hands trail down my stomach until they find my belt loops, and she pulls my hips more firmly into hers. She rocks her pelvis against mine in one undulating wave, and I remember what it was like to wake up to her sighing my name, grinding against me; the memory of growing hard beneath the movements of her body.

But I don't have to rely on memory for long.

Because this is all that and more. Because, unlike the last time, this is all very willing, very intentional on her part. She *wants* this. And I've never wanted anything more than this.

My fingers dip beneath the fabric of her skirt until I can feel the elastic band of her panties where they meet her thigh. I slide my hand around the smooth curve of her ass, squeezing it with each roll of her hips against me.

She breaks away from me suddenly, as if coming up for breath. Her pupils are blown wide, her lipstick smudged. It may just be the hottest damn thing I've ever seen. And she looks at me, wide-eyed, as if a realization has suddenly come to her. Something big and life-altering.

Then she leans in again, her lips brushing my jaw, her voice low. But her tone is steady, certain, when she whispers, "Take me home."

For a beat, I just stare at her, convinced I have hallucinated. Because those three words are too good to be true. I must be dreaming. It certainly feels like something beyond my wildest dreams.

"Silas?" she whispers again, quieter now, a little uncertain.

My throat tightens. "Are you sure?"

I don't know when exactly I lost all sense, when I decided to second-guess a woman asking me to take her home. But this isn't just any woman. It's the woman who has completely captivated me for months, who occupies every conscious and unconscious thought I possess. The woman who assured me —kindly, but firmly—that she could not have feelings for me, could not consider me emotionally, physically, or otherwise. Not now, at least. Not with Paris looming ahead of us, both a dream and a threat.

There's no way she could have said those words. No way that she would ever reconsider.

And yet, she repeats, "Take me home."

CHAPTER 13

Palmer

This is a very bad idea. I know with certainty that someone will end up hurt. Maybe everyone will, I don't know.

But maybe my intuition is wrong, this time. Maybe the universe will let us have this—this one beautiful, borrowed night together. One night untouched by consequence. One perfect night where I can pretend that we don't have an expiration date.

But I should know by now that perfect doesn't exist.

I'm standing in the arched doorway of the hotel, waiting for Silas to pull up in his truck, when I hear it—

"Palmer?"

My heart leaps at this voice. Familiar. Startling. Warm.

I turn to see Grant leaning against the stone wall, his tie loosened and hanging from his neck. He has a glass dangling lazily from his fingertips.

"Grant," I breathe. "What are you doing here?"

He glances up at the gold script above the doors, the words *The Barlow Hotel* glowing in the warm light. His implication is clear—he belongs here.

Instead, he says, "I could ask you the same thing."

A nervous laugh stutters out of me. "I don't mean, what are you doing *here*—" I gesture vaguely to the hotel lobby. "I mean, what are you doing outside? Alone? Shouldn't you be inside with Bennett?"

"Needed some air," he replies. His gaze drops suddenly over me, trailing deliberately down the length of my dress, lingering far too long. I feel the weight of his attention with the echo of a tingling sensation down my spine. I cross my arms, as if it'll stop me from feeling so suddenly uncomfortable and exposed.

"What *are* you doing here, Palmer?" he asks. "Have you been at the party this whole time?"

Except for the part where I was pinned against a wall, in the very garden where you'll soon be married. Kissing someone who isn't you.

I say instead, "Bennett invited us."

"Us?" he echoes. Then, "Oh." A muscle in his jaw jumps. "*Us.*"

"She had an open table to fill," I say too quickly, sounding defensive, feeling for some reason that I owe him an explanation. "It was last-minute. Jenna, John, Evan—they're all still inside."

As if he might want to run by and say hi to my friends, for old times' sake. He never seemed to enjoy being around my friends, even when we were dating.

"You're not staying with them?" he asks. His expression doesn't change, per se, but a calculating glint flashes in his eyes. As if he's doing the math—constructing the night he wasn't there to witness, realizing he doesn't like the way things are adding up.

I shake my head. "I was... tired."

The words sound incredibly lame. They sound like a lie— one that I'm certain Grant can detect from a mile away.

As if summoned by fate, Silas's truck pulls up into the curved drive in this moment. He parks and jumps out before the engine even settles, his eyes instantly locking with mine. That easy, boyish grin stretches across his face. He doesn't even notice Grant, standing just a few feet away.

He walks toward me like he's approaching something he wants. No hesitation. No restraint. Like I'm the center of his whole world.

"You ready?" he asks, his voice warm. His hands find my hips like it's second nature, tugging me gently into him.

He seems completely unaware of the tension in the air, so thick I feel like I'm swimming in it.

And I can't help it—I warily glance over at Grant, my breath hitching in my throat.

He isn't looking at us—his eyes are pointedly fixed on the ground, at nothing. Like he won't have to admit he is seeing this if he doesn't meet my eyes.

When I look back at Silas, my resolve wavers for the smallest moment. His smile falters, and the change in his expression almost physically hurts me, somewhere deep in my chest.

When I look once more at Grant, he lifts his gaze, his eyes finding and holding mine. And for the first time in over a year, I see him clearly. Not as the man who broke my heart. But as someone who might still believe he has some claim on it.

There's something desperate in that look—like he's silently begging me not to go. Not to walk away with someone else.

But then I turn back to Silas.

And there it is again—that quiet ache in his eyes. That simple, wordless plea: *Come with me. Let him go.*

I'm frozen with indecision for one endless second.

But then my muscles thaw.

I pull out of Silas's arms.

I extend a hand.

"Let's go?" I ask softly.

Silas's fingers close around mine, warm and certain and victorious, and he leads me into the night.

I don't look back.

When we arrive at his apartment, it isn't the frantic discarding of clothes that I initially thought it might be. Maybe it's the unexpected run-in with Grant. Maybe the heat of the moment simply cools with increasing distance from the party. But whatever the reason, a wave of nerves hits me the second we're together, alone, in his place.

He seems to sense my hesitation. "You want anything to drink?"

"Just some water," I request. I had more free drinks at the gala than I probably should have.

He ambles in the direction of his kitchen, and I can hear him opening the cabinet to fetch a glass, filling it with ice.

In his absence, I wander toward his photoshoot setup, inspecting the white backdrop hanging from the ceiling, the umbrella lights, a rack of sample clothes. A pink chest sits at the base of the clothing rack, looking like it would belong to Pirate Barbie. I kneel to unbuckle the lid and lift it open, only to find it filled to the brim with lace and satin lingerie.

"Silas?" I call out warily. "Why do you have a treasure chest full of thongs? Please tell me this is not the spoils of previous conquests."

I hear his cackle of laughter from the kitchen, and he appears with my glass of ice water. I take it from him and take a grateful sip, my mouth feeling incredibly dry.

I nod at Barbie's underwear collection, asking, "So what's the story there?"

He grins. "*Ever After* did a feature on boudoir photography. The lingerie company liked the pictures so much, they asked me to do some work for their website too. They sent me that as a thank you, in case I want to use samples for boudoir shoots for my own clients."

I lift a red satin bra out of the treasure chest. The cups are completely open, with a wide satin ribbon clearly meant to be tied in place of actual bra cups. I set down my glass of water and hold it up to my chest curiously, peering up at Silas from the floor.

"Do you do boudoir shoots often?" I ask, and I can't help it—my tone is just the slightest self-conscious at the question, the tiniest bit *jealous*. As if it's not enough that he photographed hundreds of models—lingerie models at that—the idea that he also gets paid to take pictures of random women naked gets under my skin. I think of the very normal, black cotton underwear I'm wearing beneath this dress with dismay.

"Not often," he replies. "On request, I will. Usually with clients who have known me for a while, who know they can trust me with something so... intimate."

He looks down at the red bra I'm still holding up to myself with a curious smile. It's probably the alcohol that's still blurring my senses, filtering my inhibitions, but the craziest idea suddenly pops into my mind.

I grin at him, quoting my favorite movie, "Jack, I want you to draw me like one of your French girls."

He closes the lid of the pink treasure chest with a laugh and offers a hand to help me off the ground.

"Cute," he says. "Very funny."

I purse my lips, my brows furrowing. "I'm not joking."

He lets out another laugh, only this time it sounds uneasy, nervous even. He doesn't meet my eyes as he says, "You don't know what you're asking for. It's not a good idea."

I frown, dropping the bra to my lap, feeling dejected. "I know I'm not one of your models, but—"

"*No,*" he interrupts me firmly. "Do not think it's because I don't think you would look good in... that. God help me, I'm certain you would."

"Then why not?" I ask.

"Palmer, I have been dreaming of the *exact* scenario you just asked for since pretty much the moment I met you. Day and night, conscious and subconscious, my brain is *obsessed* with the thought of taking pictures of you in something like that." He points to the delicate piece of fabric to emphasize his point. My breath hitches in my throat at his tone—he sounds pained, anguished by the thought.

I take his outstretched hand, using it not only to lift myself off the ground but to draw my body close to his, until I'm pressed into him. I'm gratified to find his body reacting to my suggestion exactly the way I want it to, the front of his pants growing tighter against my hip.

"You asked to come over," he whispers, running his fingers through the hair at the base of my neck. "This night is already better than anything I could have imagined. I couldn't possibly expect you to play out my wildest fantasies, too."

A shiver of longing ripples through me. I know with absolute certainty that I *want* this. I want more of him—everything he's willing to give me. And I want to do this for him.

This might be a terrible idea. But I realize that I don't fucking care.

"Where can I change?" I ask, my tone steady, resolved.

He exhales sharply, a low groan escaping his throat. It's nearly a whisper, but it rakes down my spine all the same.

He clears his throat, as if it is suddenly difficult to speak. "Are you *sure*?"

"Completely sure," I confirm.

He steps away, and I immediately miss his body heat. He gestures in the direction of his bedroom. "The bathroom. My bedroom. Wherever you're most comfortable."

I draw away from him. I go back to the treasure chest and

find a matching pair of bottoms in my size. I grab my discarded black heels and head in the direction of his bedroom. As I change, I try not to dwell on what I'm about to do. I know if I stop to think about it, if I give myself a chance to consider the consequences, that I'll talk myself out of it.

Once I've slipped into the lingerie, I realize that I have nothing to wear over it. The idea of walking across his apartment in this—of offering myself up completely from the beginning—makes me hesitate. I open the door to his closet, spotting one of the black button-downs he wears to weddings. I grab it off the hanger and yank it over my head. It falls to my mid-thigh, and it smells like him. It helps me regain some of my confidence.

When I emerge from his bedroom, he has his back to me. His umbrella lights are on, and there is a black chair in the middle of the white backdrop. He is fiddling with his camera settings when I approach. My heart pounds at the sight of him, so carefully setting the scene.

"Where do you want me?" I ask, angry with myself when my tone doesn't sound cool and confident and sexy. It is painfully soft and unsure.

He turns, his eyes dark as they sweep over me, wearing his shirt. He points to the chair. "Facing the back."

I start to unbutton the shirt, but he stops me. "Not yet. Keep it on."

I obey, walking slowly over to the chair, straddling it to face the white backdrop. The chair is cold against my skin, and the combination of the chill and the nerves and the delicious anticipation sends goosebumps rippling across my skin.

"Now start to unbutton my shirt slowly," he orders. "Let it start to fall over your shoulders. That's it."

I hear the steady *click* of his camera as he directs me, his voice smooth and reverent. "Look over your shoulder. Chin up. Part your lips just a bit... Beautiful. Just like that."

Each click of the shutter makes my pulse thrum impossibly harder.

"Lose the shirt," he commands, and I hesitate for just a moment. It's draped at my elbows, barely there, just covering my lower back. But still, losing it feels like I'm giving away the last bit of armor I have.

But I obediently let the shirt fall and toss it to the side.

"One hand on the chair. The other in your hair," he guides, his voice washing over me like warm water. "Arch your back a bit more. God, you look amazing. So perfect."

A steady heat has been pooling between my legs all this time, but it becomes nearly unbearable at his compliment. Memories flash across my mind of every time in my life a person has seen my naked body. I think of how self-conscious I have felt in the past, obsessing over every crease and curve of my stomach and thighs and hips.

But in this moment, all those feelings of embarrassment and self-consciousness have fled. I have never felt so desirable. Never felt like my body was so worthy of attention. Never felt more perfect than I do right now.

"Now face me," he commands softly.

I take a deep breath, steadying myself, knowing that as soon as I stand and face him, he'll finally have the full view. I rise slowly, hyper-aware of everything: my ragged breaths, my pounding heartbeat, the thin fabric that barely covers me. I lower myself onto the chair once more, facing him, but avoid making eye contact, my cheeks flushing.

But he's having none of that.

"Eyes on me," he says.

And my eyes immediately lock on him, unable to deny him. For a second, he keeps his camera lowered, as if it pains him to block his direct view of me as he looks me up and down. And I do the same, noting with a lurch of my stomach just how taut and bulging his pants are already. An involuntary whimper escapes me at the sight of him, huge and nearly perfectly outlined by the fabric.

It's gratifying to know his body is reacting as strongly as mine. I don't think I've ever been so turned on in my entire life. The need coiling in me is all-consuming in its intensity.

He collects himself again, lifting his camera once more. "Head back. Really arch your back. Extend one of your legs and point your toes."

"You have a bucket of water?" I tease with a breathy chuckle, as I realize how he's posing me. "We can do the 'Flashdance.'"

"Shh," he scolds, but his tone is teasing when he says, "No talking. You'll ruin the shot."

I sigh in mock offense. "Yes, sir."

I swear I hear him groan at the phrase, and I smirk in delight.

"Now spread your legs."

I do as he says slowly, keeping my eyes locked on his as I let my legs spread. Again, he seems to lift the camera with great difficulty, reluctant to block his view.

"Put your hands on the bow," he says. "Pretend you're about to undo it."

I take the two strands of red satin ribbon in my hands, putting tension on them as if I'm about to undo the bow. His camera continues to fire away as I look up into the dark lens.

And suddenly, I can't bear it any longer. My desire for him is so intense that it is painful to resist. I *need* him. I need him like I've never needed anything, anyone before.

My hands pull on the ribbon until the bow is released, and my breasts fall free of their confines.

He lowers the camera suddenly.

"I thought I told you to *pretend* to undo it," he says, his tone dark and disapproving.

I flash him a truly wicked smile. "Oops."

He puts his camera down carefully, and the breath is knocked out of my lungs as he crosses the space between us in three slow, deliberate steps. No more playing games, I think. My stomach flutters with anticipation.

He steps into the space between my parted legs, reaching down to gently grasp my chin.

"Remarkable," he whispers, turning my face gently from one side, then to the other. "Sometimes, I look at you and can't believe you're real."

I nearly laugh, to play it off—but nothing about this feels like a joke. I'm trembling beneath the weight of that stare.

He lets go of my chin, and I realize suddenly that I'm perfectly at eye-level with his belt buckle and the swell of him beneath the zipper. My jaw has dropped open, and I close it, worried I might just start drooling on myself. I consider reaching out to run my hand along it, but before I can follow through with the idea, he sinks down to his knees before me.

He puts one hand on each of my thighs, moving them slowly upward. I curl my hands around his neck.

His eyes smolder into me, but there's just a glimmer of amusement there when he says, "Remember when you said you didn't think we'd need a safe word to meet the terms of our arrangement?"

I gasp a soft laugh, but nod. My laughter is steadily dying as his hands slide resolutely up my thighs.

"The terms have changed since then," he says, taking his hands from my thighs to undo the tie from around his neck. He pulls it from his collar with a snap of the fabric. "Would you like to establish one now?"

A bubble of panic rises in my throat. I have no idea what to expect, don't know how serious he is about this. But his tone sounds dark and demanding and *incredibly* serious. Every cell in my body is coursing with electricity, wanting to find out just how serious he is.

"I... I don't think so?" I say, but it comes out as more of a question.

He takes my wrists and gently guides them behind my back, and my eyes go wide at the action. When I agreed to play out his fantasy, I wasn't really expecting *this*.

"You sure about that?" he teases.

I swallow hard, my attention focused entirely on the feeling of him wrapping his tie around my wrists, fastening my hands firmly to the chair.

"Yes..." I whisper. His hands reemerge, and I give an experimental tug against the restraints, noting with an equal mix of trepidation and excitement that they are tied good and *tight*.

He reaches up to stroke my cheekbone sweetly, as he says, "I need you to be absolutely *sure*."

"I am," I reply immediately. "I want this. I want *you*."

His breath catches. He kisses me—slowly, reverently.

"Good," he murmurs against my lips. "Just in case, though... the safe word is *cupcake*."

I can't help it, I laugh. "Seriously?"

"You won't forget it," he replies, before smothering my laughter with a kiss. His thumb grazes the outer curve of my breast, and I arch instinctively into his touch. I've been waiting for this, waiting for him to stop looking and *finally* touch me. But he's not giving me nearly enough, his hand moving so slowly across my skin, far too patient for my liking.

I squirm, pulling against my restraints, to no avail.

He kisses me softly, chuckling against my lips.

"You're always in control, at all times," he muses. "Just let go, Palmer. Let me take care of you."

My heart is pounding so loudly in my chest, I'm certain he must be able to hear it. It's growing impossibly damp between my legs. I've never done anything like this before, but I can't deny that this feeling, the concept of letting go of control, feels good. Feels right, with Silas, knowing that I can trust him.

I nod, swallowing hard.

"Okay," I whisper. "I'm letting go."

His lips curl upward in a wide grin. He says, softly, "Good girl."

The words send a violent shiver straight down my spine.

He lowers his mouth to my neck, his teeth grazing the sensitive skin just beneath my ear. His hand traces the shape of my breast, his touch feather-light, before his thumb circles my nipple, coaxing it into a stiff peak. I gasp, my back arching, my wrists pulling against their ties.

"Beautiful," he murmurs against my collarbone. "You have no idea what it does to me, seeing you like this."

I glance down between us, to the sight of him straining against his pants. "I think I may have some idea."

He grins wickedly, then ducks to take my nipple into his mouth. My whole body lurches at the contact, fire coursing through my veins. He flicks his tongue against it, my nerves going taut at the sensation. He draws involuntary moans from my throat that I couldn't suppress even if I tried.

I want so badly to reach out, to run my fingers through his hair, to bind myself to him. My instincts tell me to act, to reclaim control. But the restraints prevent me from doing so, and it somehow makes every sensation more intense, more deliciously sharp.

His hand slides down my stomach, the heat of his touch leaving a trail across my skin. His hand dips beneath the red fabric.

"*Fuck*," he swears. "You're so wet for me."

"Silas, please," I beg, but he doesn't keep me wanting for long. He dips two fingers inside my wet, aching center before sliding upward, making slow, deliberate circles around my clit as his tongue runs along the inside curve of my breast.

"Let go for me, Palmer," he whispers against my skin. "Come on, Baby. Just let go."

I obey his commands. I let go. It feels like barely a minute passes before I shatter around his touch, my body pulsing with the release. I cry out as wave after wave of pleasure rolls through me. My head falls back, chest heaving.

When I come down from it, trembling and breathless, he rises to kiss me on the lips once more. He unties the knot at my wrists and releases them. As I reach up to loop my hands around his neck, I notice the faintest traces of red circles around my wrists from fighting against the restraints.

He pulls me into his arms, cradling me against his chest like I weigh nothing. I trail kisses along the edge of his strong, beautiful jaw as he carries me into his bedroom.

The room is dim, moonlight pouring in from the windows and casting long shadows across the floor. He lowers me gently onto the bed.

He starts to undress himself, his eyes running over me, like he's trying to burn this image into his memory. When he's done undressing, I reach for him, longing for the weight of him, the warmth of his skin. He denies my request, but just long enough to take a condom out of his nightstand and put it on.

When he joins me in bed, his lips crash into mine, our mouths moving in a desperate rhythm against each other.

My hands trace the lines of his chest, the firm contours of his stomach. His knee nudges between my thighs, coaxing them apart. He kisses down my neck, my collarbone, the valley between my breasts. While his kisses are light and gentle, his fingers are rough, shoving the thin triangle of red fabric aside to put delicious friction on my clit. I thread my fingers through his hair and pull, earning a low groan from deep in his chest.

As he shifts his hips to align himself with me, the heavy, solid weight of him drags across my thigh. I slip my hand between our bodies, curling my hand around him. He draws in a sharp hiss at my touch. I trail down to the base, learning the shape of him, feeling him involuntarily twitch into my palm. There's just so damn *much* of him, I can't help but wonder how he will ever possibly fit.

Guess there's only one way to find out.

I hook my thigh around his hip and guide him to my entrance. He pauses, his eyes fixed on mine, as if to give me an opportunity to say something—wait or stop, perhaps. But I nod, wanting to feel him filling me. He enters me slowly, deliberately, never taking his eyes off mine. My breath hitches, my jaw clenching against the twinge of pain. It feels impossible, but he inches his way forward, letting my body slowly open and mold around him.

"I'll never get over this," he whispers, brushing the sweat-dampened hair out of my face. "The way you feel. The way you look right now."

I lift my hips to meet him, to drive him the rest of the way home, my jaw falling slack at the stretch of him buried inside me to the hilt. He pulls back and drives forward again, tilting his hips so he somehow reaches impossibly deeper. A gasp escapes me, my head falling back into the pillow.

He finds a rhythm—slow at first, deliberate—each stroke building on the last until I can feel the tension coiling inside me. The room fills with the sound of our ragged breaths, the whisper of his skin against mine, the soft creak of the bed beneath us.

"You feel incredible," he says against my ear, his voice low and guttural. "Like you were made for me."

I can hardly deny it. Every movement of his body against mine feels so exquisite, I wonder idly if I *was* made for him. It's an inane thought, but his touch has stripped me of all reason.

His hand glides down the length of my leg, until he grips my calf and suddenly shifts it onto his shoulder. With his next thrust, he feels somehow deeper, fuller, and I cry out, clutching his shoulders.

I'm so close again. The tension in my belly is winding tighter and tighter. His thrusts grow rougher, less controlled, his breathing more erratic. And I can tell he's right there too, on the precipice with me.

"Say my name, Palmer," he commands, the grit in his voice sending a fresh shiver through me.

And I want to comply. I really do. But I can barely breathe, much less form words.

"How am I supposed to know who you want if you don't say my name?" His words rasp against my cheek. "Say it."

"Silas," I manage, the sound drawn from my throat like it has been ripped free. And the moment his name escapes my lips, pleasure detonates inside me. The force of it is blinding, all-consuming.

He tenses at the sound of my voice, his body pulsing deep inside me as he tips over the edge with me. The heat of his release against my tightening walls is so sublime that it keeps the waves of pleasure rolling through me until long after his body finally stills.

In the wake of it, his body is heavy against mine, our limbs tangled, our breaths rising and falling in a quiet, unsteady rhythm. My fingers trace idle patterns across the slick skin of his back. He presses a kiss to my shoulder, then another and another, as if he can't quite stop. I hum contentedly at the feeling. It's the first time in a long time that my brain has felt quiet and settled, with nothing clouding my thoughts.

He eventually shifts, easing out of me slowly, then pulls the comforter over our tangled bodies. I curl into his side, resting my cheek against his chest. His hand finds the small of my back and lazily traces up and down the length of my spine.

I listen to the thundering of his heartbeat as it gently slows. When I open my eyes, I catch a glimpse of the swirls of black ink encircling his left bicep. I prop myself up on my elbow to get a better look.

"What's wrong?" he murmurs, eyes still closed. His entire body has gone limp with a contented exhaustion.

"I've been dying to know what your tattoo is all this time," I say, practically crawling across his chest to get a better look. "I've only seen glimpses of it."

He chuckles, rolling to give me a better view. "Seriously? You could have asked. I'd have shown you."

"There just never seemed like a good opportunity," I admit.

I inspect it in the dim moonlight, tracing the lines with one fingertip. It is striking against his skin, mostly abstract swirls and geometric shapes, following the curve of his deltoid and biceps, down to the crease of his elbow. But at the center, there is a minimalist outline of an owl in flight. Hanging from its talons is the only pop of color in the tattoo—a loose ribbon in a dull teal color.

I'm not sure what the symbol is for ovarian cancer, but if I had to venture a guess, I would think it is a teal ribbon.

"Is it for your mother?" I ask.

He nods, tucking me back in below his arm. "Got it about a year after she passed. She loved owls. Said they were protectors, that they look over everything. And that's what she was for our family."

I look up into his face, catching the flicker of emotion there. "You miss her."

"Every day," he replies. "But this helps, you know? Makes me feel like she's still watching over me. Over Emery."

And suddenly, I regret my curiosity. Because the tattoo is a bitter reminder that this isn't just a one-night thing. That I care about Silas, care about his family. That the Howells have been repeatedly left by the people they love—always unwillingly, of course—but left, nonetheless. And how dare I be another source of pain for these people?

I'm lost in thought over it when I feel Silas's breathing steady beneath me with sleep. It takes several long minutes of trying to calm my racing thoughts before I let sleep overcome me.

When I wake in the morning to the sunlight pouring through his tall windows, Silas is still deeply asleep, the rise and fall of his chest rhythmic with his breathing.

I realize with surprise that I didn't budge an inch during the night.

It used to irritate the hell out of Grant, how much I would toss and turn in my sleep, surrounding myself in a cocoon of sheets by the morning.

But here I am, still nestled into the crook of Silas's arm, using his chest like a pillow, listening to his heart beating.

My eyes wander up the contours of his chest until they settle on his left arm, to the lines of his tattoo. The dark, knowing eyes of the owl almost seem to be staring back, boring a hole straight into my soul.

A bubble of panic rises suddenly in my chest.

What am I doing? This is *exactly* what I told myself I wasn't going to do—get Silas and me so irrevocably tangled up in each other that it would kill either of us for me to leave. Because I *know* what this is, this uncomfortable ache I feel whenever he looks at me, this unbearable longing to always be near him.

I know what it is, so why does it have to be happening at the worst possible time?

I have a chance to fulfill my wildest dreams. I can't let anything—any*one*—hold me back from that.

My heart starts to pound.

Before I can talk myself out of it, I untangle myself from him, slowly, so as not to wake him. I tiptoe across his room, grabbing my dress and shoes from the floor, the guilt already curling in my stomach.

I catch an Uber back to the bakery.

When I'm back in my apartment a short while later, I receive a text from Jenna.

JENNA

That didn't look like a "fake" walk of shame to me.

CHAPTER 14

Silas

I wake to find my bed empty and a single unread text message on my phone.

PALMER

Had to head back to the bakery early. This was fun.

This was fun.

This. Was. *Fun*.

The words echo in my mind like the clanging of bells, resonating, nearly painful with their intensity. As if last night could ever be described by such small, trivial, casual words.

I can come up with a hundred words to describe last night, each more desperate and profound than the last: Incredible. Earth-shattering. Beautiful. Life-altering.

Last night wasn't merely the best night of my life—it redefined the meaning of the word best. It made every previous experience pale instantly and entirely by comparison.

Yet she called it *fun*, as if it were nothing more than an amusing but momentary distraction. Something pleasant, but ultimately forgettable; it terrifies me to my core, thinking that

that's all it might have been for her. The thought is gut-wrenching.

I have never felt anything like this before—this ache clawing at my chest. This obsessive desire to be with her again, to touch her again. To hold her close and lose myself entirely in her once more, never resurfacing, never needing anything as trivial as air or light again so long as I have her.

Nothing in my life has ever compared to this. Nothing ever *will* compare to this again. I'm certain of it.

Historically for me, the thrill has always been in the chase. Once I slept with someone, the anticipation faded, and my interest waned. I would walk away satisfied and resolved, happy to continue with my life without ever returning to the same person.

But not this time. Not this woman.

I would do anything to be with her again. I'd fall to my knees and beg her to stay; beg her to understand how deeply she has altered me. I'd worship her like a fucking deity, dedicate my life completely and utterly to *her*.

She has me locked in her grasp like a vice grip. I am completely at her mercy. And she doesn't even know. Maybe she does, and that's why she's pulling away. Maybe she feels it too, and it terrifies her. Or even worse—maybe she's still pining for her ex.

He was there, talking to her, when I picked her up from the hotel. She may have left with me, but there was a *moment* —something intense that passed between the two of them for just an instant before we left. I chalked it up to the history between them at the time, but maybe I was wrong.

The following days are torture as I mull over these possi-bilities. I try to distract myself in any way that I can. I spend nearly as many hours a day in the gym as I did in college, wondering if it might be possible to burn off some of this rest-less energy, to no avail. I try to bury myself in work, but nothing keeps her out of my mind. I can't even hold my camera without it reminding me of her anymore.

The worst part is that I have the very best reminder of her I could ever imagine—her pictures. Proof of what we had for one perfect night.

I tell myself I'm in a healthy place when I sit down at my desk to edit her photos—not that she needs much editing. I do nothing at all to improve *her*, but I fiddle obsessively over the tone and contrast and saturation of the images, if only to look at them a moment longer. Guiding my cursor over the curves of her body is a sick reminder of the real thing—one that I can't stop subjecting myself to.

Eventually, I know what to do. I have to get rid of the pictures, for my own good. Looking at them another day might just kill me. I print them, upload them to a flash drive, and put all the evidence into an envelope. Then I delete every remaining trace of them from my hard drive.

It feels like a God damn crime. A crime against art, against beauty. A crime against myself, depriving my eyes of the ability to ever look at them again. A part of my mind screams in protest the whole time as I go through and methodically remove them one by one. But I know it is the right thing to do. They're not mine to keep.

I head resolutely to the bakery that same afternoon.

Sweet P is as bustling as I've ever seen it, multiple patrons inside sitting at the tables enjoying treats or scanning the glass display case for the options. Jenna spots me and does a double-take.

"Silas?" she asks. "I didn't expect to see you here."

Every look Jenna has ever paid me tells me that there are no secrets between Palmer and her best friend. I'm certain she knows everything—every sordid detail of the last five months. I know it in the slightly pitying way she looks at me, like she knows her best friend might just ruin my life.

"I was hoping to see Palmer," I explain. "I know she's busy. It'll just take a minute. Do you think you could tell her I'm here?"

She disappears behind the kitchen door for a long minute, far longer than I would expect she would need to inform Palmer of my presence. But eventually, they both emerge.

Palmer steps from behind the counter, wiping her hands on her pink apron. Her hair is pulled back into a braid. Her eyes are bright and expectant as she surveys me with a soft, sheepish smile.

"Hi," she says.

I smile, but it doesn't meet my eyes. The pain of the last week intensifies in her presence.

"Hey," I respond, my voice rough. "Do you think we could talk outside for just a second?"

She nods, following me out front.

I don't stall, don't dance around the purpose of my visit.

"I wanted you to have these," I say, handing her the envelope. When she goes immediately to open it, I put my hand over hers.

"Maybe later?" I suggest, glancing back at the window of her bakery. "Those are your, uh, *pictures.*"

She stills. "Oh."

I take my hand from hers quickly. "I deleted the original files. Those are the only copies. They're yours."

She presses the envelope to her chest. "Silas, you didn't have to—"

"I wanted to," I interrupt, though it's a half-truth. "I didn't want you to worry about them ending up in the wrong hands or in front of the wrong eyes. But you should have them. They're beautiful pictures."

Her throat bobs with a swallow.

"I never—" But whatever she was about to say chokes off in her throat. Instead, she whispers, "Thank you."

I nod once. And even though the ache in my chest is still there, I feel a little better, knowing I've done the right thing. I take a step away from her, back in the direction of my truck.

"I'll let you get back to it," I say.

"Bye, Silas," she says to my back, and I wave a hand over my shoulder without turning to look at her.

When I'm back in the truck, she still hasn't turned to head into her bakery. She stands on the curb, clutching the envelope to her chest. I wonder, for a second, if she'll stop me from going. But she simply watches me drive away.

I have no plans today, other than moping at home and editing photos from the last few weeks of weddings. Neither sounds particularly appealing at the moment, so I find myself in front of Full Proof instead—if I'm going to mope, I might as well mope with a friend.

The bar is predictably empty on a Wednesday afternoon. Just Cal behind the bar today, scribbling something into the black ledger he uses to track payroll. I sink into the stool across from him and sigh heavily.

Without glancing up, he mutters, "You sound miserable."

Cal is the best friend I've ever had. One of his many talents —apart from making the best Old Fashioned in South Carolina—is knowing how to sit with your pain without crowding it. He has the inherent bartender ability to moonlight as a therapist. He never pushes. If I want to spill my guts, he'll listen. If I want to sulk in silence, he'll pour me a drink and sit with me.

I just can't seem to decide which I need more.

Eventually, I say, "I think I like someone a lot more than she likes me."

Cal guffaws like this is a very funny joke, but when I don't join in his laughter, he looks up from his book, alarmed. "Do my eyes deceive me? The mighty Silas Howell, reduced to a lovesick puppy?"

"Fuck off," I grumble, but there's no heat in it. I rub a hand down my face. "I'm serious, Cal. I'm spiraling."

"Well, surely, you're talking about the side piece you've yet to introduce me to," he comments wryly.

I narrow my eyes at him, a surge of anger flaring hot in my chest. "What? No. I'm talking about Palmer."

"*Our* Palmer?" he demands. "Palmer Sullivan? The woman who sat across from me at the gala just a few nights ago, looking at you like you hung the moon for her? Who couldn't keep her hands off you? *That's* the woman who isn't into you?"

I groan and bury my face in my hands.

"I wish someone would look at me the way a woman looks at you when she's not into you," he muses.

"It's hard to explain," I grumble.

"Didn't you two leave together that night?" he asks, incredulous. "You Irish goodbye'd us halfway through the party."

"We did," I admit.

"And?" he urges.

"And..." I hesitate, wondering how much I should tell him. "She left before I woke up the next morning. Texted me, *this was fun.*"

He stares at me dubiously. "You're acting like it's the first time you two slept together or something."

I meet his eyes for half a second before looking away, saying nothing. I knew I should have just silently brooded instead of talking.

"Holy shit," he swears. "That was the first time you two slept together?"

I don't respond, but my silence speaks volumes.

"No wonder you're feeling like she's not into you," he muses. "You have been together for what, six months? It's none of my business, of course, but was it a purity thing or some shit? Wasn't she with her last boyfriend for like, five years?"

"Three," I correct, sounding irritated. "And it wasn't a purity thing." The words sound gross even to say. "It's really hard to explain."

"Try me," Cal offers. I consider it, long and hard. We promised not to tell our friends and family... aside from Jenna and Evan, now that I think about it. It suddenly feels so isolating, to keep this kind of secret for so long, with no one to share it with, especially now that things have gotten so complicated. If Palmer can tell her best friends, why can't I?

I think Cal senses my resolve breaking, because he comes around the bar and takes the seat next to mine, settling in for what he realizes will be a long story.

The second he sits down, I break—I tell him everything. From the time I took a picture of the beautiful baker at the Barlow engagement party all the way to this afternoon, sparing only the most intimate details. When I finish the story, Cal whistles.

"Wow," he says. "That's a lot."

I nod miserably.

"But you're like... really together now, right?" he asks.

I shrug. "I don't think so. She won't commit to anything until after this interview in Paris, and if she gets it—"

"You're fucked," he completes.

"Completely," I mutter on a sigh.

"And you helped her get the interview?" he asks, bewildered.

"The irony isn't lost on me," I grumble.

"So go with her," he suggests simply.

"What?" I ask in surprise.

"Go with her," Cal insists. "If she gets into pastry school... move to Paris. Eat croissants. Go to museums. Speak the language of love, and all that shit. I'm certain you can find some stuff to take pictures of."

"I can't just... I can't just upend my entire life and follow her to another country," I argue, a bubble of nervous laughter in my throat.

"Why not?"

"I have a life here," I retort. "An apartment. A career. I have Emery to think about—"

"Don't pull that big brother shit," Cal scolds. "Emery isn't seventeen anymore. She's getting married in three months. And she can take care of herself, with or without Charlie."

He senses my hesitation and huffs in annoyance. "Look, Silas, I've known you a long time, right?"

I nod.

"I have never seen you feel this strongly for anyone before," he observes. "If she means this much to you, don't let her get away just because the timing is inconvenient. If she's your person, just figure it out. Build your life around the people that matter."

I wonder idly how Cal, who seems to be so much better at this relationship stuff than me, can possibly still be single. Probably because he never leaves this bar, if I had to venture a guess.

He claps a firm hand on my shoulder. "You're already in deep. Might as well see it through."

I smile feebly. A small, hopeful part of me wants to listen.

CHAPTER 15

Palmer

Summer is our busiest time of year. But no matter how busy I keep, no matter how many orders I fill, no matter how many cakes I decorate and deliver to blushing brides all over town, I'll never be busy enough to stop thinking about him.

I've been throwing myself headlong into work with no reprieve from this ache. The only thing that made it go away was one impossible night where I simply stopped resisting. Where I let myself pretend that I could have this, have him, and have everything I always wanted.

It was like I was Cinderella—one beautiful night, only to turn back into a pumpkin promptly at midnight. I woke before the sun rose the next day, and the panic hit me like a freight train. I promised myself I wouldn't hurt him, not like I hurt Grant.

And I managed to do it anyway. I snuck out like a coward. Texted him, "this was fun," which was such a laughable understatement, I haven't stopped feeling disgusted with myself ever since.

I try in vain to pipe a neat border onto a cake, but the

work is sloppy. My head isn't in it—my thoughts are miles away from the bakery this morning.

"Okay, the shop is closed," I hear Jenna's voice call from the door. "Spill."

I look up from my cake, unable to wipe the miserable frown from my face. "Spill what?"

"The *tea*," she insists, dragging a stool beside me. "Tell me why you have been moping for weeks. Why Silas Howell is coming around looking like someone kicked his puppy."

I sigh, turning my eyes back to the cake before me, even though I have no desire at all to continue the work. And it makes me even more miserable, knowing I *can't* tell Jenna, even though she has harbored every secret I've possessed since I was eighteen. Because I haven't told Jenna about *this* secret, about my interview for École Deschamps. I've been trying and failing for weeks to work up the nerve to tell Jenna about my upcoming "vacation" to Paris, but I've chickened out every time I've tried. I haven't taken a single vacation in five years— she's not going to buy that this is just a casual getaway. I was lucky that she didn't seem suspicious when I refused to take any big jobs for that week, believing when I said I would need a reprieve after the Barlow event.

How do I tell her that I want to leave? Only temporarily, but still.

"There's no tea to spill," I murmur, too quietly.

"Okay, fine. Don't tell me why you're both so miserable," Jenna responds, pausing for just a moment before she says, "At least tell me what this little package is that he dropped off for you."

Jenna plucks the manila envelope from the counter beside me, and my heart instantly lurches in panic. She takes several purposeful steps away from me, holding the envelope in her hands.

"Jenna," I warn, shooting up from my stool. "*Don't.*"

I launch toward her, but she sidesteps me easily. My hand grasps at the air that the envelope once occupied as she pulls it out of my reach.

"What is it?" she teases. "A love letter?"

She grins, slowly undoing the clasp.

"Jenna," I groan, lunging for it. She dances back another step, playing keep-away.

"Do the contents of this envelope have something to do with how you've been avoiding him like the plague?" she asks, flipping open the tab.

"I swear to God, Jenna—" But she is already sliding one of the photos steadily out of the envelope. When half the picture is visible, she stops, abruptly, her jaw going slack.

"Oh my God," she croons.

My cheeks turn unbearably hot and flushed. I hadn't had time to run the envelope up to my apartment since Silas brought them by, but I am deeply regretting it now. I hadn't worked up the nerve to look at them either, so I can only imagine what Jenna is seeing at this moment.

"Palmer Anne Sullivan," she says, but surprisingly, her tone isn't harsh and disapproving, as I would expect. If I didn't know better, I would venture to say she sounds... impressed?

Jenna stares unabashedly at the picture—one that I'm certain is graphic and in high definition. A slow, wicked grin crosses her face as she says, "You bad girl."

I groan and cover my face, completely mortified. "Please kill me."

"Why?" she demands with an incredulous laugh. "If I looked like this naked, you wouldn't catch me wearing clothes ever."

It wasn't so much the act of Jenna seeing me naked that bothered me—we lived together for years, had seen each other change hundreds of times. But this didn't feel like her seeing me naked; it felt more like I was showing her my sex tape.

"Man..." Jenna says pensively, her tone wistful. "This guy really loves you."

My hands fall from my face abruptly, my panic ebbing. "What?"

She hands me the photo before taking out a second from the envelope. "Look at how beautiful these are. This guy is obsessed with you."

I accept the offered picture and take a good look at the glossy image, expecting to feel embarrassed or exposed. But I don't.

Because it isn't just a picture—it's a heartbreakingly beautiful reflection of how Silas saw me. How he *sees* me, as something soft and strong and beautiful and... loved.

A painful breath courses through my lungs, my chest tight with the effort. Jenna hands me one picture after the other, and all my embarrassment and outrage over her seeing the pictures fades away. Because she's right.

"Look, I don't know what happened after this—" she waves one of the photos like a flag, "and you don't have to tell me if you don't want to. But I'm worried about you. You're doing that thing again."

"What thing?" I ask absently, unable to look up from the picture in my hand. This one doesn't even show anything below my shoulders. It's a close-up of my face, looking over the curve of my bare shoulder. The look in my eyes is so warm and happy and so very *alive* that it makes my heart hurt, when I feel the exact opposite now.

"The thing where you turn into a baking robot, working so much you can't feel human emotions anymore," Jenna explains. "You did it last year when Grant broke up with you, too."

A tear falls from the corner of my eye before I can stop it.

"Yeah, well. It's not working nearly as well this time. I still feel like shit."

She gathers up the pictures and puts them into the envelope, placing it back into my grasp. She puts one hand on my shoulder as she says, "I think we both know why it's not working this time."

I'm looking down at the envelope in my hands, considering her words, when we both startle suddenly at the sound of the bell chime over the door to the shop.

She jogs to the kitchen door. I hear her say, "I'm so sorry, we're closed—Oh. Bennett?"

My heart leaps at the mention of that name. What on earth is Bennett doing here? I quickly set the pictures on the counter, moving to the door.

I guess Jenna hadn't locked up yet, because Bennett is standing there, just inside. She greets me with a tentative wave.

"Hi," she says.

I wave back, confused. "Hi, Bennett."

She pulls a white envelope out of a brown Birkin bag—a real one, I'm certain—in the exact same caramel-brown shade as her skin-tight dress.

"I brought your check." She waves the envelope at me.

My pulse increases instantly at the sight of that envelope. If you ignore the fact that she has a $30,000 purse hanging over the opposite wrist, the amount of money she holds in her hand is enough to make me salivate.

This is it, I realize. The end of the charades. Once that check is in my account, there's no going back. She can't take it away. She can't fire me anymore because of personal issues.

Assuredly, things with Silas are complicated. There's a lot to consider—Paris, first and foremost. But that check frees us from the ulterior motives, from the ruse. Let's us just do what we want, without the strain of proving anything to anyone. I realize, at the sight of that check, that I want that desperately.

I turn to look into Bennett's eyes, saying curiously, "You know you can complete the payment online, right? You didn't have to come all this way."

She breathes in deeply, the check lowering. "I know... I came because I wanted to talk to you."

Bennett glances at Jenna and back to me, clearly wary of continuing in her presence. I shoot Jenna a look, and she frowns a little but flees through the kitchen door, giving us privacy. I gesture for Bennett to sit at the little white table by the window, and I join her.

Even when we're seated, she doesn't speak immediately. She has her purse in her lap; the envelope held in both hands.

"What did you want to talk to me about?" I prompt.

She takes a deep breath. "It's two weeks until the wedding, and I just have this... worry. In the back of my mind. That I can't seem to get rid of."

My gut sinks at her words. She clenches the envelope a little tighter, and I wonder idly how much tighter she would need to hold it before it would start to tear beneath the pressure.

"It's normal to have a little case of cold feet before your wedding," I reassure her calmly, belying the unrest that I'm hiding beneath the surface.

"It's not just cold feet," she says. "It's more than that."

"Okay?" I respond, unable to hide some of the wariness from my tone.

"I keep thinking, maybe it was too fast? He started things with me before you had even moved out of the house," she explains.

I'm honestly surprised she was aware of this fact, that she willingly started dating Grant, knowing my belongings still haunted the corners of his home like the ghosts of girlfriends' past. It feels like a lot, to ask me to make her feel better about this, but I've already proven that I'll move heaven and earth to keep this damn job. I simply never imagined, in my wildest dreams, that I would spend this much time convincing a woman to marry my ex.

"You don't think it was too soon?" she probes.

"I don't know what you want me to tell you, Bennett. It was soon after we broke up, but sometimes the right person just... creeps up on you." I smile a little at the thought, my brain instantly conjuring an image of Silas. "Sometimes the timing isn't ideal. But you make it work when it's the right person."

"You're probably right," she relents. She puts the check down on the table in front of her, but I notice she doesn't lift her hand from it. She keeps it pinned beneath her palm, not moving to hand it to me.

"I think I would just feel a little better about everything," she says slowly, carefully, "if I knew why you two broke up."

I drag my gaze up from the check to her face, my brows lifting. "He hasn't told you why we broke up?"

She shakes her head. "He just says you wanted different things."

I nod, agreeing, "We did want different things."

She sighs dramatically. "But what does that even mean? What did you want that he didn't, or vice versa? What if he wants something that I don't want, and I haven't realized it yet because we've only been together for a year? But you did realize it because you were together for three years? And I just haven't realized that we don't want the same things, because we're rushing into this too quickly?"

She is starting to ramble, getting frantic. She grips the envelope, curling the edges of the paper inward, and I wonder idly how wrinkled the check can be when I cash it before the bank teller will decline it. Why can't she just hand me the damn envelope already?

I put my hand over hers on the table, trying to console her, but also trying to keep her from abusing my money.

"Bennett," I stress, in what I hope is a reassuring voice. "I'm certain that if you wanted something fundamentally different from Grant, you would know it by now."

She leans in, whispering, "Was it something... sexual? Have I just not seen the red room yet?"

I can't help it—I laugh. The tension I feel releases, just a little, with the action. Bennett's lips pull into the start of a very tentative smile at the sound of my laughter. I lift my hand from hers to wipe tears of laughter from my eyes.

"No, nothing like that," I say, my tone still amused. "Okay, fine. You really want to know why we broke up?"

She nods, her blue eyes wide, desperate for this knowledge.

"Grant wanted marriage and kids," I explain, "from the very beginning of our relationship."

I know I'm downplaying it, just a bit. What really happened was that Grant wouldn't *stop* talking about marrying me—from our very first date. He talked about the future he carefully planned for us like it was a foregone conclusion, like it wasn't a discussion we needed to have *together*. And the more he talked about rings and white picket fences, the more trapped I felt.

But that was a me problem. Bennett clearly doesn't fear commitment to Grant, not like I did.

"Isn't that what you want, too?" I ask.

She blinks at me, as if the truth is entirely underwhelming. "That's it? He wanted marriage and a family, and you didn't?"

"It's not that I didn't want those things ever," I clarify, a little defensively. "I do think I want those things eventually. But I'm twenty-eight years old. He was talking about marrying me when I was twenty-four. I had just bought the storefront. I was just getting my business off the ground, and it was all I could focus on at the time. Not only was I doing all the baking and all the decorating, but I had to go to the wedding expos and advertising events. It was just Jenna and me trying to promote the shop back then. And Grant started to feel a little... neglected."

I realize I'm the one who is rambling now, and I take a deep breath to slow my pace. Bennett doesn't comment or interrupt while I gather my thoughts. "I was working so much back then. All day, every day. Weekdays and weekends, day and night, trying to make something of this place."

I look around the shop fondly, admiring the green wallpaper with pink florals that Jenna and I hand-picked; the tea tables and chairs that we thrifted one by one. Every inch of this place tells a story about the life of our business, but also about Jenna's and my friendship.

"I couldn't devote the time to Grant that he wanted," I admit, then quickly amend, "that he deserved."

Silence stretches between us for a moment before I continue, "I don't blame him for that. But the thing that really ended it between us is that he didn't understand *why* I did it. He couldn't understand why I wanted to wait for things like marriage and children until after the business was more successful. He told me he would support me and any children we might have. That I'd never have to worry about making enough money to support myself. And I just... couldn't do it."

Bennett looks confused at this admission, and I'm not surprised. The financial part of it would be hard for her to understand. She hadn't had to watch someone not meet their potential, to be held back by financial reliance on someone else.

"I couldn't let myself rely on someone else," I explained. "I wanted to be able to support myself, by myself, without needing to fall back on anyone. I couldn't settle down with Grant unless I had that first. And he didn't like that answer."

She sits with this information for a long time, processing. She shakes her head. "But your business is successful now?"

I nod slowly, not sure what exactly she's implying. "Yes, we're far more stable now than we were back then. I still work long hours sometimes, but I've been able to hire employees to help."

"So that means you are in a good place now for a relationship?" she asks, her voice timid. She very subtly, almost imperceptibly, slides the check off the table, back into her lap. I swallow with difficulty, my heart racing.

"Yes..." I say carefully. It's only now that I remember to bring up the ruse. "I have Silas now."

But the words don't mollify her this time. She doesn't look convinced. God, how much more did I have to prostrate myself before this woman before she would believe me?

"What's stopping you from getting back together with Grant?" she asks.

The words hang between us, demanding. She locks her gaze with mine, her eyes narrowing with suspicion. I can feel that same panic, that same desperate desire to get Bennett off my back. It's like I'm standing before her and Grant at their engagement party all over again, but this time, Silas isn't here to help. No one can bail me out of the situation. And the check is there, sitting in her lap, held captive unless I can give her an answer that might finally satisfy her.

"I'm moving to France!" I blurt out.

She flinches with alarm at my volume, but her lips begin to slowly curve into a smile.

"You're moving?" she asks, and her tone is more than assured now—it's practically gleeful.

I sigh with relief. "It's not for sure yet. But I have an interview for pastry school. I leave the day after your wedding. If I get it, I'll be spending most of next year in Paris."

I don't tell her that I have every intention of coming back

after the completion of my studies. She doesn't need to know that part, especially when it seems like this news has finally satisfied her. She plants the check back on the table, and this time, she begins to slowly slide it across the table toward me. I clench my fists in my lap, forcing myself not to reach out and grab it

"How exciting!" she exclaims. "You're going to love Paris!"

Her bubbly voice is back, as quickly as it had fled. This woman's mood swings are going to give me whiplash, I'm certain of it.

She stands from her seat, holding the check toward me. I stand and take it, hesitantly, afraid that she might snatch it away. But she doesn't. Even more alarming—she draws me in for a hug the second the check is in my hands. I freeze in her arms, unnerved by the gesture.

"I'm so happy for you," she says warmly, and I can't decide whether her words are genuine. Something tells me they are—that she is genuinely happy for me. The woman just needs to learn how to express herself without giving me a heart attack in the process.

I wrap my arms around Bennett and return the hug. "I'm happy for you too, Bennett. I really do wish you both the best."

She pulls away and shoots me a radiant smile. "Thanks, Sweet P."

She winks and heads for the door. When it closes behind her, I let out an enormous breath, feeling like I have been holding it for the entire interaction. I look down at the envelope in my hand with relief.

It's finally mine. All the lying and pretending can stop now. I can live my life however I want to live it. Spend my time with whoever I want to spend it with.

If I'm being honest with myself, for once... I know who I want to spend it with.

I'm still staring at the envelope, lost in thought, when I hear Jenna's voice.

"Were you planning on telling *me* at some point that you were moving to France?"

I look up to the door of the kitchen, my eyes going wide with panic.

"You heard?" I ask, though it's a stupid question. I can't believe I didn't even think of Jenna, always lurking on the other side of that door. It was my own fault for not assuming she would be listening before I went and blurted it out.

She moves from behind the counter to stand before me, crossing her arms. "Of course, I heard."

"Jenna, let me explain—"

"What's there to explain?" she asks, her voice rising in anger. "You just said it. You're going to Paris for an interview, and if you get it, you'll be spending next year in France!"

"Jenna, please. I hadn't told you yet because it's not a sure thing," I try to explain. "I didn't think I was even going to get an interview when I applied, and the chances of getting in are—"

"Don't," she warns. "Don't do that false modesty thing with me, Palmer Anne Sullivan. We both know you're going to get in."

I reel back from her, shaking my head. "It's not false modesty, Jen. It's the best pastry school in the world—"

"And we both know damn well you're one of the best bakers in the world," she says, and if she didn't sound so angry with me, I might have been flattered.

"I wanted to know for sure before we made any decisions," I reply.

"We?" she accuses. "Don't you think I should have been at least aware of your grand plans to invoke the word *we*?"

I take a deep breath and let it out. I know she has every right to be angry at me.

"What is your grand plan, anyway?" she demands. "You go to school, and then what? You frolic in France for the rest of your days?"

"No, that's not—I didn't—I haven't really worked out all the details," I sputter lamely. "I wasn't even planning to apply this year, but Silas encouraged me—"

"Oh, so I have Silas to thank for this quarter-life crisis?" Her voice has gone shrill, her face nearly red.

A hot rush of anger surges through me, powerful and unexpected.

"Don't," I warn her. "Don't blame him for this. This was my idea. I've been dreaming about this for years. I just —" I choke on an angry sob. "I was just afraid to tell you, Jen."

She deflates beneath these words, some of her anger dissipating. It takes her a long time to decide what to say next, but she says the last thing I expect.

"I understand."

My anger fizzles out instantly with my surprise. Jenna doesn't forgive so quickly, not ever. She doesn't hold a grudge —I know she will forgive me, eventually. But seeing her let go of her anger within minutes is unnerving.

"You do?" I ask, still unsure.

She nods, and I am horrified to see tears spring to her eyes. Jenna isn't a crier, either. This is strange. Uncanny.

"Jen, what—"

"I'm pregnant," she says.

The word takes on its own life, forming into an entity that seems to stand between us. It's huge and demanding. I look down at her stomach at the loose-fitting shirt she is wearing. And I realize suddenly that she has been wearing baggier clothes. She has called out sick more than once, after years of never calling out. She didn't drink when we went to the gala, despite the endless supply of free, high-end alcohol. I didn't notice any of these things in the moment, but it all comes flooding back to me now, with perfect clarity.

I've barely paid her any attention these last few months, I realize. The thought makes my chest hurt.

I'm an awful friend.

"You are?" I asked, my voice cracked and distraught.

She wipes tears from beneath her eyes and nods. "Yeah. Fourteen weeks."

"And you've known for how long?"

"A long time. Too long," she answers with a rueful laugh. "I've been trying to figure out the best way to tell you, but I was afraid."

"Afraid?" I repeat, confused. "Why would you be afraid to tell me? This is... Jen, this is amazing!"

I amble forward to draw her in for a hug. But my heart sinks when I can feel her trembling with more tears.

"Jen, what's wrong? Why are you crying? Aren't you happy?"

She pulls out of my embrace, wiping at her eyes and her nose like she's annoyed with herself as she says, "I promise I am. It's all these damn hormones. I feel like a mess all the time."

I motion for her to sit at the table in the window.

When I'm in the seat across from her, I ask, "Why were you afraid to tell me you're pregnant? Were you not planning for this to happen?"

She sniffles, laughing. "No, it was very much planned. We tried for a few months before it stuck."

I shake my head, wondering how the person I have shared everything with since we were eighteen could have possibly held this secret from me for so long. A part of me wonders if I should be offended, but I can't find it in myself—the concern for her, the guilt over not telling her about my own plans stifles any offense I can muster.

"Then why are you so upset?" I ask. "Why were you afraid to tell me?"

"I was afraid you wouldn't be excited," she admits, her voice small and vulnerable.

"Jen, how could I not be excited for you? You're my best friend. And you're growing my mini best friend. How could that be a bad thing?"

She explains, "I was worried, if I told you, you'd be more concerned about the bakery than excited for me. I'll have to take at least two months off when the baby's born. And after he's born, I won't be here running the shop nearly as much—"

"He?" I repeat in wonder. "It's a boy?"

She lets out a watery laugh and nods. "Yeah. It's a boy."

I wrench myself out of my chair and throw myself at her, awkwardly bending over to hug her while she's still seated.

"I'm *so* mad you didn't let me make you one of those dumb gender reveal cakes," I mutter against her hair.

She laughs in my arms, rubbing my back. "I knew you would be. I'm sorry."

"No, I'm sorry," I say thickly, pulling away from her and wiping at my own tears. I take the seat across from her again. "I'm sorry that I was so caught up in my own world that I didn't realize—"

"It's not your fault—"

"It is my fault," I insist. "And we'll figure out the bakery. We'll hire a little extra help once the baby gets here."

She shoots me a pitying look. "I think we're going to need a *lot* of help if both of us are gone."

I press my lips together, quiet, unable to argue with this logic. We sit in silence for a long time, both of us coming to terms with what the future holds.

This can't be the end of Sweet P, the business we built from our blood and sweat and tears. That was never what I wanted from this. I wanted to get better, to learn from the best, so I could come back and truly make this place every-thing it could be. I never really thought pursuing *my* dream would mean putting an end to *our* dream.

But this thought experiment is premature, I tell myself. I haven't even gone to the interview yet.

"Let's see what happens with the interview, and go from there," I say quietly.

Jenna nods, but there's a sad, knowing little smile on her face, like she's saying, *we both know how the interview is going to go...*

CHAPTER 16

Silas

I'm disassembling and unpacking all my equipment in my apartment after an engagement shoot, thinking idly to myself that the next event will be *the one*—the Barlow extravaganza. I should be feeling excited, maybe a little nervous, about the prospect of shooting the biggest wedding of my career in just two days. But all I can think about is the fact that Palmer is getting on a plane to Paris the day after.

My phone rings in my pocket and breaks me out of my moody reflections. I peer at the screen for half a second before accepting the call from Cal.

"Dude, are you busy?" he asks, not bothering with pleasantries. "I could really use you here at the bar. We're slammed."

"For real?" I ask. "You haven't needed me at the bar in so long, I'm not even sure I remember how to make a vodka soda."

His deep, booming guffaw answers my joke.

"What's happening on a Thursday night, anyway?" I ask.

"This big group of dudes came in out of nowhere," he explains, "and they're draining me of every top-shelf whiskey I have. Do you think you could pick me up a couple bottles of Macallan eighteen-year on your way?"

I may not need to tend bar anymore to make a living, but I imagine the tips on a tab that includes a few of those bottles must be good.

"I'll be there in a bit," I reply with a laugh.

An hour later, I make it to the bar with all the Macallan one can find within a twenty-mile radius. I hand the bags to Cal, helping him unload the bottles onto the shelf.

The group that has taken over the bar for the evening is hard to miss—a dozen or so rowdy guys, probably around my age, maybe a bit younger, all in sport coats, throwing back expensive scotch like it's cheap tequila.

Cal immediately gives me a list of tasks to do—shelves to restock, drink orders to fill. The waiters have been swallowed up by the main group, so I do a quick sweep of the rest of the tables, checking in, filling orders. After an hour of hustle, I've helped Cal catch up with the demands of the crowd.

I set about cleaning glasses, tending to rows after rows of snifters to replenish our supply. I'm nearly finished with the work when I see two guys settle in at the barstools closest to me. I dry my hands off on a towel before lifting my gaze to greet them.

"Hey, what can I get—" My voice cuts off with a strangled croak as I realize who is sitting in front of me, wearing a tilted plastic crown on his head. Grant Foster.

I hadn't given the group of men a good scan when I arrived, keeping my head down just to get the work done. But Grant Foster's bachelor party is happening in *my* bar. And somehow, I volunteered to help serve him.

God, how did this wedding manage to invade its way into every aspect of my life? Who isn't involved, at this point? The Barlow wedding feels like a black hole, sucking everything in its vicinity farther and farther in. The deeper I get, the more it seems to consume everything around me, stretching me to my breaking point.

I glare at Cal's back, cursing him for doing this to me. But I doubt he knew what he was doing when he called me tonight. Cal would never do something to hurt me. I doubt he had any inclination that he threw me to the mother fucking sharks.

"Well, if it isn't my favorite photographer," Grant slurs, his voice carrying easily over the background roar of his posse.

My body feels like it is being slowly petrified, but I force myself to resume organizing the glasses, desperate for something—anything—to keep my hands busy. I keep my eyes fixed on my work to avoid locking eyes with Grant.

"Hey, guys," I greet them, my tone much calmer than I feel. "What can I get you?"

I glance up for just a moment to find Grant's eyes narrowed on me, his stare calculating. "I didn't know you tended bar."

"I do, from time to time," I reply, my tone neutral. "What can I get you?"

Grant's buddies are still firmly in the rowdy, fun-loving stage of drunkenness. Grant, on the other hand, has already passed that stage, moving on to the quiet, contemplative part of inebriation—as if the whiskey coursing through his bloodstream has suddenly turned him into a philosopher.

"I imagine you've probably given me enough as it is, don't you?" he ponders. "You've given me beautiful pictures of my fiancée. Given me plenty of good alcohol. And you've even taken in my little lost ex-girlfriend."

My hands falter, just for a second, in their movements. God, this is a setup for danger. The self-preservation instincts are all blaring loudly in my mind, telling me to get myself out of this situation. But I'm a pretty level-headed guy. Drunk frat bros don't usually get to me. Then again, it's not usually Grant Foster I'm dealing with.

"Anything else I can get you to drink?" I stress, trying to maintain some semblance of professionalism.

Grant and his friend ignore my question. He leans back in his barstool, appraising me with slightly glossy, squinted eyes.

Just walk away, my brain warns. *Ask Cal to help them instead of you.*

I put a few feet of distance between us, close enough that they can easily call me back in the event they need me to do my job, but still far enough away that I'm not engaging in their conversation. But it doesn't mean I can't hear them, in their drunken stage-whispers.

Grant sighs heavily. "I just don't understand it. Palmer leads me on for years. But goes all doe-eyed over a bartender?"

His buddy snickers, and the grating sound feels like it is scratching some irritable place in my brain. "You sure she isn't just trying to make you jealous?

"I wish it wasn't fucking working," he swears.

"That means she still has feelings for you, man," his friend eggs him on. "No way she's actually into him. Come on— you're you."

Yes, he is. He is Grant Foster: the guy who fumbled the single greatest woman either of us has ever known. And I want to throw it in his face, to gloat. But then I remember that I have no room to brag. I haven't won her. I haven't locked her in, in any more permanent ways than Grant had. I have spent one incredible night with her that, if it's the last night I ever spend with her, will haunt me until I am an old man on my deathbed.

Grant had her for three whole years. Spent countless nights with her. And clearly, it haunts him too. I honestly can't blame him. Some of my anger toward him fizzles out at the thought.

Just for a split second, though.

"You know," Grant muses, "if she wanted to prove she was over me, she could've at least picked someone believable."

The words hit me like a punch to the gut, hitting some sensitive, insecure place I wasn't aware that I had. I know Palmer doesn't feel this way or think I'm not worthy of her. But having someone say it makes me realize that a part of me has always felt less than worthy of her. And it's a shitty way to feel.

I rinse out a glass that doesn't need rinsing, trying to distract myself, the doubts buzzing around in my brain like pests I can't swat away.

I remind myself that Grant is drunk, that he is grasping at the last threads of whatever fragile ego he has left. That he is trying to pick a fight with me, to rile me up. And I *cannot* let him get to me.

"Come on," Grant calls, his voice louder, purposefully seeking me out now. No longer pretending I can't hear him. "Level with me, Howell. Just between you and me—what's the situation here? She rope you into some kind of deal?"

And, like the shit icing on top of the shit cake he's spewing, he adds, "How much did she offer to pay you?"

I bark a laugh. I don't mean to do it—it just comes out, short and sharp and bitter. Of all the inane things this guy could have said, this just seems like the dumbest. I don't acknowledge him, just continue my senseless cleaning.

But Grant is relentless.

"You can tell me!" he cajoles. "Is it, like a long con? Or is she keeping you around until she gets bored, like she did with me?"

My jaw clenches painfully, holding back retorts I know I can't say.

He takes a brown leather wallet out of his pocket and

slowly, clumsily, takes out several bills from inside, one at a time. He slaps the pile of money on the bar between us.

"I bet I can beat whatever she promised you. I will give you a thousand dollars right now," he offers, his voice slow and deliberate, "if you'll just tell me the truth. If you'll admit that you two made this up. That you're faking it for my benefit. Come on. I need to know."

I peer at the stack of bills—hundreds, I register dimly—and anger wells inside me at the sight. The heat of it pools in my belly. I've never had much patience for people who act like they can do and say whatever they want just because they have money.

The anger is flooding my senses, taking root in my brain and driving all logic out of it. A small rational voice in my mind tells me not to engage. It tells me that not only is this man single-handedly keeping my best friend's business in the black for this month from just one night out with his buddies, but he's also my employer.

But, despite that logical voice telling me to stay quiet, not to let him and his money and his words get to me, I can't help it. I brace one hand on the bar, using the other to slide the pile of money slowly back in his direction.

I lean in close, whispering, "I think you'll find Palmer is doing far less faking it than you remember."

Grant stands from his barstool, sending it scraping against the wood floor, tottering unsteadily from the sudden movement. He squares his shoulders, glaring daggers at me, his hands rolling into fists like he wants to take a swing. From the way he's wobbling, I would bet good money he'd miss.

And for one reckless moment, I consider letting him take the swing.

I've never been a violent man, not even in college. I worked out whatever inclinations I may have had during football. Never fought anyone except to bail my buddies out from time to time. But there is a part of me that just knows I would feel better if I punched Grant Foster in the face. Just one time.

He looks like he would certainly like to hurt me, and more than once.

I feel Cal's hand settle on my arm, squeezing it firmly.

"Hey," he urges, "I think they're winding down. Why don't you head home? I can take it from here."

I make a displeased *hmph* noise, my eyes never wandering from Grant's face as I back away from the bar. I know Cal's right, even if a part of me screams in disappointment at the thought of not following through with the idea. But I think about how upset Palmer would be if she found out I punched her ex-boyfriend—and current employer—and the anger fizzles out of me.

I walk away from Grant, heading briskly toward the back exit.

Cal calls after me, "Thanks, Si. I'll split things up at the end of the night and bring you your money later."

I wave my hand, not turning to acknowledge him, not really caring about the money. The money feels tainted anyway, almost as tainted as if I had accepted it straight from Grant Foster's hand.

When I'm in my bed a little while later, I lie there wide awake and staring at the ceiling, my mind reeling, thinking about the interaction with Grant.

I need to know, he said. But why did he need to know if we were faking it or not? Why did he care so much? What difference did it make if we were faking the relationship, when he was getting married in two days? Tomorrow, really, since midnight has passed.

Unless he was questioning his choices. Unless he was still in love with Palmer. Unless he was considering backing out of the wedding.

The thought sinks uncomfortably into my gut, like dead weight.

He's considering backing out of the wedding, I realize. He's still in love with her. And I can't say with any amount of confidence that Palmer isn't in love with him too.

The thought sickens me. I stare at my ceiling, gut roiling at the thought of them being together. They aren't right for each other. And I'm not just saying that out of jealousy. *I'm not.*

I've been around Palmer for six months now. I know Palmer. And I know that it's more than them wanting different things that sabotaged their relationship. Grant didn't understand Palmer, not like I do, and he doesn't deserve her. I don't necessarily know that I deserve her, but I know that if he goes to her, he'll only bring her down. I can't let that happen.

She has to know. She has to know what she means to me. She has to know that I don't want this to end, even if the ruse is over. I don't care if she's flying to France or not. She has to know how I feel about her; how crazy I am about her.

I wrench myself out of my sheets, pulling on the jeans and t-shirt I discarded on my bedroom floor. Not even two minutes pass before I am in my car, driving to her. I know it's two in the morning and she will likely be asleep, but this can't wait. She needs to know.

CHAPTER 17

Palmer

A violent *bang, bang, bang* startles me from my focus. I look toward the kitchen door, my heart racing. I can't imagine who would be banging on my bakery door so late, and I'm instantly on alert, sensing danger. I grab the heavy marble rolling pin from my counter. I stalk toward the door slowly, my weapon raised.

Bang. Bang. Bang. Bang.

As I approach the kitchen door, I hear a voice accompanying the racket.

"Palmer? Palmer, let me in, please! I know you're in there."

I swing the door to the kitchen open an inch, just far enough to see the front door of the shop.

When I see him, I sigh heavily, putting my weapon down. My fear dissolves into annoyance. I push through the kitchen door and rush to let him in before he breaks my door down.

"Grant Foster," I scold as soon as he stumbles through the unlocked door. "What are you doing here?"

My immediate impression of Grant is that he is exquisitely drunk. His shirt is half-tucked into his slacks, and his tie is coming undone. He smells of whiskey, and his cheeks are flushed. He points at me, accusing, "I knew it. I knew you'd be working. You always work ungodly hours before a big wedding."

My eyes narrow. "Well, this one is as big as they come. You should know."

He lets out an amused guffaw. "Good one."

I shake my head at him. I repeat, "Grant, what are you doing here?"

He points out the window. "I was with my buddies a few blocks away at the whiskey bar. It's my bachelor party."

"You walked here?" I ask, incredulously. "From your bachelor party?"

He nods. "I needed to see you."

"Why?" I ask, a sense of dread and unease growing inside me at the question. I know I probably do not want to know the answer, but I cannot help but ask it anyway.

"Because," he says, like a small child wanting to get his way.

I sigh, crossing my arms over my chest, impatient. "Because?"

He inhales dramatically, steadying himself as much as he can be steadied. He wobbles a little from side to side, and I imagine the room is probably spinning in the alternate universe created for him courtesy of Crown Royal.

"Because," he continues, "this is my last chance. My last chance to talk to you, before it's too late."

I definitely don't want to hear whatever he has to say. But I am paralyzed, unable to stop him as he clamors on.

"I want you to look me in the eyes, Palmer," he demands, pointing two fingers to his eyes to emphasize his request. "And tell me I should get married tomorrow."

I roll my eyes at the drunken melodrama. "You should get married tomorrow, Grant."

He pauses, confused for a second, as if he genuinely hadn't expected me to say it so easily. He regroups and tries again.

"I want you to look me in the eyes and tell me that this is what you want," he says. "Me with Bennett, and you with this... Silas... dude."

"This is what I want," I echo, again without hesitation.

He frowns deeply. I take his hesitation as an opportunity.

"You should get back to your party, Grant," I urge. "And I will get back to making your wedding cake."

He lets out an exasperated sound, almost like a growl, and starts pacing the shop like a restless animal.

"I'm not going anywhere until you tell me why," he says. There's something about the rigid lines of his posture, the way his hands grip at the roots of his hair, that's alarming. Grant has always been the calm, level-headed type, and it's not like him to get so agitated, not even while drunk.

I try to keep my tone steady when I ask, "Why what?"

"Why you could never really love me," he demands.

"I did love you, Grant," I reply softly.

"Bullshit," he spits. "We were together for three years. We lived together. I thought we had something good, Palmer."

"We did," I whisper. "I was devastated when you broke up with me. I drowned myself in my work for a year just so I didn't have time to think about you."

His head tilts backward with a derisive scoff. "Come on now. You drowned yourself in work *long* before we ever broke up. That was always the problem."

This stirs some emotion inside me that I can no longer keep down—something hot and burning that erupts in my belly.

"You're right, my work was the problem," I retort. "This place was my dream, Grant. And you treated it like it was a cute little distraction, like it was some girlish hobby. This place was everything to me, and you acted like every second I spent here was a personal slight against you."

He pauses suddenly in his frantic pacing, wobbling with the sudden arrest of momentum.

I sputter a laugh. "Of course, I couldn't love you, Grant. Not when you could never truly love me. Not all of me, at least. Not the parts that weren't convenient for you. I tried so hard to squeeze myself into the space you made for me in your life, to be the person you needed. But in the end, I was a square peg."

"What?" he asks, the metaphor lost on his drunken brain.

"A square peg? In a round hole?" I ask.

His face contorts with confusion. "You're calling me a round hole?

I rub my face, exasperated, some of the anger fizzling out of me with the ridiculous nature of this discussion. "Forget it."

"Does he, then?" His tone is quiet but demanding.

"Does he what?" I ask, not following his train of thought.

"This guy you're with now," he explains. "You're saying he loves all of you."

"He does," I retort immediately, the instinct to keep up the charade deeply ingrained in me after all this time pretending. But as Grant is sitting in front of me, demanding answers from me, I suddenly lose the will to pretend any longer. God, it has been so exhausting. I'm so sick of lying, of pretending.

But then I think of Silas. I think of these last six months with him, pretending together. And every moment when we were together under no pretense at all. Getting to know him. Growing close to his friends and his family. Letting him not only into the parts of my world that I share freely, but even those parts of my life that I have held secret in my heart. Sharing my wildest dreams with him. Letting him see the most vulnerable parts of me and finding for once that it didn't hurt to let someone in. There's an incredibly warm feeling growing inside my chest at the thought.

"He does," I repeat, this time for myself, a wide, genuine smile breaking across my face at the thought. I cannot speak for Silas. I cannot elucidate on his feelings for me, but what I do know is this: he knows me. He has taken me all this time for who I truly am, not asking even once for me to pretend to be anything more or less than the truest, most fundamental version of myself. Which is ironic, considering how much we've been pretending for everyone else.

"He loves all of me," I test the words quietly, marveling at them with a soft smile on my lips. "And I love all of him."

It's the first time I've let myself even think those words, much less say them out loud.

Why did I have to figure it out here, with Grant, of all people?

I turn, preparing to ask Grant if I can call him an Uber, when I realize that he has closed the distance between us while I was lost in thought. I look up into his face; he's hovering over me, his deep blue eyes glassy and a little unfocused.

My spine turns to ice, my mind going frozen with panic at his proximity.

I shake my head frantically as he leans in. "Grant, I don't—"

But before I can finish the thought, he throws himself at me in a desperate last-ditch effort. His lips crash against mine, so hard it is painful. The taste of whiskey on his lips is so strong that I feel that I could get drunk on it. And the world seems to freeze. The unexpected contact sends my brain instantly into a panicked spiral, working through a medley of conflicting emotions, all at the same time.

This cannot be happening. I cannot let this happen.

He's getting married tomorrow.

God. *Bennett.* Say what I might about Bennett Barlow,

but she doesn't deserve this. Despite my best efforts, I realize that I have come to like her. And I don't want to hurt her. This would kill her if she knew.

But he's drunk. He doesn't know what he's doing. He doesn't want this. I don't want this.

The memory of wanting this is there—it's there in the back of my mind, like searching for the name of a movie I loved once upon a time but have long forgotten. I know this was once everything I wanted, and not that long ago. For Grant to love me again. For Grant to kiss me again.

I can remember that feeling, after he broke up with me, when the hurt was so very fresh and raw, the regret of not knowing that our last kiss had been our last. I remember lamenting the fact, wishing I could have just one more kiss, for closure.

And here it is—the closure I sought. The kiss I know for certain will be our last.

When did it happen? When did Grant's kiss become something so wholly uninteresting to me? When did I, unknowingly, get so completely over him?

I step back, breaking the contact. Grant leans forward, nearly falling, as if my lips were the only thing keeping him aloft. I steady him by the shoulders.

"Grant," I scold softly, with all the patience I can manage. "I think you should go."

"No, Palmer, *please.*" He leans in for a second time, unrelenting.

I close my eyes, bracing myself, but before he can kiss me again, he staggers backward abruptly.

It takes me far too long to realize that he didn't retreat of his own volition or from his own drunken lack of balance.

It was Silas who pulled him away.

He's here, looking impossibly large and menacing, looming over Grant. The sight of him is so unexpected that it temporarily puts me into a dazed stupor. I am relieved and surprised and confused to see him, all at the same time.

"I believe Palmer said she wanted you to go." Silas's words are so low and menacing that they send a cold chill rippling through my body, raising goosebumps across my skin.

"Fuck," Grant swears. "Not you again."

Silas shrugs, but the stiff rise of his shoulders is anything but nonchalant.

"Yes, me again."

He still has one hand clenched onto Grant's shoulder from wrenching him away from me, and in the next second, he uses it to brace for the punch that he lands squarely across his cheek.

The sound of it turns my stomach—the crunch of knuckles against skin and bone, the involuntary grunt of pain that it drags from Grant's throat. Grant crumples to the floor with the impact—not knocked out but certainly knocked free of whatever sense he had remaining.

Silas flexes his hand, shaking it out at his side.

Grant rolls over on the floor with a miserable groan, clenching his face. I kneel beside him, moving his hand so that I can see the huge red welt blooming just beneath his left eye. I look up at Silas, and when our eyes lock, I know mine are wide with panic.

"Silas," I breathe, my voice shaking. "What did you do?"

His chest and shoulders deflate, like the anger has been leeched from him in an instant. He sputters for words, but none come to him.

"Help me get him up," I command, putting one of Grant's arms over my shoulders. Silas moves to help me, taking the brunt of the work in getting Grant off the floor and into one of the chairs at the table by the window.

I run to my kitchen and fetch a bag of frozen berries from the freezer. When I return to the shop, I force the bag into

Grant's hand, helping him guide it toward the rapidly expanding swollen area below his eye.

"Stay here, Grant," I instruct. I fix my gaze on Silas. "You and I need to go outside to talk."

I lead Silas out the front door, the bell chiming over us, far too merry a sound for the scenario. I wonder idly how I could have missed the sound before, when Silas barged in. I imagine the kiss, and the associated panic clouding my mind, probably impaired all my senses at the time.

I turn on my heel suddenly, and Silas nearly runs into me.

"How could you do this, Silas? Grant is probably going to have a black eye."

He appraises me for a long moment, like he couldn't have heard me correctly. A disbelieving laugh falls from his lips.

"Grant?" he asks. "That's who you're worried about?"

"The wedding is tomorrow," I say through clenched teeth. "There's no way we're not getting fired over this."

"You think I give a damn about the wedding?" he asks.

"I do!" I retort. "You know I care! That's what this has always been about, hasn't it? Everything between us. We had one goal—just to get to this damn wedding. And you had to go and ruin everything!"

"Ruin everything? Palmer, I—" he pauses, momentarily fumbling the words, "I was just trying to protect you."

"I don't need protecting, Silas! I'm an adult. I can take care of myself."

"I know you can," he replies, then hesitates. He looks up at the stars above us, as if searching them for answers. "That's the problem, isn't it? You're never going to let anyone else take care of you."

The words strike exactly where I expect them to, in the most painful possible place in my heart, right in the center of my deepest insecurities. The ones I told Silas, in confidence, trusting that he would never use them against me, the way Grant always did.

I shake my head, feeling hot tears start to form in my eyes. "I think we're done here, Silas. It's about time we stop pretending."

He recoils as if I've struck him with my words.

"You don't mean that." His tone is pleading, but the hurt in my heart is vindictive and lonely. It reaches out for him, wanting to envelop him in its depths, so he can hurt just as sharply and terribly as I do.

"I do," I tell him, wiping at the tears as they stream down my face. "I think you should go. I'm going to go back in there to talk to Grant; see if I can salvage something from this mess."

The sheer amount of pain in Silas's eyes as he slowly backs away makes it clear that I'm losing so much more than I could ever possibly save.

CHAPTER 18

Silas

I am sitting hunched over the bar, nursing the last dregs of a glass of whiskey, when Emery finds me.

"Oh good, you're here," she says, slamming her huge wedding binder down beside me on the bar. "We have a minor crisis."

I look at the binder for just a moment, then back to my glass. I have been trying so hard to be involved in this process, but right now, the sight of that damn binder is the last thing I want to see. It has been my goal for the last eight years to bring Emery happiness. But sitting here at this bar, drowning in misery, I just can't bring it upon myself to do it this time.

Emery does not seem to notice my lack of engagement in the latest wedding-related crisis. She carries on, "My friend Abigail is no longer available to be a bridesmaid."

I swish the last remaining swig of whiskey around in my glass pensively. I ask off-hand, "Is she the bitchy one or the pregnant one?"

She scoffs at my assessment, but replies nonetheless, "She was the pregnant one. She unexpectedly delivered last night, three months early. She has a baby in the NICU to think about. Which means you need someone else to walk down the aisle."

"I thought I was walking you down the aisle," I retort.

"Yes, you're walking me up the aisle," she says. "You need someone to walk with down the aisle. When I'll be with Charlie."

If that's Emery's idea of a crisis, then I'm gravely unimpressed. "I'll walk myself."

"I have an even better idea," she says, her voice reaching an impossibly high decibel with her excitement. "What if Palmer were in my wedding party?"

I swig the last gulp of whiskey and place the glass back on the bar with some force. I shake my head resolutely. "Not gonna happen."

She frowns deeply. "Come on, you don't think she'll do it? I know we only just met six months ago, but I feel like we've really bonded. And you two are so great together!"

Her words feel like several tiny daggers stabbing into my chest, one at a time. I wave Cal over for another drink.

"Leave it alone," I tell her gruffly. I hand Cal my glass, silently asking for a refill. He fetches the bottle off the shelf and pours a generous dram.

Emery's lip juts outward in a dramatic pout. "Come on, let me just ask her. I bet she would—"

"Emery," I say with force. "Palmer and I aren't together. Let it go."

The words finally hit her. She scrutinizes me suddenly—my face, my hunched posture, the cloud of whiskey and misery surrounding me. She watches Cal stoically slide the glass toward me across the bar.

"What happened? Did she break up with you?" she demands.

I sputter out a laugh. "Why is that your first assumption, that she broke up with me?"

She narrows her eyes. "Have you met Palmer? She's awesome. Way out of your league."

God, did I know it. The reminder just rubs a heaping pile of salt in the open, festering wound.

Emery looks to Cal, as if my lack of immediate response is not good enough for her. "Did she break up with him?"

Cal raises an eyebrow at me, clearly wondering if I'm going to tell her the truth.

I let out a beleaguered sigh. I just have to tell her. Rip the band-aid off.

"We were never really dating," I admit. I watch her face as these words register in her mind. Her expression passes from confusion into surprise and finally settles into amusement.

"What do you mean you were never really dating?" she asks.

"It was an act," I insist. "She needed to prove to Bennett Barlow that she didn't take the job to win back her fiancé. And I needed a cheap baker."

Anger flashes across her features immediately. "Are you telling me you pimped yourself out for my wedding cake?"

I cringe. "Kind of, yeah."

She shakes her head, pointing an accusing finger at Cal. "And you knew about this?"

He raises his hands in the air, pleading his innocence. "He only told me like a week ago."

Emery narrows her gaze on me, her eyes settling on the fresh glass of whiskey I hold between my palms. Her anger suddenly dissolves, as easily as mist, and a self-satisfied smirk settles on her face instead. "Do you always drink your sorrows away over a girl you were never really dating?"

I glare at her. "I was into her, sure. But she's not into me like that."

Emery lets out a pealing laugh. "Excuse me? Palmer is head over heels for you."

"She's not."

"She is."

"And how the fuck would you know?" I'm not sure if I have ever taken such a harsh tone with my sister in my life.

She pauses, inhaling sharply, before she seethes, "Palmer is my friend. I hear her talk about you. I see the way she looks at you. She loves you, Silas."

This is just too ridiculous to even entertain. I can't handle this anymore. I do the mental math over my tab and toss a couple of twenties on the bar for Cal. I turn on my barstool as if to leave.

"That's not what she said last night," I retort, standing from my barstool to leave.

She lifts the giant binder and uses it like a shield to halt my progress in leaving. I glare at her over it.

"What happened last night?" she asks. I try to step around her, but she slides over, halting me again with her binder shield.

"For once in your life, can you please just mind your own God damn business?" The words are harsh and unkind, I know. But I'm not in a particularly kind mood today.

Emery's grip on the binder loosens with surprise, and I take the opportunity to pluck it from her hands. I hold it out of her reach and step around her, only placing it back on the bar when I'm several feet past her. I use the advantage of my longer stride to head purposefully for the exit.

"Bye, Cal," I yell over my shoulder.

"Later, Si," he replies.

"Silas!" Emery calls. "Silas, wait!"

I make my way out onto the street and in the direction of my car. Though Emery might have interrupted me before I got to finish my second drink, at least I can safely drive myself home to mope.

"Silas Matthew Howell, you stop right there," she demands. For just a moment, the petulant tone of voice gets to me. I turn on the spot, letting her catch up.

"Not this time, Em," I tell her coldly. "I have always let you get your way. You've always gotten everything you've wanted. Before Mom and Dad died, certainly, but even since then. I've put my entire life on pause trying to give you the world. But not this time. I can't do it. I'm not letting you put my heart on the butcher block to get sliced open. Not so you can have an extra bridesmaid."

She stops short, looking as stricken as if I slapped her. "You think that's what this is about? Getting my way?"

"Isn't it always?" I ask dryly.

"You think this is what I want?" she spits out. "You think I wanted Mom and Dad to die, leaving us alone? You think I wanted to be a burden on you?"

I roll my eyes. "You were never—"

"You think I want my fiancé to feel rushed to marry me and put babies in me right now, so that I don't fucking die of cancer first?"

I try to say, "I don't think—"

She lets out a laugh, but it's an angry, cruel sound. "You think I even care if I don't have one of my bridesmaids? Or a fancy cake? I don't fucking care about any of it, Silas. At this point, I'd be just as happy eloping with Charlie in Vegas. All I wanted was for you to have another excuse to spend time with this beautiful, amazing woman who is enamored with you."

I stay quiet, letting her speak. She realizes I'm not going to yell or run away from her, so she pauses to regroup, taking a deep breath.

"I know you say I wasn't a burden to you, and I appreciate

you for that. But I was. You were barely out of college when Mom and Dad died, and you have spent every second of your life since then worrying more about me than yourself. And I love you for it. But I honestly thought, when Charlie and I got engaged, that it would get better. That you wouldn't feel the need to put aside your own life to worry about mine. That you would finally do things that made you happy. But it didn't get any better. In fact, it almost got worse, in that you now find it necessary to sacrifice everything you have to give me the perfect wedding. But Silas, I don't care about having the perfect wedding. I just want to be with Charlie. And I deeply, desperately want you to get a life. Because, maybe, if you get a life, you'll stop feeling the need to help me live mine."

I shake my head, letting out a chuckle.

She grins, taking my hand. "I want you to listen to me when I say this, Si."

"I'm listening," I say softly. All the anger seems to have fled my body.

"I have never seen you live quite like you do when you're with Palmer. And I want that for you, desperately. I want you to have someone who reminds you to do what makes you happy, instead of devoting your whole life to me."

I look away from her, white hot embarrassment bubbling in my belly. "Well, I don't know if I can fix it anymore. I epically fucked everything up last night."

"What happened?" she asks again, more gently than before.

"I went to talk to her. To tell her how crazy I am about her. But when I got there, I saw her kissing Grant through the window of her bakery."

She frowns, processing this new information. "They kissed, or he kissed her?"

"Well, he kissed her," I relent.

She tilts her head, her eyes narrowing with suspicion. "And then what happened?"

I sigh, running my hands through my hair.

"Then what happened, Silas?" she repeats, more sternly this time.

"I may have... punched him," I mutter through a cringe.

She closes her eyes, inhaling deeply to gather her patience, and the gesture is so very much like our mother that I almost smile at the reminder. "You do realize you could have been arrested? You may still get arrested."

"I know," I groan into my hands. "I know. It was so fucking stupid. But I couldn't just stand by and do nothing."

"And how did Palmer react?" she probes.

"That's the worst part!" I complain. "She got mad at me, like she was defending that piece of shit for assaulting her."

"For Christ's sake, what was she supposed to do?" she demands. "Throw herself into your arms and cry, 'my hero!'?"

"That would have been preferable, yeah," I mutter lamely.

She settles a disapproving glare on me.

"I know she had every right to be mad," I explain, my voice small and vulnerable, "but it wasn't just that. She also said we had to stop pretending. She basically acted like what we had was never real. And it was, Em... I know it was."

She looks at me kindly, putting a comforting hand on my arm. "I'm sure she knows it, too. I bet she was panicking. And scared. And upset about the situation. With good reason."

I'm not ready to admit that she's right, so I remain silent.

"I know what she said hurt you," she says. "But I'm begging you just to go talk it out with her. Because if you don't fight for her? If you just stand by and let yourself lose the best thing that ever happened to you, you'll never forgive yourself. And I'll never forgive you, either."

I sigh. "You really think I should go talk to her?"

She rolls her eyes. "Obviously."

"What if she doesn't want to talk to me?" I ask, my voice timid.

"Give her a good reason," she suggests with a wink.

I take a deep breath, suddenly resolved.

I shoot Emery a tentative grin before I turn to head down the street in the direction of Sweet P. I walk briskly, naturally picking up the pace to a light jog. By the time I can see the pink facade with the green and white awning, I am running. I push into the shop with force, the bell chiming, announcing my entrance. I'm sweaty and out of breath and instantly regretting not just driving my car the half mile, but I'm here. Running to her had seemed a lot more romantic in my mind.

Jenna is in her usual spot behind the counter, helping an older woman and a young girl, probably her granddaughter, box up some cupcakes from the display case. She peers at me through the glass, her eyes locking onto me like the targeting system for a missile. She draws her attention back to her customers, her tone almost painfully polite as she pointedly ignores my presence.

I step aside to let the customers leave the bakery, never taking my eyes from Jenna. When we have the room to ourselves, she leans against the counter, peering at me.

"You look sweaty," she remarks.

I look down at myself, seeing the dark stains in my gray t-shirt. "I am."

"And desperate," she adds.

"That, too," I admit, unable to stifle a grin. I gesture to the kitchen door behind her. "You going to let me in there to talk to her?"

She arches an eyebrow. "I don't know if I should. Sounds like you really put your foot in it last night."

I approach the counter, my hands in my pockets. "I did. I'd like to try to get my foot out of it, if that's even possible."

She smirks but gestures for me to come around the counter.

Before I can push through the door, however, she puts her hand in front of me, barring my entry. "For the record, Howell, I never thought Grant was right for her. Never. You, on the other hand…" She looks me up and down, her stormy gray eyes appraising. "I've been rooting for you."

Something warm spreads in my chest at these words, at the fondness in her expression as she peers up at me. Hearing those words from Jenna Rhodes, of all people, gives me all the confirmation I could ever need that I'm doing the right thing. I could ask for no greater blessing to be in Palmer's life.

Jenna adds, "I know Palmer is angry about what you did last night, but I'm not."

"You're not?" I ask, surprised. "Aren't you worried about losing the Barlow wedding?"

"We didn't lose anything," she replies, and I'm certain she can tell from my expression that this is news to me. "But even if we did lose it, it wouldn't change anything for me. Money comes and goes." She jabs one thumb toward the kitchen door. "That girl in there is forever. She matters more than anything to me. I can't be mad at someone else trying to protect her."

I take a deep breath, bracing myself. I'm about to push through the door when she adds, "Don't embarrass me by fucking it all up, 'kay?"

I sputter a laugh. "You got it."

When I enter the kitchen, Palmer is seated at the center of the room, facing away from me, leaning over her old silver worktable. Her hands are steady as she pipes a border onto the most massive single tier of cake I've ever seen in my life. There are two other enormous, though slightly smaller tiers beside her.

I look around the kitchen, but Evan must have finished

the baking already, because he is nowhere in sight. It's just the two of us.

"Palmer?" I call.

Her hands stutter to a sudden stop, the last shell in the pattern coming out just slightly larger than the rest. But she pauses for only a moment before she continues her work, pretending like she never heard me in the first place.

I cross the space until I'm beside her.

"Palmer?" I say again. "Please, stop decorating the damn cake and talk to me."

Her eyes flit to me briefly before focusing back on her work. Her frown deepens, and her brows knit together.

"I don't have time, Silas," she murmurs, barely loud enough for me to hear. "The wedding is tomorrow."

"Two minutes," I plead. "Just give me two minutes of your time. Please."

She stands from her barstool with a huff and sets her piping bag down beside the cake with some force. She brushes her hands on her apron.

"Two minutes," she repeats, crossing her arms over her chest as she peers up at me expectantly.

I take a deep breath. "I need to apologize."

Her eyes narrow. "You think?"

She is not going to make this easy on me. I don't deserve for her to go easy on me, I know, but a man can dream. "I'm sorry. I'm sorry for barging in here. I'm sorry for punching Grant, threatening this job that I know is important to you. And above all else, I'm sorry for what I said to you after. I never wanted to hurt you like that."

Her nose scrunches, her mouth working like she's chewing on the words. She scrutinizes my expression, and I can only hope it looks as sincere as I feel.

"Fine," she says, barely louder than a whisper. "Apology accepted."

She turns back toward her barstool to resume her work on the cake, but I hook one hand around her elbow to halt her. She glares back at me over her shoulder.

"I need to get back to my cake," she insists. "Let me go."

"I'm not letting you go," I say firmly. "We need to talk about this."

She wrenches her arm free, glaring at me. "You want to talk? Why don't we talk about what I had to do last night, to fix what you did?"

I clench my jaw, too afraid to ask her to elaborate, knowing in my heart she's going to tell me anyway.

"First, I had to talk Grant off the ledge. To make him realize he was just having cold feet, so he didn't cancel the wedding. Then, I had to convince him not to fire both of us. At least, he realized he owed me that much, after being a total ass. And then, to top it off, I had to convince him not to press charges against you for assault, Silas."

"How did you manage that?" I murmur, dreading her answer with every fiber of my being.

She crosses her arms, looking down at her shoes, before she admits, "I had to promise not to tell Bennett." She fights an angry sob as she says, "You know how shitty that feels? I like Bennett. She came to me for advice when she was having doubts about Grant, and I'm the one who made her feel better about it."

She shakes her head, laughing bitterly. "I really, desperately didn't want to be the one to hit the detonate button on this explosive situation. But I would have told her, because it's the right thing to do. I wouldn't have let her get married to him without knowing what he did. But I don't have that option anymore. Because protecting you is more important to me."

"I'm sorry you had to do that," I say immediately. "I never wanted to put you in that position."

"And you know what the worst part is?" she asks.

I know the question is rhetorical, but even so, I ask, "What's the worst part?"

"Before you came, before Grant kissed me, there was a moment where everything was so perfectly clear," she explains. "Grant was saying all the words I once wanted him so desperately to say. Fighting for me the way I used to dream he would. Making this grand gesture. And for a moment, I was afraid that I would want him again. But I didn't."

She sounds surprised by the idea, as if this is an entirely new concept to wrap her mind around. "I realized that I had finally gotten over him. Completely over him, without even realizing it. I realized that his words, his kiss, meant nothing to me. That nothing he could say could ever win me back. I told him he should marry Bennett, because she loves him, and I don't. I told him I love—"

She pauses abruptly, and my heart lurches at the implication. Her green eyes are wide and watery, searching my face desperately. I close the gap between our bodies with one step, taking her face in both my hands.

"You told him you love...?" I probe, wanting—no, needing —her to finish that sentence. Needing her to say it.

"You," she whispers. "I told him I love you."

I let out a shaky breath, my thumb brushing her cheek. "And did you mean it? Or were you just keeping up the act?"

She shakes her head ever so slightly. "I meant it. I love you, Silas. I'm sorry it took me so long to admit it, but—"

I kiss her before she can say another word, because I don't care how long it took. I don't care what made her realize the truth. I'm just so fucking glad that she did.

Her hands curl around my neck, drawing me down to her, pressing her lips more firmly against mine.

Out of everything running through my mind in this moment, the most overwhelming feeling while kissing her is relief. I thought that I would never again get to kiss her, never again get to feel her. I have been mourning the loss of her—grieving. I realize now that she had me, either way. Even if she still had feelings for Grant, I would have groveled at her feet for a chance to do this again, even once.

But she isn't in love with him. She is in love with me.

And with this thought, the relief gives way, leaving room for this incredible new emotion; this magnificent, heart-exploding sensation that I can no longer deny. I break away from her, realizing I haven't actually said it yet.

"Palmer, I love you," I gasp.

She beams at me, whispering, "Thank God," before crashing back into me.

I kiss her desperately, frantically, like I'm taking my dying breath. I've seen a world where I don't get to kiss this woman, and I want nothing to do with it. I only want this. Only want her.

My hands maneuver down to her hips and lift her, settling her onto her worktable beside me, bringing her closer to my height. I kiss her neck, working my way down to taste the skin just over her pulse. It's nice not having to hunch down to kiss her, but a devilish voice in the back of my mind adds that it would be even easier if we were horizontal.

But the next second, something indescribable happens. I hear a sudden loud snap, and I feel Palmer suddenly sinking in my arms. The table below us starts to fall, and I act on instinct, pulling her into my chest to keep her from falling with it. The corner of the table sinks down to the floor beneath its snapped, rusty leg, turning it into a ramp. And we both watch in horror as three beautiful tiers of cake slide slowly and purposefully down the ramp toward us. We are dumbstruck at the sight, unable to comprehend what we are witnessing, unable to stop the progress as the cakes plummet forward.

Plop. Plop. Plop.

One by one, they slide to the floor, making a horrible

squelching noise as pounds and pounds of cake and frosting smash on the tiles below.

We stand there, still tangled in each other, staring in horror at the scene, unable to speak.

But Jenna, who has returned at the sound of the crash, has no problem finding her words.

We flinch as she says, "What the fuck did y'all do?"

CHAPTER 19
Palmer

There's a dull ringing sound in my ears, drowning out the sound of Silas and Jenna bickering at each other. I desperately want to tear my eyes from the sugary carnage smeared across my kitchen floor, but I can't look away.

My mind is frozen, stunned. But I force it to thaw, to start problem-solving.

The wedding starts at six o'clock tomorrow. For a cake of this size, in addition to the hundreds of desserts they ordered for the dessert table, I'll need multiple hours for set-up. At the very latest, I'll need to arrive at the venue at two o'clock. That leaves twenty hours to recreate half of the largest cake I've ever constructed before—the cake I've been working on painstakingly for days.

I start to take shallow, painful breaths, feeling like my lungs have stopped expanding to their full extent.

Silas realizes I'm starting to hyperventilate and stops arguing with Jenna. He places a warm hand on my back, moving it in soothing circles.

"Hey, it's okay," he says, though his voice sounds just as panicked as I feel. "We'll figure this out—"

Jenna sneers, "You can't bake, Howell. How are you going to be any help?"

Silas shoots her a glare. "I can follow instructions. I can help."

He turns to me again, his voice frantic. "Just tell me what to do, Palmer. We can fix this."

But I can't seem to breathe anymore, much less bake. The lack of oxygen is making me dizzy. I sink to the floor, wrapping my arms around my legs and resting my forehead against my knees.

"I'm calling reinforcements," Jenna declares.

"Me too," Silas says.

This starts another argument between them, but I can't process anything they're saying in my current state.

Fifteen minutes later, Evan arrives, and shortly after, Emery and Charlie follow.

I look up at them from the floor of my kitchen, dazed and watery-eyed.

Evan puts his apron on and approaches me. He offers a hand to me on the floor, grinning down at me. "Come on, Boss. We've got work to do."

I take his offered hand. I stand and brush myself off, my eyes scanning my friends, lined up in a row in my kitchen like soldiers waiting for their assignments.

Emery chooses a weapon—a whisk—and smiles at me. "How can we help?"

The sight of all of them here, in my kitchen, looking at me with so much love, breaks something inside me. I burst into tears. All five of them rush forward to surround me in a group hug, with me, the sobbing, hysterical nucleus in the middle.

When I manage to stop crying, Evan says, gently but firmly, "Yes, yes, we all love Palmer. But we really do have to get to work now."

After that, Evan takes command like a military sergeant,

directing his unwitting sous-chefs through creating my recipes. Finally, I pull myself together enough to get to work.

We toil all through the day and steadily into the night, hardly stopping for breaks. Around midnight, we get to the point where the remaining tasks are all fine detail work that only Evan and I can pull off, so Emery, Jenna, and Charlie head home. I try to tell Silas he needs to go too, to get rest before the wedding, but he stubbornly refuses. He sits beside me, talking with me and telling jokes to keep me awake through the early hours of the morning. Eventually, I convince him to go home around four in the morning.

Jenna returns to open the shop at nine, and I'm stable enough to take a nap before getting the supplies ready to head to the Barlow Hotel.

Once I'm in the ballroom that afternoon and the setup is complete, I take several steps back from the table, needing the space to take it all in—the lavish decorations; the array of tiny, ornate petit fours; the trays of delicate cookies; and at the center, the tallest, most majestic creation that has ever come from my mind and my hands. Seven towering tiers of cake, buttercream, and fondant. My crowning achievement. Half of which we frantically recreated overnight.

My chest rises in a deep inhale, and when I release the breath, it carries with it months of tension and stress that have been steadily building up inside. A part of me is reluctant to let those feelings go, to admit that I actually pulled this off. A part of me waits for the other shoe to drop, for the universe to pull the rug out from under me and prove once and for all that I don't have what it takes. But the proof that I can do it is right in front of me—enormous and beautiful and undeniable.

Admittedly, I may not have been able to do it alone. But for the first time in my life, relying on the people who love me doesn't feel like a weakness.

Click.

My lips widen with a very tired, but genuine smile. I turn at the familiar sound, watching Silas appear from behind his camera. He surveys the preview for the picture he just took, and a brilliant smile lights his face.

"There's no way that could have been a good picture," I insist with a chuckle. "I must look so sleep-deprived right now."

He raises an eyebrow, challenging, "Take a look."

I move toward him, inspecting the preview for myself. And it's almost annoying how good it is, how talented he is. The picture should paint me as a zombie, lifeless and wan, but he somehow captured me—a little tired, maybe, but beautiful and proud and strong.

How does he always manage to bring out the very best in me?

I take a moment to get a good look at him, and my breath catches in my throat. Though he has spent most of the night with me, not sleeping at all (and not in the fun way), he has managed to pull himself together in spectacular fashion. No one has ever worn a tux so well, I'm certain of it.

"You look amazing," I breathe. He looks so good it physically hurts, deep in my chest.

He looks down at himself and back at me with a pleased smile.

"So do you," he says.

I let out a disbelieving laugh. I look down at the clothes I haven't changed out of in twenty-four hours, covered in smudges of frosting and sugar.

He notices the skeptical look and reiterates, "My camera doesn't lie."

I argue, "Maybe not, but I'm starting to think it may exaggerate the truth just a little bit. Come on, tell me—do you or do you not put an Instagram filter on that thing?"

He barks a surprised laugh. He puts his camera down and

reaches out to snake his hand around my waist, drawing my body into his. "You insult me. How dare you imply such a thing? Me? Put a cheap Instagram filter on my work? Blasphemy."

I laugh at his mock-offended tone. "Okay, okay, I'm sorry to offend your artistic sensibilities!"

He cups my cheek with one warm hand, and I lean into it instinctively, feeling my whole body sink into his touch. I suspect that I could fall asleep in his arms, even standing straight up. I close my eyes, relishing the feeling; wanting this day to be done, so we can be together, without all of today's pomp and circumstance. I want to be able to talk to him, to hold him, to touch him, with this day behind us, without another soul to interrupt.

A throat clears behind us, and we break apart. I look behind Silas's shoulder and see Grant, standing there in his tux, watching us.

To the untrained eye, Grant almost looks like his normal self. Whoever did his makeup this morning truly did a fantastic job, covering what I'm certain must be an impressive bruise. If his left eye were only able to open to the same extent as his right, it would be completely unnoticeable.

Grant's eyes pointedly avoid me, looking only at Silas. "We're ready for shots of the groomsmen now."

Silas peers at Grant, saying nothing, but I can almost feel his distaste for Grant like a palpable heat radiating from him.

Silas is a professional though, so he grabs his camera anyway. He smiles at me. "I'll see you after the wedding."

I nod, smiling back at him. "See you later."

He plants a kiss firmly on my cheek before striding past Grant, toward the lobby of the hotel. Grant doesn't immediately follow. He looks up at the towering cake beside me and whistles, long and low.

"You've outdone yourself," he says quietly. "The cake is perfect."

"Thank you," I reply, not sure what else to say. My brain unhelpfully replays his visit to the bakery, and I cringe at the thought.

"You two seem good together," he says.

I flash him a small smile. "Thank you."

I pick up my bag of supplies to leave, but Grant hurriedly adds, "I'm happy for you, Palmer. I really am. I'm glad you found someone who... loves all of you. And I'm sorry I couldn't do that for you when we were together. I'm sorry for everything. Especially for being a drunken mess. I'm ashamed of how I acted. Toward you, of course, but toward Silas, too."

I stride toward him slowly, reaching out to place a hand on his arm.

"Thank you, Grant. I hope..." I pause for just a moment, considering. His remorse means something, but it's not enough. Part of me wants to ask if Bennett knows—if he has told her about the kiss. I want to know that I'm not letting another woman walk into a marriage built on a lie.

But the question lodges in my throat. I'm too afraid he'll lash out and take Silas down with him.

"I hope you and Bennett have a beautiful life together," I finish. He nods silently in thanks, and I walk away, the guilt twisting in my chest.

When I am back outside the Barlow Hotel, I inhale deeply, breathing in the sea air and letting it fill my lungs.

I did it. No going back now.

I need sleep desperately—more sleep than I can fit in my day. There is still packing to do for my trip. My flight to Paris leaves first thing in the morning, and I need to see Silas before I go. We need to figure out where we are, but the cake and the wedding have gotten in the way of that.

Sleep first, though.

I take three steps toward my van when I see her across the street, sitting on a bench. I might not have noticed her, if she didn't stand out quite so starkly—if she didn't look like some sort of fallen angel, perched in her white gown.

Bennett.

Damn it. I suppose sleep will have to wait.

I cross the street.

"Bennett?" I ask hesitantly when I'm within earshot. She turns, looking at me over her shoulder. Her mascara is streaked down her face, only adding to the image of a Greek tragedy that she paints.

"Hey, Sweet P," she greets sadly, and I fight a little smile at her persistence in not calling me by my name, even now.

"You doing okay?" I ask, even though it's a dumb question. She is clearly not okay.

She sniffles, laughing pitifully.

"I've been better," she admits.

"I can see that," I remark. "What happened? Where are your bridesmaids?"

"You mean my cousin and a couple girls from my sorority, who I'm pretty sure only showed up for the Louis Vuitton bridesmaid gifts?" she asks bitterly. "They're inside, fighting over the last mini champagne bottle."

I ponder the Louis-Vuitton-for-bridesmaid-gifts thing for only a few baffled seconds before my brain focuses on the more important task.

"Why are you out here alone?" I ask. "On your wedding day?"

She takes a shaky breath. "I don't know if it is my wedding day anymore."

I can't help it—even though concern for her is at the forefront of my mind in this moment, there is also a flickering moment of panic. There is a moment where I am convinced, even though the check is in the bank account, the dessert table is completely assembled, and I have one foot already on the plane to Paris, that this is the end. That she is going to call everything off and demand the money back. And I know that I don't have to do it—I have a contract stating that I don't have to give the money back, not when the work is done. But I know that I couldn't do it. I couldn't take her money, knowing the role I played in her less-than-happily-ever-after.

"Don't worry," she says, reading my mind. "You can keep the money. Silas too. My family's money has done far worse than support a couple of deserving small business owners."

I resist the urge to breathe a sigh of relief.

"I wasn't worried about the money, Bennett," I lie. "What's going on? Why are you reconsidering?"

I suspect, from her profoundly miserable appearance, that I know the reason why. But I need her to tell me that she knows. I swore to Grant that I wouldn't be the one to break the news to her.

"Grant told me," she confirms. "He told me that he went to you last night. That he kissed you. He didn't want me to find out from anyone else. Besides, he knew he wasn't going to be able to hide the black eye from me for long."

Relief floods through me, knowing Grant did the right thing in the end. I take a deep breath, searching for the words to respond to Bennett's revelation. But before I can find them, she says, "It's my fault, I know. I practically threw the two of you together."

I sputter out a small, surprised laugh. "Bennett, you didn't—"

"I knew," she says quickly, with finality. I snap my lips together, processing, unsure what she means. When my brows furrow, and I have not come up with the answer, she adds, "I knew who you were from the beginning, Palmer. I knew you were Grant's ex-girlfriend when I hired you."

It hits me that this may be the first and only time Bennett has ever said my real name.

"You did?" I ask, a little dumbstruck.

She nods, wiping another trail of watery mascara from beneath her eyes. "I did. I hired you *because* you were Grant's ex. He told me he had just gotten out of a three-year relationship when we met, and I did some digging. I found out who you were. When Grant proposed, I wanted to test him. To make sure he really was over you. And I guess I got what I wanted, in the end. I proved he never truly loved me. It was always you."

I exhale sharply. "That's not true, Bennett. He does love you. He certainly doesn't love me. When he came by the bakery, I think he was just scared and having cold feet. And he was very, very drunk. But he doesn't love me. And I don't love him. I promise you that. I love Silas."

Bennett laughs, but the sound is high-pitched and a little hysterical. "I cannot believe you pretended to date my photographer for all this time."

I blink in surprise. "You knew?"

She nods. "Of course, I knew. You are a terrible liar."

I sit down next to her, putting my face into my hands. Before I can control myself, I begin to laugh. And then, I can't stop. A fit of giggles overtakes me. I'm probably delirious from the lack of sleep, but it all just seems so hysterically funny.

"You're telling me," I sputter out through laughter. "I never fooled you... for even one second?"

She grins despite her situation. "It was really, really obvious."

She starts to laugh too, and before long, we are both shaking with laughter beside each other, unable to stop for several minutes.

When we are finally able to compose ourselves, still wiping

tears and breathing hard from our fit, she asks, "So when did you realize you were actually in love with him?"

I wonder for a second if she is asking about Grant, but then I realize, she's asking about Silas. "You know, you play the ditzy heiress thing far too well for someone who is so smart."

She smiles wickedly, showing all her perfectly straight, brilliantly white teeth. "People love to underestimate someone who is rich and pretty."

I sigh, shaking my head. "You know what, Bennett? I like you. This whole time, I've been thinking that we could have been friends, if not for the fact—"

"That I'm about to marry your ex-boyfriend?" she finishes my sentence for me.

"Are you?" I ask, a little surprised.

She shrugs. "Jury's still out."

I shake my head at her casual tone, and silence settles over us for a long moment.

"Why can't we?" Bennett finally asks.

"Why can't we do what?" I respond.

"Be friends?" she asks, her voice hopeful, almost shy. "I'll be honest. I have kind of struggled my whole life to make friends. Especially girlfriends. I'd like to be yours, I think."

I laugh, disbelieving. This woman has been manipulating me for months, stringing me along to test her boyfriend's devotion to her. I should be angry. Furious, even, for the strife she has put me through.

But I can't find it in myself to be angry with her. If not for Bennett, I never would have applied to pastry school. I wouldn't be leaving on a plane to Paris tomorrow morning. I wouldn't have modeled in a bridal magazine. I wouldn't know Emery or Cal or Charlie.

And most importantly, I never would have met Silas Howell.

As twisted as it might be, I owe Bennett for everything.

I say, "You know what? I do."

Her brows shoot up with surprise. "You do?"

I nod. "I think we could be friends. You don't think Grant would mind?"

She frowns, dismissing this concern. "He kissed another woman before our wedding. He doesn't get to decide."

"Have you decided what you're going to do?" I ask.

She shakes her head. "I have no idea. And I have—" she peers down at her dainty silver wristwatch—"less than an hour to figure it out."

I pat her hand, standing from the bench. "You have to do what's best for you, Bennett. Don't let anyone else tell you what's right for you—not Grant, not your mother. Definitely not me."

I turn to head back toward my van, but she calls to me, "Palmer?"

I stop, turning to look at her over my shoulder.

"I'm sorry for what I did to you," she says. "It wasn't fair to you. To anyone."

I flash her a warm smile. "I can't exactly be sorry, can I? We both lied, didn't we? And look what came out of it."

She smiles back. "Sometimes good can come from bad, I guess."

CHAPTER 20

Silas

My mom used to say you should never make any life-altering decisions without a good night's sleep. She was a logical, coolheaded woman, my mother.

But somehow, even though I'm running on very little sleep, I can't imagine she would talk me out of this decision. Not this time.

As soon as I leave the Barlow Hotel, I head straight to Palmer's apartment, still wearing the tux. I hit the buzzer on her front door and wait.

Palmer answers her door after several minutes, looking adorably sleepy in pink flannel pajama bottoms and a rumpled t-shirt. Her hair is a mess, a tangled nest of blond tendrils on top of her head.

I could *not* be more attracted to her.

"You're here," she mumbles through a yawn.

"I'm here," I agree, fighting a grin.

She looks down at her phone, noting the time—just past seven p.m.

Her eyes go wide and shocked, her sleepy expression suddenly alert. "She canceled the wedding?"

I raise an eyebrow, surprised she came to the correct conclusion so quickly. "You knew?"

"I may have nudged her toward her decision..." she admits sheepishly. "What happened?"

"Bennett showed up ten minutes before the ceremony and told Grant she needed to talk. Then she walked out and announced the wedding was off... and that was it. Grant left. The guests followed. Bennett did make a point to ask everyone to take a piece of your cake before they left, though. I make a damn good pink champagne sponge, if I do say so myself."

She groans, rubbing a hand down her face. "Oh my God. I can't believe it."

"It's not your fault," I assure her.

She winces. "I know it's not, but still. I feel responsible—"

"It's not your fault," I reiterate. I brace one hand against her doorway as I say, "Look, as happy as I am to answer all your runaway-bride-related questions, can I come inside? You have twelve hours left before you leave the country, and I don't want to spend them on the street, talking about Bennett Barlow."

"I am *so* sorry," she says with a laugh before stepping aside to let me in. "Come in."

I follow her up the stairs to her apartment. I realize, with some surprise, that I managed never to come up here in the last six months. She had been to my place a couple of times. She always described her place as simple, but it's perfect for her —neat and cozy. It smells like caramel and vanilla—scents that I'm sure never leave this place, never leave her. Her bed is covered in soft green linens. In the corner, there is a kitchenette with a table for two.

I take off my jacket and drape it over the back of one chair, then loosen my bowtie, letting the ends hang around my neck.

Palmer turns on a lamp and sits across from me at the kitchen table. She watches me with a curious, guarded expression.

"Where to begin?" she asks with a tired smile.

Her words draw me suddenly back to that first day, sitting across from her in the bakery, going over the rules for our new arrangement. I think of how far we've come since that day, the crossroads we're facing now.

I don't hesitate when I say, "I love you, Palmer Sullivan."

Her lips curl instantly into a smile, like she has been waiting to hear those words again. "I love you, Silas Howell."

I reach over and grab the leg of her chair, dragging her to me until her knees touch mine. I lean in and kiss her. The hours that have passed without being able to kiss her have felt far too long.

She breaks away from me with a quiet sigh. "It's terrible. But a part of me is kind of hoping that I don't get into École Deschamps. It would make the decision easier."

I shake my head, threading our fingers together. "Then let me make the decision easier for you: you're going. You have worked too damn hard for this not to give your all at that interview. You're going to show them how amazing you are. And whether you get accepted or not, I'll be right there—still in love with you, still cheering for you, either way. Whether you live across the street or across the Atlantic."

She squeezes my hand, but I can see the fear still burning in her eyes.

"Long distance almost never works," she warns. "I could barely maintain a relationship when we lived ten minutes away from each other. This is several thousand miles—"

"I'm not Grant," I retort. "*We* can make it work."

She purses her lips, looking unconvinced.

I flash her a wry smile. "We just need ground rules."

She laughs. "Like what?"

"Ground rule number one: we tell everyone. No more

pretending. I want everyone to know that I'm yours. Shout it from the rooftops."

"I'm pretty sure everyone who matters already knows," she teases.

I shake my head. "Not just our friends. I don't want a French man to get within six feet of you without knowing you have a handsome American boyfriend—one who used to tackle dudes competitively."

A startled laugh erupts from her, her eyes twinkling. "Okay. What's the next one?"

I place a hand on her flannel-covered thigh, my voice dropping low as I say, "We keep things as unprofessional as possible until you leave. I have six months of holding back to make up for. If I'm going to spend another nine months away from you, I want to have your body committed to memory by the time you go."

Her cheeks flush, and she leans in to kiss me again, smiling against my lips. "I think I can get on board with that."

"Ground rule number three," I mutter between kisses. "Scheduled video chat dates. I don't care if it's two a.m. We make it happen."

"Okay," she agrees.

"Final ground rule," I say, my heart thrumming painfully in my chest. "We have to be honest with each other. Always. It's the only way we're going to make this work."

"Deal," she says.

She leans in once more to seal the agreement with a kiss. When she parts her lips a little wider, I pull her off her chair and settle her on my lap. She wraps her hands around my neck and angles her lips over mine. While I'm greatly looking forward to starting the work of memorizing her body, I suddenly remember the conversation I had with Cal weeks ago, the advice he gave me.

I pull away from her, and her eyelids flutter open,

surprised that I stopped the kiss so abruptly. I cup her cheek in my palm, considering my words, before I suggest, "Or... we forget about long distance... and I move to Paris with you."

She blinks several times before a nervous laugh stutters out of her. "You're not serious."

"Completely serious," I say, more certain. "Let me come to Paris with you."

I know I should give her time to sit and think about it, to consider this offer, but I don't. I honestly don't *want* to give her time to think about it. Letting Palmer overthink things is never a good idea. I'm certain that distracting her is far more likely to work in my favor.

I kiss her again before she can argue. I stand, cradling her against my chest, never breaking our kiss. I lay her down on her bed and crawl over her, holding my weight off her with one elbow.

"Let me come with you," I whisper, brushing her hair back from her face.

She shakes her head, but her fingers are steadily undoing the buttons of my shirt, pushing it open, and smoothing her hands over my chest. Her mind and her body are clearly having two very different, opposing conversations.

"You don't speak French," she argues.

I paint a line of kisses down her jaw. "Neither do you. We'll learn together."

"You'd be leaving your whole life behind," she protests, her hands running over my chest and my stomach. She starts to undo the buckle of my belt.

"You are my life now," I murmur into her skin, my lips brushing against the hollow of her throat, down the line of her collarbone.

Her breath catches. "Silas."

I push her shirt up over her ribs, and when she lifts her

arms to help me take it off, it feels like a form of surrender. A quiet, glorious surrender.

"I mean it," I urge, kissing the soft swell of her breast. "Let me come with you."

She arches up into me when I close my lips around her hardened nipple. And I know she's losing the battle. With each gasping breath, she's giving in. Her fingers thread into my hair, gripping it at the roots.

"You're not playing fair," she gasps, trembling beneath me as I trail kisses over the soft skin of her stomach.

I grin against her skin. "Not even a little bit."

I grasp the waistband of her pajama bottoms and pull them down slowly. Her breath shudders out of her.

I kiss the crease of her thigh. "Say yes."

She bites her bottom lip hard, as if trying to hold back the response I know she wants to say.

"Say yes," I repeat, "and I'll make sure you never regret it."

I pull her legs over my shoulders. Whatever retort she might have been considering is lost in a gasp as I bury myself in her. I lick a trail up her center, before making slow, delicious circles around her clit. She whimpers with the motions of my tongue. Her hips arch off the mattress.

I once thought that Palmer's desserts were the greatest things I had ever tasted or would ever taste in my life. But I was *so* very wrong. Nothing could ever be as sweet as the baker herself.

"Silas, you can't—" but whatever she thinks I cannot do is stifled when I sink one finger inside her, feeling her clench and spasm around it. The feeling of her slick against my skin, the taste of her on my tongue is so intoxicating, I nearly come right then and there.

I slip another finger inside her, stroking inside her several times, until I feel her clench around me with her climax. Her thighs tense, and I lap at her until she melts into the sheets.

I look up at her from between her legs, panting, "Let me come with you."

She laughs shakily, her head falling back against the pillows. "You are incredibly persuasive."

I slip out from beneath her thighs and slide up her body. I kiss her, the taste of her still on my lips. "Is it working, then?"

She doesn't respond, but she runs her hand down my stomach, shoving the waistband of my pants and boxers down past my hips. She runs her hand along my length, and I groan into her mouth at the sensation.

Though it kills me to stop, even for a moment, I force myself to pull away long enough to say, "I'm sorry, but I don't have a condom."

"I'm on the birth control ring," she insists. "Don't you dare stop."

"I've been tested, too," I tell her. "All clear."

"What part of *don't you dare stop* did you not understand?" she demands, winding her fingers through my hair and pulling me back down to her.

I grin. "I kind of like being bossed around by you."

She stifles my words with another kiss, clearly having little patience for my jokes.

I run a hand down her waist, across the curve of her hip, hooking her thigh around me. When I'm poised at her entrance, she thrusts her hips forward suddenly, burying me inside of her. I pause for the briefest moment, relishing the feeling of her.

But she shifts her hips impatiently, clearly not wanting to wait. And I give her exactly what she wants. I make long, languid strokes inside her as I say, "I want to wake up with you. I want to cook you breakfast in a tiny apartment overlooking the Seine. I want to walk you home from the metro after class. I want to photograph every inch of you on a beach somewhere on the Azure Coast. I want that life with you, Palmer."

She moans softly, her hips lifting to meet mine. "Silas…"

I'm *so* close to coming undone, but I don't want to—not yet. Not until she says it.

"Just say it," I whisper. "Say I can come with you.

I can feel her body clenching around me, and I know she's close again. I thrust deep and slow, holding her gaze.

"Come with me," she begs, her voice breaking.

My heart explodes with triumph.

"Say it again." I cup her cheek with one hand, wanting to look into her eyes when she says it. Her pupils are blown impossibly wide, just a sliver of her emerald irises remaining.

"Come with me, Silas," she pleads once more.

And in the next moment, I do. I come undone with her name on my tongue, knowing she is exactly where I want to be, because wherever she is will be my home.

When the music shifts, I take a deep breath and start walking down the aisle. The rows of guests turn to me, smiles on their faces as they watch me approach the altar. The faintest fluttering of nervousness stirs just behind my navel, but I put a huge smile on my face, pleased when it doesn't feel forced. It's easy to be happy today.

This day feels magical. The church is beautiful, with white pillars lining the pews and soft light trickling through blue stained-glass windows. Picture perfect.

I hear the click of cameras following me, and my first instinct is to turn toward the sound, to find the face behind the camera. But I look resolutely forward, knowing he's not behind the camera today.

I make it to the altar, shooting Charlie a wink. He seems nervous, rocking back on his heels, but smiles back at me warmly.

The other bridesmaids fall into place in front of me, then Charlie's nieces emerge, tossing pink petals onto the aisle with reckless abandon. The room giggles and coos at them in their adorable white tutu dresses. Charlie's sister-in-law collects them and plops them beside her on the front pew, just in time for the officiant to ask for all to rise.

Then, Emery appears, looking breathtaking in her Livie Laurent gown. I beam at the sight of her standing silhouetted in the doorway, pausing as everyone takes in how stunning she looks.

I've seen thousands of brides, but I don't think any of them has ever quite held a candle to Emery Howell. I'm usually not one to cry at weddings—probably because I've only been to a handful for people I care about. But as soon as I see Charlie break, as soon as I witness his face crumple into tears, I lose it too. I regret not carrying a tissue in the pocket of my blue satin bridesmaid dress as the tears fall.

The next second, I see Silas, blurred through a layer of tears, but splendid, nonetheless. He falls into place at Emery's side, hooking her arm through his elbow.

He looks brilliantly handsome in his light gray tux, illuminated in the soft glow of light. His gentle smile widens at the sight of Charlie, the man who is so wildly in love with his little sister. But then his gaze immediately scans the row of bridesmaids in matching blue satin and finds me. His smile is brilliant when he sees me. He shoots me a wink, then fixes his gaze back on the center of the church as he and Emery make their approach.

Seeing Silas and Emery walking down the aisle, looking so alike and so blissfully happy, it's like I can feel their parents in the room with us. It's an odd, entirely foreign feeling for me. I don't go to church. I have never ascribed to angels or afterlives before, but it's like I can *feel* their presence in this room.

There are two empty spots in the front row on the side of the church closest to me, held in honor of Matthew and Renee Howell. Emery had placed two framed pictures of their parents on the bench, and I glance at the picture of their mother, with her kind, toffee-brown eyes. Suddenly, the tears

266

can no longer be suppressed. They flow endlessly, without respite.

I've never prayed in earnest, never really learned how. But in this moment, I silently ask Renee Howell for her blessing to be in her son's life. To be in *both* her children's lives. To not waste this opportunity to love and be loved by the people she raised.

I don't know how an angel would respond to such a request, but an incredibly warm, peaceful feeling settles over my heart.

Once the vows have been spoken, the rings exchanged, and Charlie has kissed his bride, I follow the line of bridesmaids as they pair up with their assigned groomsmen. And last, but certainly not least, is—

"Bonjour, ma chère," Silas greets me, the words sounding natural in his deep voice.

My cheeks hurt from the force of my smile. He offers his arm, and I take it.

"You've been practicing," I compliment through my smile, trying to maintain a camera-ready expression.

"Every day," he agrees, leading me down the aisle, through the sea of smiling faces and camera flashes.

The reception goes unsurprisingly perfect, as all things do when planned by Emery Howell (now Emery Howell-Zhang). We dance the evening away and cut the beautiful three-tiered cake covered in delicate blue flowers that Emery always envisioned. Finally, we crowd into Full Proof for the after-party.

Even though we're surrounded by dozens of wedding guests, we pile together into the center booth, like it's any other boring Tuesday night.

"Voulez-vous coucher avec moi ce soir?" Cal croons to Silas and me as he slides in beside us, handing the bride and groom their drinks.

"Do you even know what that means?" Silas asks with a laugh.

"Nope," Cal replies, popping the P. "I imagine you'll be able to tell me soon enough."

"Will you go to bed with me tonight?" I tell Cal, yelling the translation over the roar of the crowd and the music.

"I thought you'd never ask, Darling." He waggles his copper red eyebrows at me suggestively, leaning over Silas to get closer. Silas whacks him on one massive arm and attempts to push him away.

I giggle. "No, that's what it means! Will you go to bed with me tonight?"

"Jesus, can't you two keep your hands off each other for two seconds?" Emery complains with a groan, leaning forward just in time to hear the tail end of our conversation. Charlie has his arm wrapped around her lazily, his fingers laced with hers. "You would think it's you two going on your honeymoon tomorrow, not us."

I let out another exasperated sigh. "Never mind!"

"How is the preparation going for the move to Paris?" Charlie asks.

I smile brilliantly, unable to suppress my joy. "Really good. We found an apartment to rent overlooking the Seine, and—"

"Palmer Anne Sullivan!"

I look up, alarmed, at the sound of Jenna's voice. She approaches our booth with purpose, her pretty, yellow dress showing off her burgeoning baby bump.

"What could I have possibly done to be in trouble?" I demand in a whiny voice. "I've been with Emery all day!"

"Your presence is requested out front," she says with a mischievous glint in her eyes.

I look to Silas, as if he might be in on this, but he shrugs.

"No idea," he says.

He and Cal let me out of the booth, and Jenna links arms with me, leading me toward the front of the bar.

"I have an update on the hunt for a buyer for Sweet P," she says, and my heart thuds painfully in my chest.

I know this is a necessary evil. I know that there is no way we could keep the business running with me in France and Jenna out on maternity leave, despite Evan's adamant protests that he can manage the bakery all on his own. But even so, it hurts to consider selling the place that Jenna and I started from the ground up. We've been advertising for one week for a potential buyer, and a little part of me has been relieved that we haven't yet had any realistic offers.

I take a deep breath. "You found a buyer?"

Jenna squeezes my arm in delight. "Better."

I peer at her, concerned. "What's better than a buyer?"

"An investor," she says, opening the door to the bar, leading me out into the cool autumn evening.

My jaw drops at the sight of the figure standing there, looking effortlessly perfect in a black slip dress and sleek blazer. Her blue eyes are wide and expectant. Since I last saw her, she cut her dark hair dramatically, just below her chin. Of *course* she can pull off a bob.

"Bennett?" I ask, disbelieving.

She smiles, waving a little shyly. "Hi, Palmer."

I look from Bennett to Jenna and back, confused. "You're the investor?"

She nods hesitantly. "I am... If you're open to it."

My mouth gapes at the offer. Despite Bennett's request that we become friends, I haven't heard from her at all since her disastrous, canceled wedding. This is the last way I ever imagined running into her again.

To fill my stunned silence, Bennett explains, "I told my father I'm ready to play a more active role in the company. I convinced him that I'm ready to start doing something real with the Barlow name—the Barlow money. He told me to pick something I care about to invest in."

I can't quite believe this is happening, so I clarify, "And you care about—?"

"Not letting my favorite bakery go out of business," she completes with a knowing smile. "I saw that you were advertising for buyers, and I reached out to Jenna."

Jenna picks up from there, "We've worked out all the details this week. Bennett will help us employ enough people to keep the business going next year while you're in school and I'm on maternity leave. Then, when we're back to full strength, we'll start expanding."

"Sweet P Dessert Bar," Bennett supplies with a flourish. "I want one in every major city—everywhere you can find a Barlow Hotel, you'll find a Sweet P."

It is suddenly hard to breathe. I look at Jenna, who looks incredibly pleased with herself.

"You're serious?" I ask, feeling like I might just perish from heartbreak if this is some sort of elaborate, cruel joke.

"Completely," Jenna responds, squeezing my arm with delight. "This isn't the end of our little bakery that could. It's just the beginning."

With her confirmation, I completely lose it—crying big, ugly tears until Jenna and Bennett are both forced to wrap me in a hug.

Once I've calmed down, I sniffle pitifully and ask Bennett, "How can I ever possibly repay you?"

She holds my face in her hands and wipes tears from beneath my eyes with her thumbs.

"This is my way of repaying you," she explains. "You were kind to me when you had *every* reason to hate me. I want to do something nice for you, because you're my friend. Just promise me you won't become too French to come back to Charleston, okay?"

I sputter a laugh, nodding. "I promise."

"Okay, good," she says, turning back in the direction of a white Audi. "I'll stop by the bakery this week so we can work out all the paperwork. For now, I'll leave y'all to enjoy your party."

"Do you want to join us?" I ask quickly, before she can retreat.

She pauses for a second, then a brilliant smile lights her face. She nearly squeals with her delight, "I'd love to."

I watch in wonder as Jenna leads her inside the bar.

Before I can follow them, I see Silas standing just inside the door, waiting for me. He joins me outside.

He glances back inside the bar for a long moment. "Have I had too much to drink, or did I just see Bennett Barlow walk into Cal's bar with Jenna?"

"Your eyes do not deceive you," I reply, wrapping my arms around his neck and pulling his face down to mine for a kiss. "Bennett is going to invest in Sweet P. She's going to keep it going while we're away."

His face passes from surprise to delight. With a laugh, he scoops me up into his arms and spins me, the world blurring around me. My laughter spills out of me, bright and unrestrained, at the feeling of being weightless in his arms.

"That's amazing!" he exclaims.

When he sets me down, I shake my head, not quite believing my luck. "It's all coming together, isn't it?"

The look he gives me is so adoring, so brilliantly happy—like I'm the center of his entire universe. The intensity of it steals the breath right out of my lungs.

He kisses me, slow and sure, and when he finally pulls away, he says, "From where I'm standing, the future is looking pretty sweet."

Acknowledgments

1. As always, to my husband, the reason why it's so easy for me to write about true love—you show me it exists every day.
2. To my daughters, who have my whole heart. I don't know how I got so lucky to be chosen as your mom. (Also, you're not allowed to read this book for many, many years.)
3. To my unwaveringly supportive parents, who will never read my books because there is sex in it. Love you always.
4. To my editor, Hilari Cohen, my fellow stress baker. Thanks for sticking with me for my second book. And thank you for hustling to help me get this book out into the world!
5. To my beautiful beta readers. To my Columbia crew: Sarah, Ali, and Sonya. To the med school peeps: Sean, Cat, Becky, and Erica. And to my formal beta readers: Allie, Ruchi, and Millie.
6. To my cover designer, Mary Ann Smith. I don't know how you manage to come up with exactly what I want every time with so little prompt, but you are the best.
7. To my fellow residents. I love you all so dearly. You made some of the most difficult years of my life not only tolerable but enjoyable. Thank you all for being so beautifully supportive of my side-hustle!

About the Author

Jacquelynn Harbell received her undergraduate degree in creative writing from Columbia University before attending medical school. Though she maintains her day job as a doctor, she never lost hope of seeing her name on the cover of a great romance novel. When she isn't practicing medicine or writing, she spends her time with her engineer husband, her twin daughters, and her two dogs.

www.ingramcontent.com/pod-product-compliance
Lightning Source LLC
Chambersburg PA
CBHW030001010826
48973CB00007B/2114